TEMPLE OF SAND

By HR Moore

D1394528

Titles by HR Moore:

The Relic Trilogy:

Queen of Empire

Temple of Sand

Court of Crystal (coming June 2021)

In the Gleaming Light

http://www.hrmoore.com

For Atia.

FAMILY TREES

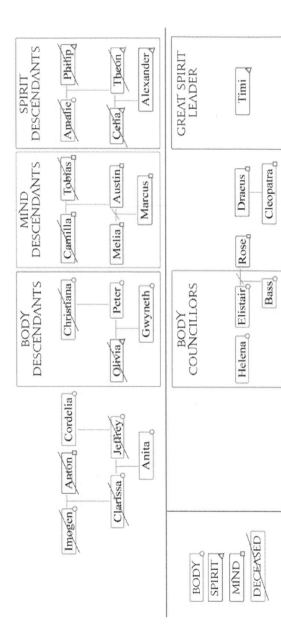

SPIRIT DESCENDANTS
Amalie — Philip
Celia — Theon
Alexander

MIND DESCENDANTS
Camilla — Tobias
Melia — Austin
Marcus

BODY DESCENDANTS
Christiana
Olivia — Peter
Gwyneth

Imogen — Anton — Cordelia
Clarissa — Jeffrey
Anita

GREAT SPIRIT LEADER
Timi

BODY COUNCILLORS
Helena — Elistair — Rose
Bass — Draeus
Cleopatra

BODY
SPIRIT
MIND
DECEASED

4

THIS FAMILY TREE CAN ALSO BE FOUND AT WWW.HRMOORE.COM/TEMPLETREE

CHAPTER 1

Light streamed in through the cracks in the ceiling, finding its way in slivers, the dust in the air floating across the shafts. She could hear people walking above, the floorboards creaking, muffled footsteps, muted voices.

Every now and again a small piece of straw would find its way through the gaps. It would float down to the unforgiving concrete floor below. Occasionally a piece would hit Anita where she lay on a makeshift bed of blankets. She watched the light, listened to the noises, and wiled away the time, wondering just why she was here.

Helena, her old mentor and friend, hadn't lingered long the previous evening, after Anita had refused to utter a single word. Helena had ordered the guards to split Anita and Alexander up for the night, told them she would answer their questions in the morning, then left.

Anita had spent the night wide eyed, staring up at the ceiling, the words, 'Let's have a chat about that cylinder in your head,' careering around, along with endless unanswered questions.

How did Helena know about the brass cylinder? What did Helena want from them? Was she cross because Anita had failed to bring Helena the information she'd asked for? Why had she taken Alexander too? Was he okay? Wherever he was, he wasn't close enough for her to read his energy. Did anyone realise they were gone? It was one thing for someone like Anita to go missing, but if the Spirit Descendent were to suddenly disappear, surely it must raise some kind of alarm...

At last, the ringing of crisp footsteps on the concrete outside her makeshift prison cell cut across the monotonous background noise. They stopped as they came level with the door, replaced by the loud jangling of metal, the scraping of a key fitting the lock. She heard a dull clunk, then the old, fragile door swung inwards. Anita stayed where she was, on her back, on the floor, turning only her head to see who was there.

Her eyes took in the nondescript, middle-aged man gingerly entering the room. He was dressed all in black and had floppy brown hair. He waited a moment for his eyes to adjust to the semi-darkness and then said in a perfect councilor-eqsue accent, 'Good morning, Anita. I hope you slept well?' He continued without pausing for an answer. 'Please come with me.'

He said it like she had a choice... but anyway, finding out why she was here was a far more entertaining prospect than remaining in this cell. She got to her feet, dusted off the stray bits of straw, and said, 'Lead the way.'

The smell of stale straw wafted around them as they walked in silence to the end of a dark corridor. They reached a wooden wall blocking the way, and the man rapped curtly on it. A hatch in the ceiling was immediately and efficiently pulled aside, a ladder with wooden rungs lowered.

Another man in black appeared at the top, this one younger, with cropped blond hair and blotchy skin. The first man indicated that Anita should ascend. The ladder had seen better days, but she climbed nimbly to the top and out into the rickety wooden barn above.

The barn's large doors had been thrown open to reveal an impressive farmhouse beyond, and a feeling of dread filled her as she realized she had been here before. The image of a pigeon flashed before her eyes. Adrenaline filled her veins as the implications hit her. The world around her seemed to blur as they worked their way through her thoughts. She hardly noticed as another man, this one burley and bearded, took her arm and steered her out into the sunlight.

They walked around the house, through an archway covered with climbing white roses and into a beautiful cottage garden that would rival even Cordelia's. A pergola extended out from the side of the old farmhouse, this too covered with climbing plants. Underneath sat several people, some lounging on sofas, others sat casually on wooden benches, eating breakfast at a rustic dining table, Alexander and Helena included.

Alexander's back was to Anita, but he felt her energy approaching before he heard or saw her, sending a silent, reassuring nudge to the edge of her energy field. Helena sat on the opposite side of the table, and Alexander waited for Helena to notice Anita before publicly reacting to her presence.

'Good morning, Anita,' said Helena warmly, as Anita and her guard approached the table. 'I trust you slept well?'

'Not a wink, but thanks for your concern,' said Anita. 'I'm very much looking forward to your explanation of what we're doing here though, if that wouldn't be too much trouble?'

Anita placed herself at the table next to Alexander, purposefully brushing his arm as she sat down. The familiar tingles had a calming effect as she helped herself to a croissant and orange juice without waiting for an invitation.

Helena wasn't riled; she liked a fight. 'Yes, of course, but I'd like to start by apologising for the way we secured your company. It was the only way we could be sure to get you both here with no witnesses and without a long persuasion process. I'm genuinely sorry, but I'm afraid we're running short on time, so it was necessary.'

'Like stealing *your* memory back from Austin was necessary?'

Helena looked down into her breakfast before meeting Anita's eyes. 'Yes, a little like that. The reason I asked you to do that was because the memory is of something I'm deeply ashamed of. Austin will use it against us if he's given half a chance. Why do you think he hid it so well?'

'I don't know, Helena, but I'd also like to know why Austin chose this place for the end of the Chase? If you and he are enemies, why would he choose here?'

'Austin knows about the Institution. He also, rightly, suspects that the man who owns this farm is one of our members. Austin used the Chase as an opportunity to intimidate us, to let us know that he knows where and who our members are.

'We didn't know what he was planning; Amber's too careful for that. As you two were reaching for the scroll, hidden away beneath the floor were several prominent members of the Institution, a lot of whom were supposedly in Kingdom at the time of the Chase.

'This has been one of our informal bases for years. In fact, your parents and I used to spend time here when we were your age.'

Anita's energy turned hostile at the mention of her parents. Parents who everyone had all but denied existed, parents who Helena had been such great friends with but had never once thought to mention. Anita wasn't certain she wanted to know about her parents any longer.

'Ah yes, the old parent carrot,' said Anita casually.

Helena waited for her to continue, but Anita didn't give them the satisfaction. Instead, she poured herself some tea and tucked into her food.

After a pregnant pause, Helena filled the silence. 'Look, Anita, I don't want to fight with you. I know I've lied to you and kidnapped you and that doesn't do much to engender trust, but now is the time for the truth. You didn't give me up when they were torturing you, so I know I can trust you. Now I need to show you I'm trustworthy too.'

'And how do you intend to do that?' said Anita. 'By casually dropping in a power play like… oh, I don't know… brass cylinders?'

Helena at least had the decency to look a little ashamed. 'I'm sorry. I could have handled last night better, but you know me, I'm dreadful with people.' She said it light-heartedly, like it was funny.

'Oh, in which case, carry on, do whatever you want, so long as you acknowledge your behaviour is deplorable.'

'Anita, I'm sorry… this isn't going as planned, so here, just read this,' she said, sliding a beaten-up leather notebook across the table. 'When you have, maybe you'll be willing to talk.'

Helena got up and made towards the farmhouse.

As she approached the back door, Alexander's chocolaty voice pierced the tense silence. 'To clarify,' he said slowly, 'do you consider us your prisoners or your guests?' He dwelled on the word guests, drawing it out, the irony obvious.

Helena turned. 'My guests, of course,' she replied. 'Roam around as you please. You'll have bedrooms in the main house tonight. The cells were a necessary measure to ensure you didn't leave before we talked.'

'And if we decide we don't want to stay?' he hypothesized.

'I can't hold you here indefinitely. If you wish to leave, then leave, but you will find no answers, no friends, no explanations waiting for you in Empire. Before you do anything rash, read the diary, I think you'll find it quite enlightening.'

Helena retreated into the farmhouse and the others gradually dispersed, off to do whatever it was they had to do on a lazy autumn morning.

'Walk?' asked Alexander, squeezing Anita's hand under the table.

She nodded; they needed to talk away from the prying ears of all these people. She didn't want anyone to see her reading the diary, at least until she knew what they were dealing with.

* * * * *

They walked out of the farmyard, through an open gate and into the field beyond. It sloped gently at first and then steeply, leading to a copse of trees that stood proudly at the top of the hill. Anita looked up at the leaves turning shades of orange.

From there they had a good vantage point overlooking the farm buildings. Nobody could approach from that side without being seen. They withdrew back past the treeline, out of site, and sank down, side by side, in the roots of the largest tree.

'I'm so sorry,' he said, looking back across the field. 'I never saw this coming.'

Anita smirked, almost cruelly, her frustration at boiling point. 'Of course you didn't, why would you? You didn't even know I was trying to steal Austin's brass cylinder for Helena until last night. I trained with Helena for years and the thought never crossed my mind that she would do something like this.'

Alexander nodded. 'No point dwelling anyway, I suppose,' he said, putting his arm around her shoulders. 'Shall we see what kind of bait we're dealing with?'

She pulled out the diary and opened its battered cover to find a page full of spidery scrawl, with no hint of who it belonged to or what story it had to tell. Anita plunged in, reading aloud.

'5th June, 1331.

Today is the day I become an 'adventurer', how exciting that sounds and yet, in reality, how terribly dull. The parents are shipping me off to the Wild Lands with them to trade and travel, which they see as one almighty good time, but I see as a waste of a perfectly good summer.

I'm nineteen and have just graduated from school, FYI, I'm a Body (most definitely), and am writing a diary on the suggestion of my best friend, Evie. Evie is of the opinion that writing about the inevitable monotony might help me escape it. So here goes nothing.

To give you some background, my name is Clarissa. My parents, Anton and Imogen, are what I'd call enterprising academics, meaning they're academics who have a talent for making money through trade. They're good at what they do, but it also doesn't hurt that Mum's best friend is Christiana, the Body Descendant...

Normally, when they venture into the Wild Lands, they leave me behind in Empire, with my aunt. But now they've decided it time I learn the family trade, hence my enforced attendance. Don't get me wrong, there's a part of me that's quite looking forward to the Wild Lands. Wild Water sounds totally up my street, Wild Fire sounds crazy, Wild Air exhilarating, but even so, I'm sceptical about how much fun a trip with the parents is ever really going to be... especially when the delicious, newly single Jason will be kicking around Empire, free as a bird, all summer.

No doubt dreadful Petunia will have her claws firmly into him by the time I get back. I'm not convinced any man is strong enough to extract those once they're in...

Anyway, shouldn't think about them. Evie keeps talking about the rugged Wild Land dwelling super men she thinks I'm going to meet. Maybe she's right, and if that is the case, things will soon be looking up.'

Anita paused as the entry came to a close. 'Clarissa was my mother's name,' she said, 'so I guess this is the start of Helena's promise to tell me about my parents.'

Alexander nodded and gave her arm a squeeze. She turned back to the notebook in her hands.

'23rd June, 1331.

So, it turns out I'm dreadful at this whole keeping a diary thing. Suffice it to say, I'm having an unexpectedly great time. The trading posts are nothing short of raucous. There are parties every night; debauchery galore.

The gossip is beyond anything I've ever known, and we've picked up a few strays along the way. They're now travelling with us and are nothing short of hilarious.

The nights we're not at a trading post, we throw up tents, build a campfire, and get drunk on the local beverage of choice. Last night was some crazy kind of rum... I'm regretting it today.

But I digress, my main reason for writing is that I feel like I'm about to explode with excitement and I have nowhere to vent my feelings but onto these sorry, good for nothing pages.

Last night, after midnight, as my parents were saying goodnight and going to bed, a stranger arrived in the camp. After a brief chat with Dad, he made his way to the fire. We were dancing around, singing, screaming, chasing each other around the flames, the alcohol's sorcery evident.

Anyway, Brunel (hilarious, short, gay, from Wild Fire - all you need to know) was chasing me and I ran straight into the new guy. He caught me, and I looked up into the fiery, toffee eyes of a man named Jeff. He looked indulgently down at me, and we both burst out laughing as he set me back on my feet. Then, he casually draped an arm around my shoulders and walked me to the fire to join the others.

We polished off the rum (naturally) but by that time it was three in the morning and too late for him to put up his tent, so he bunked in with me (all totally innocent, I assure you). However, I woke up this morning to find my back to his chest, his arm across me, his hand stroking my arm, and my energy screaming.

I rolled over, my face invading his personal space and said, 'Good morning'. He raised what can only be described as a flirtatious eyebrow, smiled, kissed me on the forehead and then got up and left without so much as a word.

He at least threw me what I'm calling a 'to be continued' smile as he departed back to the fire for some early morning coffee. But I mean, really, talk about infuriatingly exciting. Maybe Evie was right after all... although, I don't think he's from the Wild Lands...

9th July, 1331.

At last. Success. It might have taken me two weeks, but it finally happened. He gives me a wide berth when Mum and Dad are around; I suppose he's scared they'll throw him out of the travelling party. But yesterday, Mum and Dad went for dinner at the Wild Lands residence of some councillor, and left us all to it for the evening.

Jeff and I were cleaning up after supper, down by the stream, well out of sight of the others, and he just did it! He walked straight up to me, stopped, bent his head down towards mine, looked at me with brooding eyes, took my head in his hands, and kissed me.

Naturally, I dropped the tray I was holding and kissed him back. Alas, Brunel decided that was the moment to come and find me for a card game, so it was only brief. Luckily, Brunel called out from the top of the hill before we were in view, but the tension now is like nothing I ever thought could exist.

My heart feels like it's going to break through my rib cage, my energy is so high I feel like I'm skipping along on air. I can't stop stealing glances at his tall, rangy physique and into his luring eyes. Oddly, his hands are his most mesmerising part, purposeful and powerful… the way they pulled me to him… I think I'm going to burst!

10th August, 1331.

SO. BLOODY. INFURIATING. It's been another MONTH. We've been in the most romantic places on the planet: Wild Water, where the waterfalls seem to come from the sky, mist makes you see the world through a dreamy haze, a plethora of secluded caves and rivulets to explore. Wild Fire, where lava flows as the rivers do in Water, a dangerous place where the unsuspecting traveller could at any moment be spat on by an angry passing stream. A place where it would be so very easy to sneak off and get lost in the complex web of hot pools and steam vents.

Now we're in Wild Sky, where ghostly lights in heavenly colours flit and play across the sky at night. But Jeff has barely spoken to me since the kiss. I catch him looking every now and again, but every time I do, he quickly looks away. And, of course, Brunel has realised there's something wrong…

We went to toast marshmallows over a lava pit before we left Wild Fire, and Brunel came right out with it. He said we should stop messing around and get on with it; even my parents must have noticed the tension by now! The problem is, I would just get on with it, if only Jeff would make a move.

Brunel thinks I should get him drunk and pounce on him, of course. But what if Jeff doesn't like me like that? What if I make a total idiot of myself? Surely if he liked me, he would do something? And he did do something, a MONTH ago... but nothing since.

Maybe he hated the kiss? Maybe he thought he liked me and then changed his mind? But if so, why does he keep looking at me? I wish Evie were here, although she would probably be in Brunel's camp... I just don't know what to do.

11th August, 1331.

Bliss! He kissed me again!

Last night, Brunel (the darling Brunel), suggested Jeff and I come with him to a ledge that boasts the best view of the lights. Uninterrupted views across the countryside, the horizon seeming to stretch forever...

We went at sunset, naturally taking with us a good supply of dandelion wine (a Wild Sky speciality). Brunel stayed no longer than ten minutes. He poured us wine, drank a couple of sips, said he suddenly felt ill, and left us to it.

If Jeff realised this had been the plan all along (which let's face it, how can he not have?), he didn't say a thing. Instead, he looked me in the eye for the first time since the kiss and tapped the ground next to where he sat.

I placed myself down next to him, he put his arm round me, and we watched the sunset in silence, marvelling at the lights that crept into the night and danced across the sky the moment the sun disappeared below the horizon.

After a while he turned his head towards me and kissed my hair. My energy literally leapt in response. I met his toffee eyes, the lights casting shadows across his handsome face. All I could think to say was, 'Why have you been ignoring me? It's been driving me mad.'

'I know,' he said, pulling his eyes away to look back at the spectacle in the sky. 'It's been driving me mad too, but we can't do this. I'm not who you think I am... I can't commit to you.'

'Who do I think you are?'

I laughed at the melodrama and the mention of commitment. 'A traveller? A trader looking to make his fortune?'

I laughed again. 'I've been out here for months now and I'm afraid you fit neither one of those bills. You're way too purposeful to simply be a traveller. I saw you trying to barter for chocolate the other day, which tells me you're no trader, and you don't hail from any of the lands we visited so far.

'Your mannerisms and quirks are familiar to me and yet alien, because they're the tell-tale signs of an academic; my parents are prominent within the Temples, remember? I've grown up surrounded by people like you... but I've never seen you in Empire, so I'd say you're from Kingdom.

'You're a Body, but you've got Spirit in you too, like Mum. But you're not really like my parents, so I'd guess you're from the new generation they talk about in excited, hushed tones when they think I can't hear. More radical, more fanatical, more volatile, more dangerous, not willing to toe the Descendants' party line like those from Mum and Dad's generation.'

He was clearly surprised by my appraisal. 'You're more astute than I gave you credit for.'

'Have you met my parents? They'd be inconsolably disappointed if I were anything else.'

He suddenly looked worried. 'So, you think your parents know who I am?'

'Of course. I mean, they may not know exactly who you are and why you're here, but they know in general who you are. If I've worked it out, then they definitely have. Why? What are you trying to hide? Why are you here?'

He took a long, deep breath. 'I'm with the Institution...'

'Really?' He certainly piqued my interest with this bombshell.

'You've heard of them?'

'Who hasn't?'

'Anyone who doesn't have two prominent academics for parents, I should think.'

He said it defensively, so I backed off a bit. 'Yeah, sorry, I forget. So why are you here? Obviously something to do with Mum and Dad?'

He paused, wrestled, although not too hard, with what he should tell me, and in the end just came out with everything (or at least I think he did). 'The Institution sent me to see your parents, to talk to them about our cause, and see if they'd be interested in helping us.'

'Helping you with what?'

'I can't go into specifics.'

'Have you spoken to them yet?'

'No.'

'Why not?'

'Because the right moment hasn't presented itself yet.'

'You've spent loads of time alone with them. How could the right moment not have cropped up by now?'

'The right moment isn't just to do with them.'

'Cryptic,' I said, mocking him flirtatiously.

He raised one eyebrow. 'It's also to do with you.'

I blushed bright purple. Thank the Gods it was dark. 'What does that mean?'

'Once I've spoken to your parents, I won't need to stay, and I don't want to leave yet.'

'Really?' I said, smiling. 'And why is that?'

'I think you know,' he said, lifting his hand to my neck and pulling my lips to his. We kissed for ages, pulling apart every so often, just to change our minds and start kissing again. My energy was soaring, and I could feel his heart pounding through his chest.

When we did finally pull apart, we lay on the ledge, entangled, watching the lights. I woke up the following morning to find him still there, gently stroking my hair.

We returned to camp, stopping by the tiny trading post first to pick up pastries for breakfast. This way, if anyone asked where we had been, we could tell them we got up early to get breakfast for everyone.

Not that the ruse mattered anyway; Jeff didn't let go of my hand until we were standing by the campfire. He kissed my cheek playfully as I went to get mugs, and draped his arm around me as we sat on the ground, leaning back against a straw bale, eating breakfast.

Brunel's mouth actually fell open as he emerged from his tent and saw us.

'I take it you two had a fun night?' he said provocatively, helping himself to a pastry.

Neither one of us answered, but Jeff pulled me into his chest and rested his chin on the top of my head.

Mum and Dad both did comedy double takes as they joined us at the campfire. Luckily they had the good manners not to say anything. They did however throw a raised eyebrow at each other when they thought I wasn't looking.

Anyway, bliss, bliss, bliss! And again, I find myself with no one to share the details with, apart from Brunel. I don't think he really counts; he's just disappointed the story is so tame.

1st September, 1331.

It's been three weeks of walking on air; romantic strolls, secluded campfire dinners, sleeping under the stars. But today the illusion shattered, and I came crashing back to the ground.

A letter was delivered for Jeff at the trading post we're staying at. He wouldn't show me the message, but it was from the Institution and the gist was that he had to get back to Kingdom as soon as possible.

He looked almost scared as he burned the note in the fire. He sought out Mum and Dad immediately, to have the talk he'd been putting off for so long.

There was shouting. I could hear Dad telling Jeff, in no uncertain terms, that he was no longer welcome. Then Mum emerged, looking strained, heading my way.

She led me to a swinging bench suspended from a tree, a charming feature to be found all over Wild Wood, where we're currently staying.

'Clarissa,' she started, pushing a long strand of my strawberry blond hair back behind my ear, 'do you know why Jeff is here?'

I nodded. 'He's here because the Institution sent him to see if you and Dad would help them.'

Mum was shocked at both the honesty and content of my response. She concentrated for a few moments on getting some momentum going with the swing. 'Yes. Do you know what that means?' She asked me calmly, evenly. Mum was always so level-headed, unlike Dad.

'Not really. I know they're a group of young academics who have new ideas. But what that means in reality, I don't know. I thought you guys were intrigued by the Institution. The only times I've heard you discuss it, you seemed excited about them... but the shouting would indicate otherwise.'

Mum nodded. 'I can see how it could have come across like that. The Institution doesn't just have different ideas, they pursue radical concepts. They're constructing what most would consider a dangerous philosophy.

'They want to overthrow the Descendancy and set up a new political system; to forget about sending back the Relic. They want to create a world where we ignore the higher order, those who created us, those who sent us the Relic to test us and free us.

'Since Peter's birth into the Body line, and the corresponding dip in energy, their cause has grown stronger. They've found support from those who think the prophecy is broken. It's whispered that Peter himself associates with them...'

Mum looked so sad when she told me this, I stopped the swing and hugged her.

'Anyway, Dad and I are full supporters of our current system. We're firm believers that the current Descendants will find a way to return the Relic.'

'Of course you are. The Body Descendant is my Godmother, for goodness' sake. Christiana is one of your closest friends. Why did the Institution think you'd be interested in helping them?'

'We're more forward thinking than most academics. They probably thought we see sense in what they're proposing, which, of course, is nonsense. No doubt they're trying to muster support from all prominent academics who don't directly align with Tobias. The Gods only know what he would do if he thought we were in league with the Institution; he hates our research enough already.'

'Does he? Why?' This came as a shock to me. Mum and Dad spend loads of time with the ruling Mind Descendant and his wife, Camilla. I'd always thought they got on like a house on fire.

'He thinks some of the research we do is too radical, which is probably the reason the Institution sent Jeff to approach us. In reality, the work we do isn't radical at all; Tobias just hates change and anything he doesn't understand or control.'

We swung in silence for another couple of minutes.

'Did you really like Jeff?'

I nodded, then realised she had used the word 'did' as opposed to 'do'. 'What do you mean 'did' I really like him? I still do really like him.'

'Yes, but Darling, he works for a dangerous organisation. You can't continue your relationship with him. It's impossible.'

'Impossible in your eyes maybe, but not in mine. You're always harping on about the benefits of diversity of opinion; you don't get to pick and choose the opinions you like and call the others dangerous.'

'But they are dangerous.'

'Only if they get enough support, which seems unlikely.'

'It would be wrong to underestimate them; they're gaining a great deal of silent patronage.'

'But that's just it, it's silent.'

'But patronage none the less. Anyway, Jeff is returning to Kingdom and we are heading for Wild Air. This is where you part ways.'

'Unless I decide to go back with him.'

'Assuming he wants you to go back with him and he hasn't been using you to get to us.'

'Mum, how can you say that?'

'I'm sorry, I didn't mean for it to come out like that. I'm sure he does truly like you, but you've got to admit, it's a possibility.'

At that moment, Jeff appeared from the wooden cabin of the trading post. I left Mum and the swing to talk to him.

He didn't tell me much other than the obvious and said he had to go back to Kingdom. He didn't suggest I go with him, so I didn't suggest it either. He simply hugged me tightly, squeezing me protectively to his chest, kissed the top of my head, and left without another word.

Surprisingly, I haven't cried. I feel sad and drained, like the days will be more difficult to get through now. But I suppose I'd known this day would come; he'd told me as much on the ledge.'

Anita stopped reading and turned to look at Alexander. 'What was your dad's name?' he asked.

'Jeffrey, so I suppose it could be him, but then again, there are lots of people out there called Jeff. It's odd to read about them through my mum's eyes though,' she said, 'especially when they're total strangers to me. They don't sound as terrible as I'd thought they might, being such close friends with Helena.'

'You spent a lot of time with Helena too… she can't be all bad.'

'Nobody's all bad. The question is how bad. Need I remind you she knows about, and let's face it, may have planted, the cylinder in my head? She lied to get me to steal something that belongs to Austin. She withheld all knowledge of my parents when she was my mentor.

And last night she kidnapped us. I'm not ready to forgive and forget just yet.'

'I know, I'm not suggesting you do. I've certainly not forgiven her for the kidnapping, but maybe deep down she's one of the good guys.'

Anita looked sceptical. 'Maybe. Anyway, I think it's time for lunch; I'm starving.'

Alexander nodded, but instead of getting up, he pulled her into him and gently kissed her lips. Both of their energy responded instantly, pouring out of them like a tidal wave. They pulled apart and Alexander ran his thumb across her cheekbone. 'I'm not used to that yet,' he said, smiling as his energy started to return to normal.

'Me neither,' she said, getting to her feet and taking his hands to pull him up too. 'Come on,' she said, a mischievous look taking hold of her face, 'race you.' And with that, she pelted out of the trees and down the hill.

As they reached the farmyard, Alexander had almost closed the gap. She shrieked with laughter as he caught her and dragged her to a stop. He pulled her into a playful embrace, continuing to walk towards the farm and refusing to let her go, Anita having to walk backwards to stop herself from falling.

After a few paces he stopped, looked down into her grey eyes, kissed her briefly on the lips, and then released her from his hold. He left one arm around her shoulders, not wanting to completely let her go.

Alexander dropped his arm back to his side as they approached the farmhouse, hearing a clamour of cheerful voices as they passed under the archway into the garden. There were a whole host of new people noisily eating lunch at the table, a feast of soup, bread, cheese and platters of meat strewn across its length. Helena spotted Alexander and Anita and got up to welcome them, indicating to the two sitting across from her that they should shuffle up to make space.

'Good morning?' inquired Helena. She ladled steaming broccoli and Stilton soup out of the kettle in the middle of the table, handing a bowl to each of them.

'Fine thanks,' Anita replied.

Helena ignored her stilted response, instead saying brightly, 'I'd like to introduce you both to Rose.' Helena indicated towards a tall, well-built woman with blond hair and green eyes to her right. 'Rose is one of my oldest and dearest friends. She was also very close to your parents, Anita, and she is a long-standing member of the Institution. Not to mention, Rose is the mother of your close friend, Bass.'

Anita's mouth dropped open, on the inside at least; she'd been friends with Bass for as long as she could remember. She had never once entertained the idea that she would get to meet his mother. She'd only heard mention of her a handful of times.

'Lovely to meet you,' said Rose politely, energy reserved. There was something about the way she looked at Anita… like she was holding something back.

'Lovely to meet you too,' said Alexander, copying her polite tone. 'Rose, you look familiar, but I can't quite place why?'

Rose fixed Alexander with penetrating eyes, taking her time before answering. 'We've never met,' she said distantly, 'but I look a great deal like my cousin, Melia, Marcus' mother. She said it in a way that did not invite further question.

Helena stepped in, chatting about the farm and how great everyone was being at helping to keep the place running. Anita zoned out, trying to imagine what Rose wasn't saying; a futile effort, of course, given she had only just met the woman.

She turned her attention to all the other people around the table, who were chatting freely. There was no one she immediately recognised, some younger than her, many Helena's age or older, and people to represent every age in between. Their energy was relaxed; no one seemed to be there under duress. Their conversations ranged widely across an abundant number of topics, from trivial gossip, to the energy levels, to the latest fashions.

Anita wondered how they had all come to end up here. Had the younger ones been recruited by teachers like Helena? Did one of the older ones recruit Helena in the first place? No doubt she'd find out in time...

CHAPTER 2

After lunch, Alexander and Anita retreated once more to a private space, this time by the river. They lounged on the lush grassy bank, the rush of the water therapeutic after the surreal gathering at lunch.

'More of the diary?' suggested Anita, shuffling over to get comfortable.

Alexander nodded, absentmindedly stroking her back, 'I'm keen to find out what Helena wants us to uncover.'

Anita pulled the notebook out of her pocket, flicked to the page where they'd left off and started reading once more.

'9th January, 1332.

I've finally returned from the Wild. My parents decided it was about time we came back to civilisation, not least to sell all the wonderful, exotic things we collected along the way. Yesterday, we went from market stall to market stall selling the cocoa beans and spices my parents trade in. Our version of a library back home in Empire is full of jars of different herbs, spices, roots and beans, alongside books my parents have written about the properties of each. My dad has a knack for seeking out the purest supplies, and my mum has a knack for selling them - together a formidable force.

So yesterday, Mum was in her element, reeling in the younger, greener stall holders with her 'pushover woman' act. The older stall holders invited her in for tea and sweet cakes hoping if they treated her with respect, she would respect their profit margins in return.

Mum goes a bit easy on the older ones; they're people she's been trading with for years. Often they're people who helped teach her everything she knows, back when she was a child whose playground was the market, her father a stall holder selling silks. In the end, somehow or other, Mum always gets the price she wants, my father, famously, one of the few people to have ever bested her in a trade. I suspect this had something to do with why Mum eventually accepted his marriage proposal…

To celebrate a great day's trading, we went for a lavish dinner at my dad's club, ginger champagne all round, and by the end of the evening we were all quite merry. Until that was, I saw him. It was odd; the blood seemed to drain from my brain, adrenaline coursed through my veins, my energy soared, and yet I couldn't move, frozen to the spot.

He was talking to a friend as he walked past, both clad in dinner jackets, their hair slicked back, the friend offering him a tobacco roll from a silver case. He'd refused.

'Must dash,' he said to the friend, placing a warm hand on his shoulder, 'but I'll be at Monty's later. Elistair and I were thinking of playing some cards. Might see you there?'

The friend nodded. They shook hands informally and Jeff left, not looking back, so not seeing me. The friend noticed I'd been watching them as he returned to his table on the other side of the floor. He gave me a strange look but didn't say a thing.

My parents and I returned to our guest house, and I immediately headed for bed, their company now suffocating; it was a relief to close the wooden door behind me and shut out the world. I lay down on the enormous mattress, the feather duvet threatening to engulf me.

I hadn't heard from him in four months; nothing since he abruptly left the trading post in Wild Wood. In the last month or so I'd even begun to miss him less, almost believing it was just a fling, a fun way to pass the time when we were travelling. But seeing him in the club wrenched me back to those glorious weeks we'd had together. The feelings came flooding back.

I had to see him. If I'd waited until morning, I wouldn't have known where to find him, and I wouldn't have had the false courage supplied by the champagne. All I had to do was slip out of the guest house and walk the two streets to the bar.

I arrived at Monty's and they looked me up and down. I was very glad of the elegant black dress and stilettos Mum had bought me especially for dinner. The cinched in waist, puffed out skirt and cap sleeves at least made me look the part, even if the girl at the front desk could sense I wasn't at ease.

'Who are you here with?' she asked viciously, seemingly looking for a reason to turn me away. Her stance had been that of the most popular girl at school vetting a newcomer to see if they were worthy, her drop waisted flapper dress somehow adding to her passive aggression.

'I'm here to see Jeff,' I replied, trying to be confident but non-confrontational.

'Jeff?' She'd given me daggers as the name rolled off her tongue. She'd flicked her eyes over me as she decided what would happen next. 'Come with me,' she said eventually, turning to lead the way, not waiting to see if I followed.

She'd slinked up the long, wide, marble steps that led to an extravagant circular bar at the top, the columns on either side giving the place an almost erudite feel. The place oozed a weird kind of sophisticated danger; it felt like no one here could be trusted, but everyone realised that, making it part of the fun. I felt like I was walking into a vipers' nest, the girl leading me the snake charmer, the one in control of who could bite me and when.

As we reached the top of the steps, the girl turned right, away from the packed dance floor, full of couples energetically dancing to the faultless band. She took me around the circular bar *to a less busy area where there were card tables dotted here and there. She approached a group of men standing casually at the bar, sipping elaborate cocktails from martini glasses, Jeff standing in the middle, carelessly leaning back against the dark mahogany.*

He was the first to notice her, not looking to see who was trailing in her wake, and an evasive smile had spread across his lips. 'Helena,' he said obliquely, sending her a questioning look.

She said nothing in return, locking eyes with him, ignoring the others. She walked right up to him, kissed him flirtatiously on the lips and then moved her mouth to his ear, where she whispered something to him.

His eyes snapped up as she pulled away and he stayed motionless, pinned against the bar as his eyes found mine. Everyone else disappeared in an otherworldly haze as I took him in, desperately trying to read his thoughts, my heart thumping against my chest. To my relief, he brushed Helena aside and moved in my direction, pulling me into a fierce embrace.

'Hi,' I whispered in his ear, holding him tight. My turn now, *I thought smugly; I could almost feel Helena's eyes boring furiously into Jeff's back.*

'I'm so happy to see you,' he said, pulling back, pressing a hand to my cheek, kissing me firmly on the other side before pulling away completely. He took my hand and led me to the bar, where, happily, Helena no longer stood, and introduced me to the people he was with.

I have no idea who they were; I was too busy focusing on Jeff. He'd placed a drink in my hand, one of whatever it was they were all drinking, and led me a little further around the ornate, mirror-and-crystal-clad bar, to a secluded table.

'What are you doing here?' he asked, taking my hand and repositioning his chair so our knees touched.

'We came back from the Wild a couple of days ago. Mum wanted to trade our purchases, Mum and Dad need to get back to academia, and I suppose I need to work out what I'm going to do with the rest of my life.'

Jeff lifted my hand to his lips, and my stomach flipped. I was so relieved; he was genuinely happy to see me. 'When you left Wild Wood...' I started, but he cut in before I could get the words out.

'... I'm so sorry. Your dad didn't give me any choice; he said he was going to tell Tobias about my involvement with the Institution unless I left immediately. Looking back, there are so many things I should have said before I left... it all happened so quickly.'

'I haven't heard a thing from you in months.'

He lowered his eyes to the table. 'I know. I'm sorry. Your dad said if I contacted you and he found out, he would tell Tobias.'

I can't tell you how angry this made me. The whole point of going to the Wild Lands was to learn the family trade, to be treated as an adult, yet Mum and Dad are still trying to make decisions for me.

'I can deal with Mum and Dad,' I blurted, before I thought about the implications of the words. Jeff looked at me with unreadable eyes and I flushed bright red. 'I mean, sorry, you've probably moved on... you and Helena...'

He laughed. Loudly. 'There is absolutely nothing going on between me and Helena. We had a very short fling two years ago and nothing has ever happened since. She's just like that... marking her territory. She doesn't like or trust new people, especially new girls,' he said, eyes flashing as he grinned knowingly.

I smiled inwardly. 'Who is she anyway?'

'A member of the Institution, and a very gifted Body. She's about to become an academic, and is working here until then. It works well actually; there's a back room that we use for meetings. It's helpful to have someone like Helena keeping tabs on who's coming and going.'

'What exactly is the Institution?' I fired the question at him like a poisoned bullet, needing to hear in his words what all the fuss was about.

29

He took a breath, considering what to say. 'In a nutshell, it's an organisation centuries old, dedicated to preserving energy stability.'

'I thought that's what the Descendants were here to do?'

'No. They're here to send the Relic back and free the world, it's totally different.'

'But the consequence of sending the Relic back would be stable energy, so the end goal is the same.'

'Only if you believe that the Descendants really want to send the Relic back. They don't seem to be trying very hard. Austin has just made a move to ban energy research, almost certainly at the direction, and obviously with the support, of his father.'

I thought then of Christiana, my mother's best friend, my Godmother, the ruling Body Descendant. I found it hard to believe someone so just and kind would purposely fail to act on the oath she had sworn when invested in power. 'Tobias might think like that, but Christiana? Philip? Peter? Theon? I can't believe the Body and Spirit Descendants would go along with that too.'

'Well, believe it Clarissa.' A delicious shiver ran down my spine when he said my name. 'Think about it: what have they ever done to help find a way to send back the Relic?'

Now he mentioned it, I couldn't think of a single thing. I was going to defend them, to say they must take steps in private, but my mother, Christiana's best friend, had not once mentioned talk of sending the Relic back. Instead, I said, 'Is that why Peter's involved with the Institution as well?'

Jeff nodded, a slow, purposeful movement. It was rare for him to be so serious, and I wondered in silence what was causing it. Before I could find the words to ask, he changed the subject. 'What are you going to do with your life?' he asked flippantly, his usual devil-may-care demeanour back in play.

'Gods, not you too?'

My avoidance tactics are getting better since the endless tirade of questions and 'helpful' suggestions from my parents on the topic, but it didn't deter him. Instead, he used his own

*manoeuvre to throw me off guard, slowly leaning across the table
and moving his face towards mine.*

    *'I think you're evading the question,' he murmured, running
his nose across my cheek, inhaling deeply. He pulled back a little,
eyes alight and playful. 'I want an answer,' he said, placing a
feather-light kiss on my cheekbone. 'I demand an answer.' His
voice was husky as he moved to the other side and kissed my neck,
his warm breath sending shivers down my spine, the intoxicating
scent of his cologne mixed with cocktails and cigars making me
light-headed.*

    *'Maybe I don't want to give you an answer,' I whispered
into his ear, nipping his ear lobe as I pulled away.*

    *'Well then, I shall have to persuade you,' he said, taking my
hand and lifting it to his lips as his eyes poured into mine. A
newfound intensity washed over him, the mood changing, a potent,
palpable stillness settling around us. He closed his eyes, took a
deep breath and then, without another word, stood, dropped my
hand, and made his way swiftly towards his friends at the bar.*

    *I watched him go, looking dashing in his dinner jacket, the
line of his hard stomach hinted at below his crisp white shirt. He
isn't what you would call muscular, he's too thin for that, but he
has an aura of strength around him, an aura as captivating to me
as ever.*

    *He returned and held out his hand for mine, an
unscrupulous smile playing around his lips. My head was saying,
'It's late,' and, 'I should go,' or, 'I'm supposed to be trading chilli
powder in the market tomorrow, and I need to get my beauty sleep
before I do,' but the words wouldn't come. Instead, I took his
hand and stood, in a deliberate, provocative way, a salacious mist
settling around me as I met his smouldering eyes.*

    *We paused there for a moment, a spell around us, until he
turned unexpectedly away, keeping hold of my hand and drawing
me behind him. We descended the marble steps, past Helena, who
gave me another dirty look, and emerged into the cool night air,
where Jeff wrapped a warm, protective arm around me and led me
down the cobbled street.*

After a couple of minutes, as my energy was finally starting to settle, I realised we were going totally the wrong way. 'My guest house is the other way,' I said.

'Is it? That's a relief. It would be a shame to cut the evening short. It's a lovely night for a stroll down to the harbour.'

He was lying of course, and to prove it, at that moment, large splotches of rain started exploding on the cobbles around us. We laughed, and he dropped his arm from my shoulder, seizing my hand and pulling me into a run. 'Come on,' he said, 'my place isn't far from here.'

We ran through the streets, the rain so heavy that pools of water were already collecting between the cobbles, Jeff careful to avoid them. I'm not sure why he bothered, as by the time we fell through his front door, we were drenched to the bone. He pushed the door closed behind us and somehow, as though it were part of the same movement, pulled me to him, his lips hovering just above mine for several tantalising beats. My body was like a coiled spring demanding to be released, every cell silently screaming at him, as his eyes studied the lips they wanted him to kiss.

He lowered his lips to mine, pulling at the soft, impatient skin he found there, slowly at first, and then, like he was gradually winning some silent battle, building until his mouth moved with desperate urgency. His hands found the small of my back, pulling me to him, mine grabbing handfuls of his hair.

He won his inner fight, picking me up and carrying me to his bedroom, where his deft and dominant hands undid first my belt and then the zip that held my dress in place. It fell unceremoniously to the floor, along with his shoes, jacket, tie, and shirt. He led me to the bed, pushed me onto my back and climbed on top, looking down at me with unseeing, reckless eyes.

* * * * *

Afterwards, we lay in silence, my head on his chest, his hand playing lightly along my arm, when he suddenly rolled me onto my

32

back, his head above mine. 'Stay with me,' he said, 'in Kingdom. Don't go back to Empire.'

I looked up at him, considering his words as he ran inquisitive fingers across my lips, cheek, neck. 'What would I do here?'

'Any number of things… you could trade? Look after your parents' business affairs here? Or just live with me and I'll look after you.'

I couldn't help but laugh. 'No contact for four months, and then this? What about my parents telling Tobias?'

'You said yourself you can take care of them.'

I looked up at him, trying to read his unreadable eyes. 'Okay,' I said simply, easily, the word just falling out, like it had a mind of its own.

His face broke into a broad smile and he hugged me, rolling onto his back and pulling me with him, refusing to let me go. He kissed me again before allowing me to wriggle back to the comfort of his chest, arms wrapped around me like they would never let me go.

I made it back to my guesthouse early enough so only the receptionist knew of my night time absence. She smiled indulgently before averting her gaze; I took this as a signal that she wouldn't tell my parents.

I'd come back barefoot, carrying my shoes, with one of Jeff's shirts over the top of my still damp dress. He insisted on walking me back, but I'd made him leave me at the end of the road for safety, giving him a brief peck on the lips and telling him I'd see him later. He'd pulled me back for a proper, last kiss before letting me go.

I'd looked back when I reached the front door; he hadn't moved an inch, watching my every step. I rolled my eyes, smiled, and blew him a kiss.'

'Not sure I'd write all that in a diary,' Anita laughed as she closed the notebook.

'Me neither,' said Alexander, lying back on the grass and looking up at the moon that had appeared in the dying light of day. 'So, what do you think Helena's getting at?'

'I honestly don't know. I still don't think we've got to the crux of it. All the stuff Jeff says about the Institution is basically a carbon copy of what Helena told me, so I don't think that's it. It sounds like the Descendants were the same then as they are now; Tobias was just like Austin, or I guess Austin is like Tobias... what do you think?'

Anita was trying to concentrate on the matter in hand, but the base of Alexander's muscular stomach had been revealed as he lay down. Without thinking, she reached out and ran a hand over the exposed, washboard flesh.

'Not a clue,' said Alexander, inhaling sharply at her touch. 'I agree we haven't got to the good stuff yet.' He sat up so their torsos were in line, Anita facing one way and Alexander the other.

Anita shivered as the sun dipped behind the horizon, although she couldn't say if it was the cold or Alexander's proximity that had caused it.

'Do you think we should stay until we've found out what she wants us for?'

Anita took a breath. 'I don't see why not; we don't seem to be in any immediate danger, but I don't want to talk to Helena about the diary until we know what we're dealing with.' She fisted her hand in his shirt. 'And being here has its advantages...'

Alexander leaned in and kissed her.

* * * * *

Alexander and Anita eventually returned to the farm, and to their astonishment, arrived to find a barn dance in full swing. They had placed bails of straw around the sides of the barn, with a band set up at one end, people enthusiastically swinging each other around the make-shift dance floor in the middle. Just outside, a barbeque was churning out a mountain of venison burgers, chicken, halloumi kebabs, and sweet potato fries.

Anita recognised a few of the dancers from earlier. They seemed to have already consumed a great deal of the dubious-looking rum punch sitting on a trestle table by the barn door.

Anita and Alexander made their way towards the side of the barn and were just about to sit on a bail of straw when a couple came and grabbed their hands, pulling them to the dance floor. The band pounded out a manic pace, and the middle-aged man who had grabbed Anita careered around the floor, just about taking her with him, narrowly avoiding the other dancers.

Despite herself, Anita had a broad grin across her face; there was nothing she loved more than to dance, and before she knew it, she was twirling him just as vigorously. Alexander seemed to be having just as good a time with his much younger, much more attractive partner, and a pang of irrational jealousy ripped through her.

The music stopped. She thanked the man for the dance and made her way quickly to Alexander before he and the girl could start dancing again. The girl's hand rested on Alexander's arm, and it was all Anita could do not to shove her aside. Instead, she took Alexander's hand, pulling him towards her as the next song began.

'Dance?' she suggested, her voice neutral, but her actions sending a clear message to the girl, whoever she was.

Alexander said nothing, choosing instead to pick Anita up and spin her around before placing her back on her feet. Then he whirled them deftly around the floor. Anita silently scolded herself for being so ridiculous. She knew Alexander had no interest in the other girl; she could read his energy for goodness' sake, but that didn't stop her from being glad his hands were now firmly on her waist.

They danced four consecutive songs in a row before helping themselves to some of the shady-looking punch. Anita was about to pull Alexander back for more, when, to her surprise, Anderson and Bass appeared in the doorway. Alexander's energy reacted the same way.

'Anderson,' said Alexander, not even trying to hide his shock. 'I didn't realise you were a member.'

Anderson looked sheepish. 'Yeah… have been for a while, actually. Didn't think this would be your bag though?'

'It's not. Long story.'

'And you, Bass?' asked Anita. 'Are you a member too?'

'Um… I… I'm not sure yet. Anderson introduced me to the concept. I like their goal; energy stability is for the good of everyone. But I asked Dad about the Institution and he flipped. I've never seen him react so badly to anything. Ever. I said I'd come along tonight and just see what it's all about, but I don't think it's going to be for me.'

This whole thing was getting crazier and crazier… Anita downed her punch. 'Come on,' she said to Bass. 'You're the only person I know who loves to dance as much as me; I think Alexander's had enough.'

She took Bass' hand and led him to the dance floor, over the moon when Alexander's energy reacted just as negatively to her dancing with Bass as hers had when he'd danced with that other girl. Bass took the lead, confidently spinning and lifting her as they looped around the floor.

By the time they stopped for a breather, Alexander was dancing with an older woman. Bass left Anita by the punch, said he would see her later, and made his way towards Anderson, who was beckoning him, clearly wanting to introduce him to someone or other.

Anita took a seat on a bale, and watched the spectacle the other, now decidedly drunk, dancers were making.

Almost immediately, a tall, finely built woman Anita didn't recognise sat down next to her. She was strangely familiar, but Anita didn't know why.

'You two make a great couple,' said the women, in a drawling accent, her tone anything but sincere, energy on the hostile side of neutral.

'Bass and I aren't a couple,' she replied evenly, not elaborating further, feeling more than a little uncomfortable.

'I wasn't talking about you and Bass, I was talking about you and Alexander.'

Anita turned to look at the women but said nothing; she didn't know what to say. The woman didn't exude anything approaching friendliness, and clearly had some ulterior motive, so she kept quiet.

'You've caused quite a commotion; lots of interest in who you are,' said the woman, looking at the dancers rather than at Anita.

'I'm sorry, but do I know you?' Anita asked, not unkindly.

'You know of me,' said the woman, finally turning her head to look at Anita.

Anita met her eyes and her energy reacted at once; they were eyes she knew well, eyes that also belonged to another. To Marcus.

'Melia,' said Anita, guardedly, 'it's a pleasure to meet you. I've heard a great deal about you.'

'And I you. And yet here you are, with Alexander.'

'Marcus and I broke up.'

'Yesterday.'

'Technically yesterday, but it's been coming for a while.'

Melia said nothing, her unwavering eyes seeming to penetrate Anita's soul, reading all they could find there. Where Marcus' eyes were always busy, flitting from here to there seeking entertainment, Melia's eyes were serious, old, wise, grounded. They were eyes that judged, taking no prisoners.

When she had read all she could, she sat back against the barn wall, turning her gaze back to the dance floor. 'He loves you. You do know that?'

Anita wanted to get up, to leave, to tell her this was none of her business. They had only just met, for Gods' sake. She had no right to Anita's feelings...

'He says he loves me, but he's also said many things that frighten me. He's changing as the days go by. Austin is moulding him into the kind of monster he wants for a son, the kind of person who thinks he can dictate who I can and cannot see, who trails my every move. He thinks it's acceptable to demand rent from farmers when their crops are failing and they have nothing to give. You, of all people, should know why I did what I did.'

'Really?' she spat. 'Pray tell me, why is that?'

Melia's sudden change took Anita off guard, but she opted for honesty. 'Because, from what others have told me, you left Austin for similar reasons.'

'In small part you're right, meaning in large part you're wrong. At least I finally got to meet you,' she said, standing up and leaving the barn, walking with the grace of a much younger woman.

Anita was pondering the conversation when Alexander sat next to her, handing her another punch and feeling the confusion in her energy.

'Are you okay?' he asked, concerned. 'What did she say?'

'Think she's pretty pissed about me dumping Marcus, and she said something cryptic about her relationship with Austin, something about them not really splitting up because of him turning into Tobias...'

Alexander raised his eyebrows. 'Tonight's been eye opening if nothing else,' he said, draining his glass. 'I had no idea the Institution was so well attended. I never would have pegged Anderson for a member.'

'And I can't believe Bass is here,' said Anita, 'especially against Elistair's wishes. Bass never keeps things from him. Although, it seems likely that Elistair is the Elistair in the diary, which makes him a bit of a hypocrite.'

CHAPTER 3

They woke the following morning, huddled together on a pile of straw, a raft of others strewn across the floor around them. The welcome smell of sizzling bacon wafted through the air, enticing the hung-over group to their feet.

If there had been any doubt that Alexander and Anita were a couple, they'd dispelled it, Bass and Anderson throwing raised eyebrows at each other as they walked past. Anita couldn't help but feel guilty; he was putting on a brave face, but Bass' energy dropped as he passed.

'He certainly likes you,' said Alexander, before pulling her to her feet.

'I know,' was all she said in reply, pursuing the spectacular smell of breakfast, that now included freshly baked bread, out of the barn. They ate greedily and drank several cups of tea, trying to quell the throbbing headaches the rum punch had left behind.

When they'd eaten two large bacon sandwiches each, they took themselves off to the copse of trees on top of the hill. They opened the diary, hoping today's excerpts might shed more light than those from the day before.

'11th February, 1333.

So much has happened since a year ago when I last wrote. But today, I again find myself with something to say, but not a soul to say it to, so again I turn to you in the forlorn hope that spilling my thoughts onto your pages might help.

The day after my last entry, I told my parents I was going to stay in Kingdom with Jeff. They went ballistic, calling me stupid and naïve first, then trying to win me round with reasons why it was dangerous to collude with members of the Institution.

None of it worked. They agreed not to run to Tobias, although they drew the line at letting me run their business in Kingdom; it would have always been a long shot, even if Jeff hadn't been in the equation...

So they left me in Kingdom when they returned to Empire, and I haven't seen them since. I know they've been in Kingdom, trading and lecturing, but they have never once tried to seek me out, so I haven't tried to contact them either.

I moved in with Jeff and joined the Institution, which, to be honest, is more of a social club than anything else. Yes, it has ideological undertones, and yes, we get together to discuss them, and yes, we try to garner support from powerful people, but other than that, all there is, is a great deal of drinking and dancing and playing cards.

I've never met the leadership, nor do I know who they are, so I don't know if they're really as dangerous as people make out. They let us get on with our lives and don't interfere with our affairs.

There's quite a large group of us now; me and Jeffrey, Elistair (a friend of Jeff's from his time studying), Rose (a promising Mind from an influential Mind family), Helena, Celia (Helena's cousin), Olivia (Rose's cousin), and the two most surprising members: Peter (son of Christiana, the ruling Body Descendant) and Theon (son of Philip, the ruling Sprit Descendant). Everyone knows the only reason they joined was because of their respective relationships with Olivia and Celia.

Helena would love to make it a full house, and has been working on Austin for as long as anyone can remember. He's infatuated with her and she boasts she has him wrapped around her little finger, but he won't join us for fear of what his father would do if he found out. In truth, this is all anyone can accuse us of, nothing illegal or dangerous as my parents made out. We involve high-profile people in conversations about progressive ideologies. We talk of democracy, elections, true free trade, but take no action to progress in that direction. We're a debaucherous, ideological drinking club, that is all.

And I write, oh useless diary, because of late, it's got more debaucherous than ever before. Last night, we were in Monty's back room, drinking and smoking and playing poker after dinner. I was returning from the bathroom and saw Jeffrey and Melia going into the bedroom reserved for Monty's owners.

Melia had her back against the door, looking up at him. Jeff had one hand on her stomach and one hand on the handle, then swung the door open and pushed her through. I didn't say anything, nor did I do anything. It felt like an out-of-body experience, like a bad dream. I floated back to everyone else and sat quietly, trying to work out what I should do.

Jeff can be like this. He's an outrageous flirt; I suppose it was only a matter of time before something like this happened... for all I know, this isn't the first time...

Anyway, a few minutes later, the door flew open, and a barman rushed in. Tobias' men were demanding entry to Monty's, to search the place.

We fled out of the back exit and scattered, each of us taking a different route through Kingdom's maze of streets to lose them. Peter and I ran together; he knows the streets far better than me, so I grabbed his hand and followed his weaves through this archway and that turning.

We could hear boots behind us; some of the guards had been sent round the back, chasing after us when they saw us leave. He pulled me into a tiny passage between two streets and hid us behind a lip in the wall, pressing himself against me to make sure we were out of view.

The guards passed, but we stayed where we were, just in case they came back the same way. The echoes of the guards' boots fell away, the blackness swallowing us until the only thing left was Peter pressed up against me. His breath and mine were deafening in the silence.

I looked up, surprised to find him looking down at me, intensity there I hadn't seen from him before, nor indeed expected from a man who was usually so meek and mild. He slid his hand to my neck, lowering his head towards mine. I pulled my eyes away, looking down at the floor, raising a hand to his chest to fully deter him. When I looked back up, to explain, he had already moved away, making for the other end of the dark passage, leaving me to walk the short distance home alone.

Jeff was already there when I arrived, I was pleased to see without the company of Melia. He said he had been returning from the bathroom when he'd heard the alarm and fled. I didn't say I knew he was lying; I didn't really see the point.

18th August, 1334.

My entries are becoming only annual events now, and I fear this entry is dangerous to write. I hide you, Diary, so you will never accidentally be found.

A few weeks after my last entry, Theon and Celia became engaged, and the rest of us followed like a stack of falling dominos. First Peter and Olivia, then Rose and Elistair, then finally Jeff and I.

For all of us, this had always been the likely conclusion, but for Helena, the story was quite different. I don't know what she'd expected to happen between her and Austin, given the influence Tobias has over his son... but she had not been expecting the announcement of his engagement to Melia, the daughter of a prominent Mind councillor. Helena appeared unaffected on the surface, but I knew the news was eating her alive… she finally admitted to me how devastated she was.

'We were together the night after they announced it,' Helena said. 'He told me he didn't want to be with her, but that he didn't have the luxury of choice. We both knew it was a lie; he'd made his choice, and it wasn't me…'

After the marriages, our partying died down a bit, and recently, babies have started making an appearance. First Celia and Theon's son, Alexander, then Austin and Melia's son, Marcus. It's hit Helena hard. She still sees Austin, even to this day. I think a part of her hopes that one day he'll finally choose her…

Anyway, life seems to have somehow become more serious. Tobias' guards are everywhere. He increases taxes almost by the month, any has outlawed any kind of Relic research. The other Descendants are notably absent. Christiana has moved permanently to her Empire residence, and Philip is barely seen at all.

So it was a surprise when Christiana summoned me to see her a couple of months ago. I had not a clue why, the only reason I could think was that, as my Godmother, she wanted to restore my ruin of a relationship with her best friend, my mother.

I didn't tell the others where I was going, not even Jeff; our relationship deteriorates almost daily. I headed to Christiana's enormous, square manor house on the outskirts of Empire. To my surprise, Peter greeted me at the door, asking if I knew why we were there. I told him I had no idea, and we went straight to see Christiana together.

Unusually, Christiana had invited us to eat dinner with her in her suite, dishes of food already laid out on a dresser when we entered. We followed her lead and helped ourselves to roast lamb before sitting at a small, round table, sending her quizzical looks between mouthfuls.

'I'm sure you're both wondering why you're here,' she started. She breathed a half laugh when she saw our faces. 'I'll skip the chitchat and get straight to the point. As you are aware,

Descendants have particular duties, especially to fulfil the oath we swear when we are crowned, that we will strive to return the Relic and free the world from the Gods.

'You also know that the Descendants don't take this oath seriously. In fact, I'm sure you'll have interpreted certain recent events as a move in the other direction, to ensure we never fulfil our oaths. I'm afraid you wouldn't be wrong.

'I've given the Relic little focus, have been entirely unconcerned about it, in fact. My mother, Patricia, the Body Descendant before me, was a radical, as was Tobias' father. This means Tobias and I both hold views that, until now, I haven't thought to question. However, given Tobias' recent actions, I've had a change of heart.'

Peter was losing patience, not catching her drift. 'Mother, what exactly are you trying to say? It sounds like you're going to throw in your lot with the Institution, for Gods' sake.'

'Well, that's the thing, I sort of am... and, you shouldn't call me Mother... Clarissa should.' Christiana inclined her head in my direction and Peter's mouth fell open. I frowned and tried to make some sense of what she'd said.

'Sorry, what?' I replied at last, lost for something more intelligent to say.

'I'm your mother, Clarissa, not his.'

'I'm not your son?' said Peter, looking as though his world was crumbling around him, as indeed it was. 'Then whose son am I?'

'We swapped you and Clarissa at birth. Her parents are your parents.'

I sat in silence as I took in what she was saying, astounded more by the way she had broken the news than the words escaping her mouth.

'Why?' was all I could whisper, a small shadow of a word in a sea of deceit and confusion.

'As I said, my mother was a radical. Power-obsessed. She never wanted the Descendants' reign to end. So she, Tobias, and I, hatched a plan to make it so. All we had to do was put an end to one of the lines, meaning the prophecy could never be fulfilled, and we would rule forever.

'As your mother was due to give birth around the same time as me, it was a perfect opportunity to swap the babies and tell the world the line was at an end. If Peter hadn't been a boy, we would have found someone else, but as Imogen was my closest confident, it fitted together perfectly in the end.'

'My father? Did he know about this? And Peter's father?'

'No. The only ones that knew were Tobias, my mother, Imogen, and I. It seemed more likely we would succeed that way.'

'Why are you telling us now?' said Peter. 'You got away with it; nobody knows, nobody suspects. Why not just continue as you have?'

'Because I've had reason to reflect. I was a radical, but with my mother gone and her voice no longer in my ear, I've heard views from a cross section of our world, from people who look up to me, and expect me to fulfil my vow. People think I'm their only hope. They plead with me, offer to help me, send me gifts, and all the while, Tobias is playing the tyrant to an ever-increasing degree.

'Even when my mother was alive, that was never the plan. The reason for the switch was twofold: to keep the Descendants in power, yes, but also to provide stability, so people could live free lives and not have to worry about years of famine and fear like we had before. It seems to me that Tobias will single-handedly bring down that stability, entirely for his own gain, and I can't sign up to that.'

'I felt so guilty for joining the Institution, like I was betraying you and all the good things you stand for; how laughable that seems now,' said Peter, throwing back his chair and storming out. He yanked the door open so hard it slammed into the wall with an almighty crash.

I looked at Christiana, my mother, and couldn't find a single thing to say. She didn't look repentant, or sad, or angry. She was impenetrable. I have no idea what she was thinking, or if this was all just some game to her in which we, and everyone else, were insignificant little pawns.

I placed my napkin down, pushed my chair back, and left the room, following Peter down the stairs and into the drawing room. A fire blazed in the colossal hearth, Peter sitting on a pile of furs in front of it.

There was a tension in the room that seemed to slow my movements, sucking at my limbs as I entered. Even for an energy reader, I'm sure that kind of sight would be rare; the energy of a man whose identity had just been cruelly and unceremoniously wrenched away from him. And not just any identity; an identity that made him one of the most powerful people in the world. An identity with a destiny that the entire world cared about…

He had a glass of whiskey in his hand and indicated for me to join him. I walked to the cabinet and poured myself a large amaretto over rocks of ice, the crystal glass shimmering in the fire's light as I quietly sat down beside him.

We drank in silence for a while, our eyes meeting every now and again, each trying to draw something from the other. Each of us was who the other had been only minutes before, but the new roles didn't even begin to suit us. Then again, nor did the old ones now.

In a few effortless words, our worlds had changed forever; everything we thought we knew was all wrong. The rules that had bound us seemed to vanish. Peter reached up and pushed a stray strand of hair behind my ear. He stared at me as he ran his fingers down my neck, as though I were a new person to him, like he had never really seen me before. Still, his eyes told me he expected me to pull away. But behind his eyes was a reckless blankness; our worlds were upside down, so how were we to tell what was right or wrong, or good or bad, or true or false?

I leaned towards him, kissed him, then pulled back, tracing my fingers across his lips. My eyes took in the lines of his face, a frown on my forehead as I tried to find the answers my mind sought. I kissed him again, his hand moving from my neck, down my back, to my waist, where featherlight caresses dulled my mind.

Was this wrong? Did it matter? I'd never been attracted to Peter; he was a forgettable man, although I'd long suspected he felt differently about me. But then, when something as big as who you are can be a lie, what could be wrong with something so small as a kiss, or a touch?

He pulled away and drained his glass, discarding the crystal on the hearth before drawing me back to him, kissing me once more. His hands unzipped my dress, pulling it open, sliding it away from my skin as he lowered me back onto the furs. He looked down at me, his eyes cloudy and unseeing, as though this might all be a dream. Then his hands took charge, his mouth insistent, my body compliant but refusing to feel anything at all.

After that, we returned to our daily lives and said nothing to anyone, least of all each other. We never spoke of what had happened, nor did we do it again; it was as though the whole encounter was some farfetched figment of our imaginations. Until that was, a few days ago, when I found out I'm pregnant, and not only that, but Olivia, Peter's wife, is too.

I went to see Peter and told him the baby is his and that I think we should switch the babies when they're born; we'd restore the rightful bloodline and the prophecy would be intact.

'What about Olivia? And Jeffrey? We can't do that to them,' Peter had immediately objected, his true, cautious nature showing through.

I'd laughed at that. 'Do you have any idea what Jeffrey does to me on a near nightly basis? He runs to the beds of countless other women, seducing his way around Kingdom, for no greater reason than because he can. We have a chance to set things right, to do something for the good of the world. Surely Olivia's feelings aren't worth jeopardising that?'

He'd objected, throwing his hands about and making a great show, but eventually he came around. Even he couldn't justify setting aside a chance to restore the prophecy, not when the only reason not to was to spare his wife.

23rd March, 1337.

Part of me can't believe I'm writing this down... if these words were to be discovered, Tobias would kill us all. But then again, the chance that he kill me, and nobody ever know what we plan to do, is worse.

After the birth, Jeffrey, and our daughter, Mia, and I, moved to the Wild Lands to stay well away from Tobias and Christiana. In the end, Gwyneth, Olivia and Peter's daughter, arrived three days before Mia. But with her birth came Olivia's death.

Peter was so distraught at the idea of having to give away his only remaining link to Olivia that he refused to switch the children, saying instead that we can bring out the secret when they're older. I would have reasoned with him, but Jeffrey turned up, ready for us to leave for Wild Air, so I had to go, silently swearing to find a way to make things right.

We had almost three good years in Wild Air, learning a great deal from the Spirit Leader and his monks, who live atop the tallest of the many mountains there. That was until Peter sent word that Tobias is on the war path. He's become paranoid about the prophecy and wants me and Mia dead. Christiana has been doing everything in her power to deter him, but Peter thinks we should switch the children now, finally seeing sense.

Two days ago, Jeffrey and I returned to Kingdom, the last place Tobias would expect to find us, and waited for Peter to return from Empire. He's been living in the farmhouse we used to visit, keeping Gwyn away from prying eyes; nobody is allowed to visit, and he never takes her where people can see her.

They arrived today, and tonight we plan to switch the children, in the Temple of the Body, at midnight. At least I'll be able to say happy birthday to my darling girl before I give her away. After that, I'll leave Jeffrey and return to the Wild with Gwyn. I'll become someone else and Tobias will never be able to find us. Mia will be safe posing as Gwyn, and Gwyn will be safe, hidden away with me. Peter can introduce his daughter to the world, and nobody will ever know the truth.'

The diary ended abruptly with no further entries, the full weight of what she had read hitting Anita hard. This neither confirmed nor denied that she was the true Body Descendant, but either way, if Clarissa was her mother, it would seem that Peter was her father, making Gwyn her half-sister…and…Gods, meaning Cordelia wasn't her blood grandmother.

Questions hammered at Anita like a battering ram. What happened to Clarissa? Was the switch successful? Had Clarissa really died? For all Anita knew, Clarissa and Jeffrey could be living out their lives in the Wild Lands, even now…

Alexander had been watching her since she'd finished reading, waiting for her to speak. She met his gaze but didn't really see him, her eyes flitting from his left eye to his right, brow furrowed, holding her breath as she processed the implications.

He lifted his hand to her cheek, caressing her skin, the motion snapping her out of her thoughts. She raised her hand to his and pulled it away. 'Gwyn and I are sisters,' she said, brow still furrowed, the notion not making any sense to her.

Alexander suppressed a laugh. 'It would seem so. And Peter is your father. I'm not sure which is worse.'

Anita raised her eyebrows, shaking her head. 'Bitch face...my sister.'

'You're right, that bit is worse.'

CHAPTER 4

Anita and Alexander pushed open the wood and glass door to the potting shed. It was hidden around the side of the farmhouse, the entrance partially screened by an enormous trailing wisteria. As they stepped inside, Anita was struck by how light and airy the unexpectedly large space was. Roughly whitewashed walls bounced the light from four skylights above, windows and a door the other side looking out over another part of the garden. On closer inspection, the garden looked to be accessible only through the potting shed, or, more accurately, through the comfortably decked out potting room.

Down one end were two old, worn linen sofas with a low, white table in between. Bits of broken pot, jars of seeds, flower heads, and a liberal sprinkling of compost covered it. Shelves full of terracotta pots and dressers with hundreds of small drawers took up most of the wall space. Anita assumed they contained seeds and plant specimens. Potting benches stood in the middle and at the other end, each with piles of pots, compost, sand and stones.

They entered to find Helena unceremoniously dropping seeds, one at a time, into a wooden tray full of compost. She didn't look up until she had gently pressed each one down and given the tray a drenching, using a metal watering can that had seen better days. Helena placed the tray to one side, finally acknowledging her visitors by indicating that they should take a seat on one of the sofas.

Helena moved to the large Belfast sink that stood in front of the window overlooking the secret garden. She filled up an old copper kettle and placed it on the small gas ring that stood to the side of the sink. Without saying a word, she disappeared out of the door into the garden beyond.

Anita and Alexander looked at each other, bemused. 'Should we follow her?' Anita asked.

Alexander shook his head. 'I think we should wait here.'

'She seems nervous,' said Anita, alarmed. Helena had been her closest friend and mentor for almost her entire childhood. In that time, Anita could think of perhaps two other occasions when Helena had seemed even a tiny bit nervous, unsure, or out of control.

'I'm not surprised. She wants something from you and she doesn't know how to make you give it to her,' he said, cynically.

Anita gave a little shrug of her shoulders; his analysis was as good an explanation as any. They didn't have time to dwell as the door swung open and Helena returned with a large bunch of freshly picked peppermint.

Helena removed the boiling water from the stove, stuffed the mint into a large, chipped teapot, filled it with water, and swirled it around for good measure. She picked up three mugs in her other hand and joined them on the sofas, leaving the mint to infuse before pouring. Once she'd settled herself, she looked expectantly at Anita.

'I read the diary,' Anita said, 'and other than delivering the disturbing news that Gwyn is my half-sister and Peter my father, assuming I truly am one of the little girls in the diary, we learned very little. It didn't say if the child switch was successful or otherwise, and therefore neither affirmed nor denied that I'm the Body Descendant. It didn't say what happened to Clarissa and Jeffrey. It didn't explain why you had me steal a memory from Austin... it's sparked more questions, answering none of the ones I already had.'

Helena picked up the teapot, swirled it again, and poured the contents into the mugs. She ignored the stray leaves that found their way out of the spout along with the tea. She handed a mug to each of them, inhaling deeply.

'I'm sorry the diary didn't answer any of your questions. Clarissa wanted you to have it. She gave it to me before she went to the temple that night. She told me to give it to you when you were old enough to understand...'

'... which you didn't,' Anita blurted, unable to contain her anger.

'Which I didn't,' Helena agreed, tense shoulders and still body betraying her discomfort. 'You'll soon understand why.' She looked down into her tea, taking a tentative sip of the piping hot contents. 'I'll answer all your questions, anything you want to know, but I need you to open the cylinder in your mind. We believe you hold the key to saving the world.'

'I've heard that one somewhere before,' Anita said, her eyes stone cold. 'Let's start with you answering our questions, and then maybe we'll agree to help you.'

Helena sighed, visibly irritated.

'What was in the brass cylinder you convinced me to steal from Austin?' said Anita, feeling from Helena's energy that she was out of options, and furious about it.

'Okay. If that's what you want, ask away, but I'm not starting with the cylinder.'

Anita saw no point in arguing. She would get her answer soon enough, so she started with her mother. 'Fine. Whose daughter am I? Clarissa's or Olivia's?'

'Clarissa's.'

'How can you be sure? The diary said Clarissa was going to swap her daughter with Olivia's that night in the temple, but it doesn't say she was successful.'

'Peter told me and Elistair you were never swapped. Not at your birth, because after Olivia's death, Peter couldn't do it. Then, after the fire, he thought they should grant Cordelia the courtesy of looking after the child Jeffrey had spent more time with.'

'What fire?' said Alexander, his energy full of excited dread. 'The fire at the temple? The one my father died in?'

Helena turned her head to take in Alexander. 'Yes, the same fire. Maybe I should show you all I know from when Clarissa gave me the diary.'

'If you can,' Alexander nodded.

'What do you mean, show us all you know?' said Anita, confused.

'It's a relatively new technique,' said Alexander, 'where you can replay memories in a joint meditation. It's a bit like opening a brass cylinder, but the leader determines what you see.'

'Okay,' said Anita, 'if that's the best way.'

'With three of us, we shouldn't need to touch,' said Helena, folding her legs under her on the sofa, 'assuming you two know what you're doing?'

'Of course,' said Alexander, shooting Helena a look as he took hold of Anita's hand and crossed his legs. Anita followed suit.

'Good. See you on the other side then,' said Helena, all three of them closing their eyes.

Anita felt a plunging rush, her insides flipping as she came to a hurtling stop beside Alexander, in what looked like a very ordinary office. They looked around, taking in shelves packed full of books and brass cylinders. Complex academic diagrams on ragged, yellowing paper covered the white walls, and a shabby wooden desk stood in the middle of the room. Behind the desk sat Helena, already pulling a selection of brass cylinders towards her.

'Is this your centre?' asked Anita, trying to notice every detail.

'Yes, but then again, no,' said Helena. 'Once your centre has come together, you no longer have anything other than a centre.'

'All the places in your mind amalgamate into a new centre,' said Alexander. 'Sometimes they just add to your existing one, and sometimes a new place takes over, but from then on, you only have one place in your mind. That's why developing new skills afterwards is more difficult, because your centre is heavily biased towards the skills you've already developed, and there's no other place for your mind to entertain new abilities.'

'Was this your centre before?' asked Anita.

'No. I've come a long way from where I began,' she said, not elaborating further. 'Sit if you wish,' she said, pointing to two scared wooden chairs before picking up a cylinder and placing it in her palm. The cylinder unrolled, jolting them to a dimly lit sitting room. It was pokey and had mismatched furniture.

Before they could ask Helena where they were, there was a knock on the door, and a younger, more cavalier looking Helena, rushed to fling it open. She obviously hadn't expected the person who stood on the other side. 'Clarissa,' said Helena, doing nothing to hide her surprise, 'what are you doing here so late? I didn't even realise you were back in Kingdom...'

'I'm sorry,' said Clarissa, an urgency about her. 'I won't keep you long. I need to ask a favour.' She stepped through the door, making sure it was firmly closed behind her before continuing.

'Of course, anything,' said Helena, 'but what are you doing here? Tobias is on the warpath... what have you done?'

'I can't explain now,' said Clarissa, pulling a beaten-up notebook from her leather travelling bag, 'but when you read this, you'll understand.'

Helena took the notebook, almost snatching it from Clarissa's hands, flicking through it with an edge of disdain. 'A diary?' she asked, irritably. 'Clarissa, what in the Gods' names is going on?'

'I need you to look after that for me... and promise to give it to Mia when she's old enough to understand. I'm going to the Wild Lands for good, and I'm taking Gwyn with me. We need to throw Tobias off the scent.'

'Peter's coming with you too?' asked Helena, not fathoming her meaning.

'No, of course not. Peter will stay here with Mia. We're switching the girls to keep them safe and because we have to protect the prophecy. Please, just read the diary. Don't tell anyone about it, and give it to Mia when she's older.'

'Clarissa, you're not making any sense. You're leaving without Mia?'

'I have no choice.'

'What about Jeff? Where's he?'

'I'm leaving him here too. You know as well as I do that he's been sleeping with half of Kingdom. Even in the short time we've been back, he's already been with Camilla; Tobias' wife, of all people...

'I finally confronted him about it. He said he's never done anything unless it was on Institution business. He even tried to make out that his latest betrayal was because he was trying to uncover Tobias' secrets through Camilla. Ridiculous... like Tobias would ever tell Camilla anything.'

'But he knows you're leaving?' asked Helena, tentatively.

'No. He would try to convince me to stay, and I don't have the patience for another word from him. He's made his bed.'

'Who else knows about this?' asked Helena.

'Nobody. Peter and I are the only ones. Look, Helena, we found out Peter's not the true Body Descendant, I am, so we're switching the girls back to reinstate the bloodline.'

'What?'

'I told you, it's all explained in the diary.'

'Fine, I'll read the diary, I won't tell anyone, and I'll give it to Mia when she's older. I'm sure I can manage that, but are you really sure this is the only way?'

'There's something else,' said Clarissa, ignoring Helena's question and checking her watch before continuing. 'I'm planting the brass cylinder the Spirit Leader gave me in Mia's mind before I leave. I need you to help Mia open it when the time is right.'

'But you don't know what's in it!' said Helena. 'It could be something dangerous.'

'And if it is, Mia will handle it. She's already exhibiting exceptional skills, far beyond anything I've seen before, and with your help I know she'll find a way.'

Helena looked sceptical, but reluctantly nodded her agreement.

'I have to go,' said Clarissa, hugging Helena. She made for the door, turning before she got there. 'It's Mia's third birthday tomorrow,' she said regretfully. 'At least I'll be able to say happy birthday before I say goodbye, and who knows, perhaps our actions will one day change the world...'

A flash of light momentarily blinded Anita, who found herself back in the office with Alexander and Helena when it cleared. She blinked several times to encourage her eyes to refocus.

'Tobias was having an affair?' asked Alexander, frivolously.

Anita inwardly rolled her eyes; Alexander was spending too much time with Cleo if he thought that an appropriate opening question after what they had just seen.

Helena smiled. 'Yes, Tobias had a mistress for years, and when Camilla found out, she decided she could play at the same game.'

'Who was it with?' asked Anita. This was, after all, first rate gossip.

Helena's eyes twinkled. 'Anderson's mother.' She let the news sink in. 'She was quite a bit older than Tobias, but held some great allure for him; no idea what, but he kept her in a plush apartment in Kingdom, right next to his own residence. In fact, that's where Anderson lives today.'

'Wow,' said Anita, relishing the idea of what Cleo's face would look like when she relayed this to her later. 'That's why Anderson's allowed to study the Relic?'

'Yep,' nodded Helena. 'In fact, a lot of Anderson's early education was with Elistair and Jeff. He used to follow them around like a puppy, lapping up anything they said and did. Jeffrey and Elistair met because they were both conducting energy research. One day, Tobias turned up with Anderson and told them if they wanted to keep their funding, they would teach Anderson about the energy. Anderson was harmless, so they went along with it; I think they quite enjoyed someone doting on them, if I'm honest.'

'Wait,' said Alexander, 'Anderson's not Tobias' son, is he?'

Helena actually chuckled. 'I have no idea. You wouldn't be the first person to suggest it, but he doesn't look much like Tobias. Allegedly, Anderson's mother wasn't short of suitors, much to Tobias' rage, so it was more likely one of the others.'

'If Clarissa trusted you with the diary, why didn't she tell you what was in the cylinder?' asked Anita, dampening the mood as she changed the subject.

'Clarissa was adamant you were the only person who should know its contents and when the time was right, you would open it and share its message with the world. I didn't press her as she was resolute, and anyway, I don't think even she knew what was in it.'

'But that was the night of the fire?' asked Alexander.

'Yes,' said Helena, reaching for another cylinder, 'but again, it's best if I show you.' The cylinder unrolled, jolting them uncomfortably into a new memory.

They were at the alter in the Body Temple. Clarissa was crouching, Anita's toddler self sitting on a step, looking as though she were having a whale of a time, excited to see what would happen next. Clarissa pulled her into a hug, holding her tightly until she heard the thud of footsteps behind her and spun around to see who was there. She was confronted, not with Peter and Gwyn as she had expected, but with Austin and Tobias.

Clarissa's eyes went wide, knowing without doubt their intention, pushing her daughter behind her and barking at her to run and hide. The young girl's features contorted, the careless joy of moments before chased away by confused fear as her mother shoved her away. She looked up, begging for Clarissa to scoop her into her arms and hold her tightly, to tell her it was all a joke, that it was going to be okay. She was met with a stone wall of icy resolve, Clarissa directing all her energy into propelling Mia away. Mia's face crumpled.

Austin and Tobias approached Clarissa slowly, menacingly, making sure there was nobody else in the temple to get in the way. Mia finally turned and ran, the toddler out of breath from panic before she even started moving. Clarissa squared up to the Mind Descendants, forcing herself to drag her eyes from her daughter, resolved to her fate.

'Clarissa,' said Tobias, triumphantly, bloodlust in his eyes as he came ever closer. 'We've been trying to chat with you for some time.'

'Oh?' she replied, a tremor in her voice.

'And you've been nowhere to be found,' he said, a terrifying savagery behind every word.

'I've been in the Wild Lands,' said Clarissa, eyeing Austin, who was tracking Mia's course, 'with the man who's just had an affair with your wife.'

The tactic worked. Austin's eyed snapped round to look at Tobias, to watch what his father would do next, surprise plastered across his features. Without warning, Tobias stepped forward and punched Clarissa in the face, a right hook that sent her reeling to the ground, her head hitting the cold stone floor with a sickening crack.

Mia stopped in her tracks, turning at the sound, crying out when she saw her mother on the ground. Clarissa's eyes found her daughter, horror contorting her features. 'Run,' she screamed, as Tobias stepped forward to finish what he'd started, Mia sinking to the floor next to a stone bench, crawling underneath and huddling against its side.

Tobias pulled out a knife and put it to Clarissa's throat, effortlessly swiping aside her frantic protest as he took her life. Austin pursued Mia rather than look at what his father had done. He'd almost reached her, now backed as far under the bench as it would let her go, tears streaming down her face, when a loud thud sounded behind him. Austin whirled round to see, to his astonishment, his father face down on the floor, a knife protruding from his back, blood seeping from him. Austin scanned the temple to find the knife's owner, Theon stepping out of the shadows towards him.

'What have you done?' said Theon, reaching Clarissa's body and feeling no pulse. 'You've killed her,' he half whispered. He turned his head expectantly towards Austin, a look of mistrust and disbelief across his face when he heard Mia's sobs. Theon's eyes flicked around, finding Mia before turning his attention back to Austin, disbelief filling him.

'I... we...' Austin faltered. For a moment he seemed almost as shocked as Theon, but as he looked down and took in his father's lifeless form, his uncertainty vanished. He hurtled towards Theon with furious passion.

Theon was caught off guard, only just making it to his feet in time to meet Austin's assault, falling to the floor at the impact of his attacker's first punch. Theon bore very little resemblance to Alexander. Where his son was tall and muscular, Theon was average height, with a slight build and no interest in Body disciplines at all. Austin, on the other hand, was muscle clad and interested in any Body discipline involving violence, the fight between them anything but fair.

Theon never again made it to his feet, Austin on him before he could try, landing punch after punch on Theon's untrained flesh. Austin carried on long after Theon's body went limp. He was bashing Theon's head against the alter steps when a man Anita didn't recognise appeared at the back of the temple.

'By the Gods,' said the man, as he took in the scene, inadvertently alerting Austin to his presence. Austin snapped out of his blood rage, dropping Theon and snatching up the knife his father had used to end Clarissa's life.

'Stay back,' Austin shouted frantically, shooting a sideways glance at Mia, judging whether he could get to her and get out before the others reached him.

The man's gaze found Mia's terrified form. Rage took hold of his face when he saw the little girl. He plunged forwards, towards the front of the temple, towards the only adult survivor in the horrific scene.

'Jeffrey, no!' shouted Austin, as he whirled and fled, no time to pick up Mia as Jeffrey careered after him. Austin rounded a corner and grabbed a fire stand, pulling it over, throwing the flames towards the generous swathes of fabric that adorned the nearest archway.

Jeffrey didn't seem to notice the flames as he pursued, the clear night sky now visible through the temple entrance ahead. He lost sight of Austin, but kept up the pursuit. He'd almost reached the entrance when a movement caught his attention, something coming at him from behind the nearest pillar. He swerved, ducked his head, and pulled his hands up to protect his face, but wasn't quick enough to avoid Austin's blow. A solid, terrible force met with his head, his hands barley reducing the impact of the large candle stick against his temple. It knocked him backwards, his feet going out from under him, sending him plummeting to the ground.

Jeffrey tried to sit up, then slumped back to the floor. Austin appeared from behind the pillar, discarded the silver candlestick, and pounced. He pulled out his knife and dug it into Jeffrey's torso without a second's hesitation. He stabbed and stabbed, stopping only when he heard running footsteps closing in.

'You know Mia's not even your daughter,' Austin hissed, 'she's Peter's. Only right you should know before you die,' he said, smiling as he pushed himself to his feet and fled.

The footsteps belonged to Elistair, who could do little to hide his horror at the sight that lay before him. He fell to his knees next to his best friend, desperately trying to staunch the bleeding, but it was futile and Jeffrey knew it too. He caught Elistair's hand to stop him.

'Mia's not mine,' Jeffrey whispered, breathing laboured, blood trickling from his lips.

'What?' said Elistair, leaning closer to hear the words.

'Austin told me Mia isn't mine. She's Peter's.'

'He was lying,' said Elistair. 'Of course he's lying.'

'Look after her,' said Jeffrey, 'even if she's not mine, I still love her. And now Clarissa's...' his voice caught.

'Of course,' said Elistair, squeezing Jeff's hand. 'I'll look after her. I'll make sure she's safe. Austin won't be able to find her.'

Jeffrey relaxed, his eyes closing, the corners of his mouth twitching upwards to form the faintest trace of a smile before his energy finally left him, seeping away into the night. Elistair slumped to the floor, still clutching at Jeff's hand, tears rolling down his cheeks.

The memory paused, a stillness settling over the scene before another blinding white light flashed. Anita was surprised to find herself back in the potting shed when their eyes adjusted, sunshine blazing through the skylights above. Helena sat silently, looking away, sipping her tea.

Anita's eyes bored into Helena, harsh disbelief directed at the women she had formally held in such high regard, but Helena's back was to them, not ready to face them.

How could she be so insensitive? It was as if she was oblivious to Anita and Alexander's deep, personal connections to the memories. As though she were not imparting information that had been shrouded in secrecy, hidden from the listeners for over twenty years.

Anita took Alexander's hand, and he pulled his head up to look at her, his eyes hollow. She sent a nudge to the edge of his energy field, trying desperately to help. She felt him respond, so she pushed further in towards his core, closing her eyes and wrapping herself around him, willing his spirit upwards.

To her relief, Alexander pushed back, entangling their fields together. They held there for a moment before Alexander reached out and pulled Anita to him, an eruption of energy barrelling through them as their bodies collided. The impact was so strong it was like being kicked in the chest; they rebounded instantly at the strength of the shock.

Helena snapped around to see what had happened, intrigue painted across her face. 'What was that?' she asked, her previous, sad disposition chased away on the wings of her interest.

'What was what?' said Anita, meeting Helena's gaze with a challenge.

Helena looked like she was about to push the point, then dropped it, her shoulders slumping.

'So, what happened to me?' asked Anita, slipping her hand into Alexander's, entwining their fingers. 'Elistair went back and got me out?'

'Yes,' said Helena. 'The whole place was on fire, smoke everywhere; he almost didn't make it...

Afterwards, he was distraught, we all were, although the true depths of what we had lost took weeks to sink in.

'It hit Celia the hardest. She and Theon had become so complexly intertwined through meditation that it was like a literal part of her was lost when Theon died. She sank into a black hole that nobody could pull her out of. She spent days by herself, meditating, alone, and when anyone tried to draw her back, she said she was looking for Theon's energy. She was sure, if only she tried hard enough, she could reconnect with him. She never found a way, but trying sapped all of her energy.

'At the end, she meditated for days at a time, refusing to speak to anyone, or eat anything, or in any way acknowledge the real world. One day she just didn't come back. Her body was found lying on the floor as though meditating in the love pose, her right hand open by her side, waiting for someone to reach down and take hold.'

Helena was talking more to herself now than to Anita and Alexander. She got up and leaned against the door that led to the secret garden, looking vacantly out on the greenery beyond. She stopped talking, the air still, her energy sad and lonely.

Alexander's energy was the lowest she had ever felt from him; it was flat, and worse, it was empty; no life, no fight. That he was hurt and distressed was obvious; the pain radiated out of him, sucking at Anita's energy, and further deflating Helena's.

'What happened next?' asked Anita. 'After Elistair got me out?'

'Peter hadn't intended to go ahead with the switch anyway; he couldn't bear to let Gwyn go,' said Helena, still staring at the garden. 'Elistair visited Peter's residence the following day. He agreed with Peter that he would take you back to Empire, to Cordelia, Jeffrey's mother, who nobody knew anything about.'

'But surely Austin checked known associates and close family of my parents?' said Anita. The idea that Austin would let her go without proof she was dead was ludicrous.

'Of course he did. He searched the homes and workplaces of everybody he could think of, but Cordelia wasn't Jeffrey's birth mother. He was the son of her closest friend. She took him in after his mother died, protesting in one of the food riots. There was no official record to link Jeffrey back to Cordelia and none of his friends, apart from Elistair, even knew she existed. She hadn't spoken to Jeffrey in years; not since he'd married Clarissa.'

'Why?' asked Anita. 'What had my mother done to turn Cordelia against her? I've never known Cordelia to dislike anybody that much.'

'It wasn't Clarissa per se, more that she hated the Institution. The riot Jeffrey's birth mother died in was rumoured to have been organised by us. Cordelia was sure his ongoing involvement with the Institution was Clarissa's fault. She didn't even go to his funeral because she knew we would all be there.'

'If Cordelia had disowned Jeffrey and hated Clarissa, how did Elistair convince her to take me in?'

'She wasn't happy about it, but Cordelia couldn't refuse her son's dying wish. Of course, Elistair left out the part about you not really being Jeff's daughter. Elistair convinced Cordelia that he was done with the Institution. He said keeping you safe would be a kind of penance for his involvement. I think Cordelia found some solace in that. They've been friends ever since.'

'Didn't she insist on knowing what had happened?' The Cordelia Anita knew was almost as bad as Cleo in her need for gossip, even if she were a little better at putting on a respectable front.

'Elistair told her most of it, and that the only people who knew the truth were him, me, Peter, and Cordelia. He told her you'd be in danger if people realised who you were, so she never spoke about them, even to you.'

'That explains why she was always so cagey about my parents,' said Anita. 'How did the Institution survive after the fire? It sounds like most of the members were killed, or left.'

'Don't underestimate the Institution,' said Helena with a wry smile, 'its membership is bigger and more widespread than you could possibly imagine. For those in our immediate intake, you're right, it wasn't easy.

'A few years later, I moved to Empire as Head Body Councillor. I read the diary and wanted to keep a close eye on you. Rose, Melia and I were the only three left and our relationships were strained. A couple of years later, Melia and Austin split up, and since then, the air has cleared between us; we agreed to put the past behind us. We turned our efforts to recruiting the next generation of the Institution.

'I tested the water with you too, Anita, but Elistair knew what I was doing, hence why he was so keen to give you a job at the observatory. That, and his never ending hope that you might one day marry his son.'

Anita raised her eyebrows but stayed quiet; her relationship with Bass was the least of her worries right now. Helena sat back down on the sofa and drained the last of the tea from her mug.

'But how did Austin, Tobias, and the others find out about what was going on at the Temple?' Anita asked, when it was clear Helena wasn't going to continue.

Helena met Anita's eyes for a moment, looking uncomfortable, edgy, like her fight-or-flight response was kicking in and she hadn't yet decided which of the two options to choose. She was tense in a way Anita had never seen before; her energy was... scared.

'They found out because I told them.'

'What?' said Anita and Alexander together.

'The memory I asked you to steal from Austin was the memory of me telling him Clarissa was planning to disappear. It's what Austin has been using against me for years, threatening that if the Institution got too big for its boots, he would tell other key members about my betrayal. It would, he thinks—and I think he's right—turn the Institution's focus inwards, causing a split, and we can't afford for that to happen; we can't lose focus on stabilising the energy.'

'But... why? Why would you do that to Clarissa? You must have known they would kill her...' Anita could barely get the words out.

'I didn't think they would go that far, and I loved Austin. I thought if I told him about Clarissa, he would choose me over Melia, and Tobias would think I was worthy.'

Anita sat back at Helena's brutal honesty.

'Doesn't seem to have worked out quite as you planned,' Alexander said harshly, a venomous look contorting his face. Anita put a hand on his arm, feeling the ferocity of his anger.

'No. You're right. It didn't work out as I planned,' said Helena. 'Austin was pleased Tobias's vision had been fulfilled, but was beside himself at his loss. In part, he blamed me. If I'd never told them about Clarissa, none of what happened would have taken place, and Tobias, Clarissa, Jeffrey, Theon, they'd all probably still be here...'

'How did Theon, Jeffrey, and Elistair know to go to the temple that night?' asked Anita.

'Theon had been in the Temple of the Spirit. He was leaving to go home and heard something in the Body Temple, so went to see what was going on. Elistair and Jeffrey turned up because Christiana had been at Tobias' residence for dinner when I arrived. She overheard our conversation and left shortly after I did. She went straight to Peter, to tell him Austin and Tobias were planning to go to the temple. Peter told Elistair and Jeffrey. All of that took time, so they got there after Austin and Tobias.'

'Do the records say I'm dead?' asked Anita.

'Yes, and no. It says Clarissa and Jeffrey's daughter, Mia, is dead. That's what Clarissa called you until her death. When Elistair brought you to live in Empire, he created a new birth record, taking advantage of the death of another woman who had died of childbirth around the time of your birth. Her baby had died with her, but Elistair doctored the record to make it appear the baby lived, calling that baby Anita.'

'What about the baby's father?'

'There was no record of the father. Peter told Christiana the truth years later, to reassure her the bloodline was intact. Towards the end, in some moment of madness, when Christiana knew her death was near, she told Austin the prophecy was intact, that the plan had failed. That's what brought everyone to Empire, because Christiana wanted to find you. Austin played along, but his real motive was, and still is, to finish what his father started.'

Silence settled over the room for several long moments.

'And now,' said Helena, 'the energy is dropping rapidly and there are new reports coming in every day, from all over the world, that the situation is getting worse. In Wild Wood, some of the ancient trees have started to rot. In Wild Water, the fish stocks are lower than they have ever been. Here, the farmers that don't own their land outright are being crippled by debts; they aren't even producing enough to pay the rent they owe. We've got to act, now, before this goes too far. We've got to find out what's in that cylinder in your head, Anita.'

'Why do you think it contains the answer?' she asked, full of suspicion. 'What do you think it contains? Where does it come from? For all we know, opening it could kill me.'

Helena sighed. 'When your mother and Jeffrey went to the Wild Lands, they spent a great deal of time in Wild Air, right next to the Cloud Mountain, where the Spirit Leader lives. Clarissa spent virtually all of her time there meditating in the Cloud Temple. If you can believe the Spirit Leader's account of events, her meditative maturity progressed quickly, to the point where a previous Spirit Leader requested she meditate with him.'

Alexander frowned. 'I thought Spirit Leaders kept their position until they died...?'

'Strictly speaking they do, however, this particular Spirit Leader's 'death' wasn't conventional, in that he didn't fully die.'

Helena laughed at the looks on Anita's and Alexander's faces. 'He went into a deep meditation and never came back. They kept his body alive, and a few of the very skilled among them found him in meditation occasionally. He would tell them to keep him going for as long as they could; he had something important to tell someone, whenever they found their way to him.

'They kept him going for decades, new followers taking over when the old ones died, his body wasting away to virtually nothing. And then, one day, the current Spirit Leader connected with him and he requested to meditate with Clarissa. It was unheard of; he hadn't requested to meditate with a single person in all that time, so they knew Clarissa must be the one he'd been waiting for.

'She started regularly meditating with the Spirit Leader, not breathing a word to anyone about what happened in the meditations, becoming more and more withdrawn as the days went on. Then, after twelve days, she came out of his chamber and announced he was gone. He'd drifted off during the meditation, telling her it was finally his time to join the Gods.

'The monks, not to mention the current Spirit Leader, questioned Clarissa endlessly about what was said, what had happened, and the purpose of his staying alive for so long. All she would tell them was that he had given her a precious gift that she had to store until the time was right to pass it on. There was only one person who she could pass the gift on to, and if she tried to give it to anyone else, the cylinder would combust. She wasn't even supposed to tell them it was a brass cylinder. They pounced on her slip, trying to force her to impart more, but from that moment on she refused to say anything more about what had happened.

'Shortly afterwards, Clarissa and Jeffrey returned from the Wild. In the temple, on the night she'd planned to leave forever, Clarissa planted the cylinder in your head, Anita. You must be the one it was meant for.'

'Or maybe she never got the chance,' said Anita. 'What if I don't have it?'

'You do. I know that as well as you do.'

'And what do you think's in it?' asked Anita, neither confirming nor denying Helena's suspicions.

'I don't know. It must be something about how we can stabilise the energy though, or how we send the Relic back.'

'What if it's not? What if it's totally unrelated?'

'Then we start again. We turn over every stone until we find some way to stabilise the energy and save our world.'

'How do you know he gave my mother the cylinder?'

'Aside from the fact she told me, it's the worst kept secret at the Cloud Mountain; monks are surprising gossips.'

'And the rest of it?' asked Alexander. 'The memories you just showed us don't belong to you, so they must have been Austin's? I can't imagine he would have just given you the memory of the death of his father.'

'They're not Austin's,' said Helena, standing, pacing. 'For my whole academic career, I've been interested in memories. Not very conventional for a Body scholar, but then again, the mind's a muscle too. It's always fascinated me, how it can be trained and utilised.

'Anyway, quite near the beginning of my career, I found a way to extract memories from people after they had passed away. It has to be soon after, before the last trace of their energy has left them, but so long as there's something left, if you know what you're doing, you can force your way into their mind and take what you want. They have no energy left to resist. But you have to be quick, as if you're still in there when the last of their energy leaves, you die too; it's not without its risks.'

'You stole Clarissa and Jeffrey's memories?' Anita blurted. 'As if you hadn't done enough already, you violated them when they were all but dead?'

'I followed Tobias and Austin to the temples. I stayed outside to start with... I didn't want to get caught, but eventually I went inside. Clarissa was lying there, dying, and I needed to know what had happened.'

'Only to make sure your secrets were safe,' said Anita, bitterly.

'That's not the only reason,' said Helena, unable to meet their eyes.

'Why have you never documented and shared your discovery?' asked Alexander. 'It's ground-breaking research; the council would certainly want to know about it.'

'Because it's immoral, and I can't trust them not to abuse it. Imagine what Austin would do with such an ability, the things he would learn.'

'That's rich coming from you,' said Anita.

Helena looked away again, her energy full of guilt.

'Who did your orders come from?' asked Alexander. 'You said you couldn't know what the others had been asked to do. Why?'

'I don't know who the orders ultimately come from. I'm not allowed to know, nor is anyone but the very top echelons of the organisation.'

'You're not in charge of the Institution now?' asked Anita, an unsettled feeling spreading across her insides.

'No. Nowhere near. I have a handler I report to and take orders from. He, I believe, takes orders directly from our leader and sits on the Guiding Council, but I don't even know that much for sure.'

'The Guiding Council?'

'A group that advises our leader. It's surprisingly democratic; they vote on the best way to proceed, but if there's a disagreement, the leader has the casting vote.'

'And you don't know who this leader is?'

'No. I don't know who it is, where they live, what they do for a living. I think the same leader has been around since your parents were involved, but that's all I know.'

'And you've never thought to question the motives of your illustrious leader...? Why so secretive? What if they're a total psychopath? What if Austin or someone equally poisonous is the leader?'

'It's possible, but unlikely. I've been in the Institution all my adult life, and I've never been asked to do anything that contradicts with our aim of energy stability. I reported my misdemeanour and Austin's brass cylinder a few weeks after the fire, and we've been trying to recover it ever since. Melia had orders to try, I've tried, you've now tried, Anita. Everything we've ever been asked to do has been to benefit the organisation; there's nothing to suggest the leader is benefitting personally from our actions.'

'How do you know that? You don't know the orders of everyone else, you said that yourself,' said Alexander, agitated.

'I don't know for sure, but sometimes you just have to take a leap of faith, otherwise, what's the point of living? You've got to believe in something.'

'And what if I believe the way to energy stability is to send the Relic back?'

'Fine, you may really believe that, but what have you or any of the other Descendants ever done to send the Relic back? Austin banned energy research, for goodness' sake. You might be friends with Anderson, and I know you've been finding covert ways to support his research, but it's not enough. It's too little too late.'

Anita could read Alexander's conflict, but Helena was right. The Descendants had done nothing to find a way to send the Relic back. Most Descendants were greedy, selfish people who cared most about sustaining their own comfortable situations. The idea they could no longer rule by right was terrifying to them.

'Who's your handler?' asked Anita, curious who Helena had to answer to.

'I'm afraid I can't tell you that. We're not allowed to reveal to anyone the identity of the next level up. I don't know who Melia or Rose's handlers are either.'

'But everyone here at the farm knows that you, Rose and Melia are all handlers. You must be the handlers for everyone here.'

'We never confirm or deny anything to anyone. Nobody should know who reports to whom, but in reality, at this level, the secret is less important. Everyone suspects I'm a senior member of the Institution anyway, so it won't surprise anyone that I've recruited a few people.'

'And if we agree to help? You become our handler?'

'I suppose so, yes. But all it really means in practice is that I'm your connection to the leadership. I would provide the communication channel from you to them and back again.'

'And what if I only agree to help if I can meet the leadership?' asked Anita, purposefully pushing the boundaries Helena had laid down.

'Impossible,' said Helena, her eyes flashing with annoyance. 'I've never met the leadership. They simply won't meet anyone, regardless who they are or what they could do to help.'

'Well, that's too bad then, because I'm not sure I want to help someone who won't deign to provide me with the common courtesy of letting me know who they are.'

'Anita, you could have the key to energy stability, or sending the Relic back, locked in a cylinder in your head. How can you sit on that and say you won't help us?'

'Because we don't know what's in the cylinder. It could kill me when I open it, and maybe I'd rather throw in my lot with others, people whose ideologies are more aligned to mine.'

'Unlikely,' said Helena, dismissively. 'Your mother put it in your head. I doubt very much she would have given you something with the power to kill you, not after the lengths she went to to make sure you were kept safe. And who else is there to work with who has the resources to make a meaningful difference?'

Anita stood up abruptly. She'd had enough of Helena's tone. It amazed her that even in a situation such as this, where Helena was asking for help, she could be more concerned with establishing control than getting them onside. 'Well, thanks for the history lesson, but I think it's time for us to go. We can't help anyway; the cylinder is lost and won't be found. I guess you'll have to find some other way to stabilise the energy.'

Helena looked blankly at Anita, her face now tinged a greyish shade. Anita walked out of the potting shed into the bright sunshine outside, Alexander following in her wake.

When the door had safely slammed shut behind them, Rose stepped in from the secret garden, an unreadable expression on her face. 'That didn't go as well as we'd hoped...'

'... I know,' Helena snarled.

'Do you think she was telling the truth about the cylinder being lost?'

'Honestly, I have no idea.'

CHAPTER 5

Marcus stormed through the empty archway and slammed the door behind him. He stopped short when he saw Austin's brooding form slumped over the kitchen table, briefly entertaining the idea of vacating the kitchen and finding somewhere else to be angry, before curiosity overtook him.

'What's wrong with you?' he asked his distracted father.

Austin's eyes flicked up. They were a hostile pot of emotion, sneering at Marcus as he replied. 'I see that question applies equally to you.'

Marcus said nothing. It was best in situations like this to wait for his father's true agenda to be revealed. Austin never let an uncomfortable silence stand for long; it made him feel out of control, so only a few moments passed before he continued. 'I hear you've been to visit your treacherous girlfriend again, and this time, she let you in to see her.'

Normally Marcus would have been outraged by this invasion of his privacy, but, given what had happened when he'd last seen Anita, he couldn't muster the energy to fight. 'You'll be pleased to hear that Anita broke up with me, so you no longer have to worry about my 'inappropriate' girlfriend. To add insult to injury, she and Alexander have disappeared, so you were probably right; she was probably lying to me the whole damn time.'

Marcus slumped down on the bench opposite his father at the aged wooden table. The furious tension left his body, and he bowed his head forward, resting it on his hands. 'I can't believe she would do this. Not so soon after breaking up with me...'

'Unless, of course, as you say, she was cheating on you from the start. Maybe Alexander had her spy on us.'

Marcus' head shot up. 'Why would Alexander do that?'

'Or maybe Anita has been using both of you. She's been working with the Institution; it's the only explanation for her trying to steal that particular cylinder, not that she would have known what was in it.'

'For the last time, she didn't steal that cylinder,' said Marcus, agitated, emphasising each word.

'Really? You're sure about that now she's dumped you and disappeared?'

Marcus opened his mouth to defend Anita, but couldn't say the words out loud... he wasn't sure any longer. Had she been using him the entire time? Had she ever felt anything for him? 'What was in the cylinder?'

Austin dodged. 'More importantly, where is she now and what's her next move? I'm sure she'll come back, and when she does, we need to be ready for her, Alexander, and the whole Gods-damned Institution, if it comes to that.'

'What do you mean?'

'The Institution are spreading rumours that we're causing the food shortages. People are starting to believe their lies, and if we don't stop the momentum, who knows where this whole sorry business could end up.'

'What if they have a point?' said Marcus, without giving adequate thought to the words escaping his mouth. 'What if it is all to do with the energy, and it could be solved by finding a way to send the Relic back?'

Austin's fury was plain to see. He set his jaw, eyes cold, brow furrowed. 'Sometimes I wonder if you're truly my son,' he said, venomously. 'Firstly, this is not to do with the energy; there's no proof of that. Secondly, even if we wanted to send the Relic back, it's impossible; the Body bloodline is broken. The prophecy is dead.'

'What's causing the shortages then?' Marcus snapped, unwilling to roll over with the sting of his father's cruel words fresh in his ears.

'We've just had a poor year, that's all. Next year we'll be back to the bumper harvests we're used to.'

'And the fish stocks? And the dead birds falling out of the sky?'

'All part of the same problem. Bad weather affecting their food supplies.'

Marcus didn't argue further. Austin wasn't paying any attention to the actual argument; these were standard, rehearsed responses that slid effortlessly off his tongue. 'What do you suggest we do then? Nothing? Sit back and let people starve while we carry on as normal?'

'Don't be so melodramatic; it's really not that bad. People won't starve as the result of one bad year; it will take much longer than that before people really feel the impact on their lives. Next year, the crop yields will return to normal. What just need to be patient, and we need deal with the Institution before they can stir up enough of a movement behind their lies to cause us real problems.'

'And how do you suggest we do that?'

'I don't yet know, but Anita is at the centre of this somehow, so I suggest we start with her.'

* * * * *

Anita and Alexander left the farm without telling anyone they were going, walking the miles back to Empire in relative silence. They walked without touching, each agonising over what Helena had told them, Anita thinking about her parent's brutal deaths, and Alexander contemplating his own parents' demise.

They headed for Cleo's. They needed to go back over all they'd learned, and Cleo would ask the most probing questions, would pick the most effective holes in what Helena had told them. Not to mention, Cleo was one of the very few people they both agreed they could trust. She might be a gossip, but she could keep a secret when it counted.

They reached Cleo's in what seemed like no time at all, Anita not sure how they had got there. Alexander rang the bell, then surprised Anita by pulling her to him, kissing her forehead before Cleo threw the door open and hastily ushered them inside.

Cleo was subdued. She gave Anita a welcoming hug then showed them into her vast, open plan living space where Bass was already lounging on one of Cleo's enormous white sofas. Cleo lived in a converted warehouse next to The Island, the space a towering loft full of old industrial paraphernalia converted masterfully into furniture. It was spacious, light and entirely homely, managing a stylish convergence of old and new. Cleo could always be counted upon to be on the leading edge of chic.

'What's up with you?' asked Anita, Cleo's downbeat mood making her nervous.

'Several things, actually. Bass has been filling me in on the ever declining energy levels, Dad's sent a couple of letters describing the effects in the Wild Lands, and Bass mentioned that Helena kidnapped you two, which I'm pretty interested to hear all about by the way,' she said, revving up to more usual energy levels. 'What the hell is going on?'

Alexander and Anita exchanged a look, silently agreeing to tell the full story, even though Bass was present. Bass had been second on their list of safe people to tell, and at least now they wouldn't have to repeat themselves.

Anita and Alexander told them all that Helena had said and everything in Clarissa's diary, embellishing nothing and leaving nothing out. They finished the recount and waited in silence for Cleo and Bass' inevitable stream of questions, a strange feeling of relief washing over them when they'd shared all they knew.

'So, you're the Body Descendant?' Cleo ventured, after a pronounced and uncharacteristic silence.

'It would seem so,' said Anita.

'And Helena is essentially responsible for the death of both of your parents,' Bass said, weightily.

'Yes,' said Alexander, tense. Revealing so much information to relative strangers was stuffing him full of conflicting emotions. He couldn't deny it felt good to share, but his grandfather had taught him secrets were safest when locked away inside, and a lifetime of practice was a hard habit to shake.

'And the prophecy is still intact?' asked Cleo.

'Apparently,' said Anita.

'And Helena thinks the way to send the Relic back is in a cylinder in your head?' said Cleo.

'She's not sure what's in there, but she thinks it's the missing piece of the puzzle. Although, Helena's not set on sending the Relic back. She and the rest of the

Institution think it's possible to achieve energy stability without fulfilling the prophecy, but the Institution would take energy stability however they could get it.'

'Dad was part of this whole thing and never said a word about it,' said Bass.

'I'm sorry,' said Anita. 'At least it explains Cordelia and Elistair's close friendship. I guess being part of the Institution is something he wanted to hide.'

'Not to mention that it's an illegal organisation,' added Alexander.

'An illegal organisation that's stirring up bad feeling among those affected by the energy drop,' said Cleo.

Anita frowned. 'What do you mean?'

'Dad sent a letter saying those mistreated by the Descendants are becoming militant. They're holding demonstrations in the Wild Lands, complaining the Descendants are doing nothing to help anyone but themselves, saying that somebody needs to take action. Dad said the Institution were getting behind the demonstrations, building momentum wherever they can, driving people to more anger and action. The Institution want vast swathes of people to rise up against the Descendants. Even if they can't send the Relic back, they see overthrowing the status quo as the first step towards stability.'

'Helena neglected to mention that,' said Alexander, 'and doesn't it seem counterintuitive for such upheaval to lead to stability?'

'Then there's only one answer,' said Bass. 'We have to find a way to send the Relic back before the Institution builds enough momentum to overthrow the Descendants. Who rules afterwards, the people can decide, when the Descendants no longer have the right to lead. Anderson and I are already working on it, but maybe we'd make more progress if you helped too.'

'Of course,' said Anita, 'and we'll try to open the cylinder in my mind.'

'And hope it doesn't kill you,' said Alexander.

Anita gave him a wry smile. 'If it kills me, it'll probably kill you too, seeing as you'll be with me in my head.'

'We need to get Marcus and Gwyn involved,' said Cleo. 'If we do find a way to send the Relic back, we'll need all the Descendant support we can get.'

'I'll speak to Gwyn,' said Bass. Anita shot a look at Cleo: so the rumours about Bass and Gwyn were true... 'but I refuse to tell her she's not really the Body Descendant, nor that Anita is her half-sister, nor that the Institution are launching a plan to have her overthrown...'

They all laughed.

'Fair enough,' said Cleo. 'What about Marcus?'

'I dumped him the last time I saw him, so I'm probably not the best person for the job,' said Anita.

'And he'll probably punch me when he finds out Anita and I are together,' said Alexander.

'We'll keep working on it. There must be someone Marcus trusts, we just need to find them.'

The doorbell rang as Anita and Alexander got up to leave. 'That'll be Gwyn and Henry,' said Bass, getting up to answer the door, 'we're going on a double date this evening.'

Anita's eyes shot to Cleo, a mix of amusement and friendly scorn conveyed as Cleo looked elsewhere. 'Henry the councillor's son?' Anita asked. 'The one you slapped in the street for standing you up because he was on a date with someone else?'

Cleo shoved Anita towards the stairs. 'It's a long story. I'm sure I'll tell you all about it next time I see you. Weren't you two leaving?'

'Alright, alright. We won't stay where we're not wanted,' said Anita, following Alexander down the stairs. She reached the bottom step, and was shocked to stillness at the sight of Bass and Gwyn's lips locked together.

* * * * *

Alexander and Anita headed to the Spirit Temple, to work on finding the brass cylinder. It had been a while since they'd paid it the attention it deserved, and after everything with Helena, it was time to give it some focus.

They sat, cross-legged, at the back of the temple, facing each other, close but not touching, eyes closed, minds merged at Anita's centre. It was more intense than usual, Anita hardly believing that was possible, an electricity crackling through the air between them. Anita stood at the entrance of the yurt and Alexander sat on the bed in the corner. He was, as usual, shirtless, but today his body seemed to call her to him. It normally sat there, impassively waiting for her to act, but today the muscles on his chest seemed more defined, more contoured, even more appealing.

He sat silently as he watched her, smiling as he felt her energy. She moved easily towards him, all thoughts of the cylinder forgotten. She reached him and climbed, cat-like, up onto the bed in front of him, leaning forward so her lips could find his. A trickle of desire snaked around her insides, an agonising void left behind by its treacherous scales. Their skin touched and energy coursed between them like a toxic current, serving only to intensify their already charged minds. She pulled away and flicked her grey eyes to his, sending a flirtatious challenge he responded to without hesitation, rolling her sideways and pinning her to the bed with his weight.

He hovered over her as she slowly traced her fingers down the muscles at his sides, revelling in the affect the simple movement had on him. He leaned forward, brushing his lips along her collarbone, sending shivers of instant pleasure down her spine. She arched her back, and he moved his lips to her ear, murmuring, 'We're supposed to be looking for the cylinder.'

'It's not my fault you're so distracting.'

'*I'm* so distracting?' he said, kissing her neck. 'It's not me,' he said, sliding his fingers down her neck, walking them across her chest, over her now-sensitive breasts, tantalisingly across every rib. He dipped into the contour of her waist before skimming her hip bone, coming to rest on the curve of her behind. 'You're the distracting one.' He leaned in for a long, tender kiss. When he finally pulled away, he gently caressed her cheek before lifting himself off her, manoeuvring himself off the bed, and walking to the other side of the room.

Anita sat up, annoyed and frustrated, feeling a forceful desire to stamp her foot in protest, but she knew he had a point. They needed to find the cylinder, and to do that, they needed to concentrate. 'Okay,' she said, 'what do you suggest we do? We've already tried so many times…'

'We need a new approach,' he mused, keeping his eyes off her. 'We need to locate the most difficult place to find; that's most likely where it's hidden.'

'It won't be somewhere full of Body, or Spirit, so we can safely assume it's somewhere full of Mind, which will also make it most difficult for us to find.'

'Let's hope not impossible. Maybe we should start in the most Mind orientated places we've found so far and see if we can find a link from there?'

'Okay,' Anita agreed; it seemed as good an approach as any. 'The boat then.' She wasn't keen on going to the boat owned by Marcus' grandfather, but it was the only choice they had.

Alexander cleared his mind and Anita pushed them to the boat, where they sat, knees touching, in the stern, sails reaching up like wings into the flawless blue sky above.

'It's so beautiful here, don't you think?' said Anita, turning her head to kiss Alexander on the lips. She found it so liberating that, in here, nobody else could see them, or hear them, or interrupt them, and she delighted in the shivers of energy that raced through her as Alexander kissed her back, running his fingers up her spine and into her hair, pulling her ever more urgently to him. They broke apart, eyes alight, and Anita stood up, moved to sit on top of the entrance to the cabin, putting deliberate space between them.

'What now?' she asked, looking out at the crystal turquoise ocean.

'I don't know... the boat is the main Mind component here... maybe we should look around inside?'

Anita agreed, and they made their way under the beautiful teak deck into the small cabin below. They found themselves in a cramped galley with a compact table surrounded on three sides by bottle green seating. There was a stove, a sink, and a number of cupboards containing everything from navigation equipment to bits of string and old bolts, to champagne glasses, but nothing that linked them to other places in her mind.

After searching the galley, they split up, Anita venturing forwards towards the bow, where she found two cabins and a bathroom. Alexander took the stern, where he discovered a large cabin complete with a double bed and its own private bathroom. Neither found anything of interest, only berths without bedding and more storage lockers, but then neither of them was fully concentrating on the job in hand. They headed back above deck and agreed to call it a day; their hearts weren't really in it anyway.

Anita pulled them out of the meditation and they opened their eyes to find a small crowd of people nearby in the Spirit Temple, watching them from a distance. Anita didn't know why; they had never attracted this kind of attention when they'd meditated here before, but they didn't hang around to find out.

Alexander quickly helped Anita to her feet. She tried to ignore the concentrated flow of energy coursing through their fingertips. He led her to the stone in the centre of the temple that covered the steps down to Alexander's rooms. The stone slid aside as they approached, and Alexander ushered Anita in front of him before following her down the spiral steps that led to his study below.

'That was weird,' said Anita, slouching back into one of the beaten-up old leather armchairs. 'What do you think is going on?'

'I don't know. But if I had to guess, I'd say it's something to do with Amber or Austin.'

'Why?' asked Anita.

'Because until a few days ago, you were going out with Marcus, which afforded you a certain amount of… if not protection, then courtesy. Now that's gone and being seen in public with me is only going to rile them further.'

'That's ridiculous. Marcus convinced them I wasn't trying to steal anything, and they let me go.'

'That's not how I remember it,' said Alexander. 'Marcus blackmailed Austin to make him release you, and he had to do that because you were, in fact, trying to steal something.'

'Okay,' said Anita, wanting to spend as little time on that as possible, 'let's say, for argument's sake, Austin has people spying on us and reporting back. For what purpose?'

'Austin's been looking for the real Body Descendant for some time. That's why we all came to Empire in the first place, because Christiana wanted to find you, to tell you who you really were, and Austin killed her when he found out her true purpose.'

'Austin killed Christiana?' Anita repeated, shocked. 'How could you possibly know that?'

'Because I was there when it happened,' he said. 'I was on my way to see her and when I approached, I heard Austin and Christiana arguing. I hid to listen and when Austin found out what she was really in Empire for, he suffocated her with a cushion.'

'Why didn't you do anything?'

'Because Christiana was a reader; she knew I was there but didn't appeal for my help. I think she wanted me to know what happened so I could finish what she started. If I'd revealed myself to Austin, he would've killed me too, and my bloodline would be over.'

Anita sat silently contemplating his words for several minutes. 'Do you think Austin knows I'm the true Body Descendant?'

Alexander smiled, his eyes alight with a mocking gleam. 'It's not like there are a great number of candidates, and you haven't done much to dispel suspicion.'

'Well, what was I supposed to do? Lose the Chase? Shy into the background and let everyone think a bunch of Descendants had beaten me?'

'Yes.'

'Why do you persist with this crap? I'd rather put myself in danger than let them think they've won.'

'But they will win unless we get smarter.'

'What do you suggest we do?' said Anita, her energy hostile. She knew he had a point, and she wanted to hear it, but the idea that she should make herself small was infuriating.

'I don't know exactly, but we need to lie low for a while. We need time to find the cylinder. Bass and Anderson need time to find a way to send back the Relic, and we need a strategy to find out what the Institution are really up to. Most of all, you need to stay away from Marcus, Austin, and Amber, and limit how much you're seen in public. If Austin kills you before we figure out how to send the Relic back, then sending the Relic back becomes impossible, and the prophecy's over: we fail.'

A shiver of fear ran down her spine. 'Okay, fine, I'll lie low for a while. And don't worry, I promise I'll stay away from Marcus.'

* * * * *

'I thought I'd find you here,' said Austin, whispered voice menacing in Helena's ear. He placed two whisky glasses on the bar in front of her and sat down on the stool beside her.

'Oh damn, am I that predictable?' she said, the dimly lit bar hiding half her face in shadow as she continued to look forward, sipping her existing drink. It was 2am, and the bar was practically empty, but the Jazz band was still going strong, the music a mellow ripple caressing the room, a stark contrast to the frivolous volume and pace of the hours that had preceded.

Several couples danced around the floor, several booths were occupied, but everyone ignored everyone else, all enjoying the anonymity this place was famous for. Jack's was in Empire, but not in the well-to-do Temple Mews or on one of the well-manicured surrounding streets. Jack's was on the other side of the river, home to the not-quite-so-well-heeled, where unsavoury behaviour was the order of the day.

'It's where you go in times of trouble, or when you're looking for trouble, come to think of it.' He smirked as he took a large gulp of whiskey. 'Seeing as your latest ploy didn't go to plan, I didn't doubt you would be here.'

'My latest ploy?'

'You want to play games with me?' he purred. 'You and I are the only two who know what's in the cylinder Anita tried to steal from me, and I sure as hell didn't put her up to it.'

'I think all that power might have gone to your head... conspiracies everywhere... Amber bumping people off whenever a theory gets out of control...'

He shifted in his seat, anger plain to read, and Helena smiled inwardly; she still knew how to wind him up.

'Tell me then, why, out of all people, did Anita, the girl you took under your wing for so many years, find her way into my family's vault and pick up the one thing you would so dearly like to have?'

'Firstly, she is no longer under my wing. Secondly, I didn't know you had a family vault. And thirdly, she's always been too curious for her own good, so maybe that's the reason.'

'If you're going to lie, you could do me the courtesy of trying harder than that,' he hissed.

She turned her head to face him, her eyes inches from his. 'Why don't you get Amber to interrogate her?' she said. 'If Anita is guilty, I'm sure your attack dog will beat it out of her.'

Austin grabbed Helena's arm, spinning her body towards him. 'Don't be so foolish. You think you're immune because of some long-ago history between us?'

'Long ago? Darling, your memory must be failing.'

'Helena, I'm being serious.'

'I'm terrified,' she said, leaning into him so their foreheads almost touched. 'Simply shaking with fear.' She moved forward and took his bottom lip between her teeth. She bit hard enough to enrage him, but gently enough not to do any damage, smiling brazenly as he tore away, his eyes a sea of rage as he reached out and wrapped her throat in his hand.

'I know Anita is the real Body Descendant,' he said, tightening his grip, pulling her towards him.

Helena cocked one inviting eyebrow. 'That's news to me,' she said, reaching a hand up to stroke his cheek, 'but if you want to take this any further, we should probably find somewhere more private.'

Austin paused, searching her face. He pulled her lips to his, kissing her with rough ferocity before driving her away. He stood, drained his glass, and turned to leave. 'Watch your back, Helena. If you carry on like this, even I won't be able to protect you.'

CHAPTER 6

Anita met Cleo by the river. They walked Thorn several miles along the bank, the springer spaniel jumping in and out of the water after sticks they threw for him. They stopped by a section of rapids where they idly watched the frothing water make its turbulent way over the rocks. Alexander had been called to Kingdom with the rest of the Descendants and councillors for an emergency council meeting. Kingdom was witnessing protests at the rising food prices and Austin had finally relented, agreeing to start crisis talks on what should happen next.

'How are the talks going?' asked Cleo, throwing a stone into the rapids. 'Dad says not well.' Draeus, Cleo's father, was a Wild Lands trader. He made it his business to know about anything that might impact his livelihood.

'I don't know. I haven't heard a word from Alexander since he and Bass left for the meeting. Bass hasn't sent any messages back either.'

'Well, let's hope Austin finally sees sense and they do something.'

'Unlikely, but fingers crossed.'

'Have you found the cylinder yet?' asked Cleo.

'No. We've looked for it a few times but never get very far. Meditating with Alexander isn't the most productive exercise...'

Cleo laughed. 'I can imagine. Tricky predicament.'

'I'm not sure Alexander's the right person anyway. He thinks the cylinder is most likely to be hiding in the most difficult location to find, which for me, would be a Mind dominated place. We've only found Spirit and Body places, apart from the boat, but I'm not sure either of us really knows what we're looking for... and it's not like I can ask Marcus to help.'

'What about me?' said Cleo, offhandedly, as though it wouldn't be a big deal if Anita said no. She continued, before Anita had a chance to respond. 'I mean, you and I did get to the boat in a previous meditation, and if you need a Mind who's in on what you're trying to do, you're limited for options.'

Cleo was about to continue when Anita jumped in and stopped her. 'Of course; it's a great idea.'

'Really?' said Cleo, shocked. 'You're happy to meditate with me?'

'Of course!' said Anita. 'Why wouldn't I want to meditate with you?'

'I've never successfully meditated with anyone, so who knows if I'll be any use at all.'

'There's only one way to find out,' said Anita, shifting, so she faced Cleo, cross-legged on the soft earth. 'Come on. Cross your legs, close your eyes, relax and breathe deeply. Just let your mind go and I'll guide us to my centre.'

Cleo did as she was told, but when they both arrived in the meditation, they weren't at Anita's centre; they were on the boat in the middle of the ocean. 'Um... this is unexpected,' said Anita, looking around her. 'Most of the time I have to go to my centre before I can come anywhere else.'

'Weird... so... what do we do now?' asked Cleo, looking around in wonder.

Anita remembered the first time she had properly meditated with Alexander, so gave Cleo a few moments to take it all in. 'It's crazy, isn't it?' she said, instead of answering the question. 'That we're somehow in the same place in my mind. That we can talk to each other in here and nobody outside can see us or hear what we're saying.'

'Yep. Pretty weird,' said Cleo, taking one last look out to sea before turning purposefully back to Anita. 'So what now? How do we find new locations?'

'I'm not totally sure. When Alexander and I were first exploring, we found things that linked one location to another, a bit like a door. So, from my centre, a piece of leather led us to a stable containing a horse. Some canvas there led us to the boat, and so on.'

'So I should look for Mind related stuff that might link us somewhere else?'

'I think that's the best thing to do. Alexander and I tried to do the same thing here, but found nothing.'

Cleo had already stopped listening. She was rootling around, looking for anything that might be Mind related. She descended into the cabin, returning with a sextant and some dividers. 'These are the most Mind orientated things I could find down there,' she said, handing them over.

Anita took the objects and turned them over in her hands. She cleared her mind and focused on the cold metal, willing the instruments to take her somewhere new. Nothing happened. She closed her eyes and pushed her mind into the objects, forcing as much energy towards them as she could muster. Still nothing happened. She opened her eyes and looked up at Cleo, shaking her head. 'Nothing,' she said, 'sorry.'

'Don't be sorry. We just have to keep looking,' said Cleo, never one to be deterred by a minor setback.

Cleo spent the next half an hour searching every inch of the boat, working methodically through the cabins from front to back. They tried several objects: a bottle opener, a kettle, a pair of binoculars, but all to no avail.

They made their way back up on deck, where they turned their attention to various cleats, ropes, and even fenders, to see if they would have any luck with those. Again, nothing.

They sat, forlorn, on the bow, legs dangling over the side, hugging the safety rail, out of ideas as to where they could look next. Anita silently beat herself up, chastising herself for not being able to find something as simple as another location in her mind. Cleo was irritated. She kept talking through everything they had looked at, desperately trying to work out what they'd missed. She turned to Anita, putting her left hand down to support her weight. A shot of excitement flooded through her, and Anita turned as she felt the reaction.

'What is it?' she asked, following Cleo's gaze down to where her hand rested on a heavy, tarnished chain.

'The anchor,' Cleo said, brimming with enthusiasm. 'It's got to be the anchor.'

Anita reached forward and traced the chain over the front of the bow to where the anchor was hanging just out of sight. As her fingers reached the cool, wet metal, a strange tension filled the air, and the environment shifted from a breezy, salt filled freshness, to an oppressive, flat, warmth.

'We did it!' yelped Cleo, looking around at a grand, dark throne room, filled with burning torches and an enormous open fire, flames roaring angrily upwards in the hearth. Heavy throws, rugs and tapestries adorned the walls and floors, covering every inch of the bare stone below. Columns supported a balcony above that hid the sides of the hall in darkness.

At the far end of the room were two ornate thrones, but instead of shimmering gold or silver, they were a dull greyish tone, the seat bare metal, not a cushion in sight, contrasting in stark fashion with the illustrious comfort of the fabric all around. In between the thrones sat a small, plain table made of gnarled wood that looked like it had no natural place here. On top sat a wooden box, its brass latch shimmering oddly in the torchlight.

Anita made her way towards the box, a feeling of dread filling her, knowing if it contained the cylinder, they both could be in danger. She walked slowly over the soft, plush rugs, her feet being sucked into the piles, so it was an effort to take each step.

She reached the thrones and looked up at the box, steeling herself for the three steps that were all that now stood between them. Cleo looked on from the other end of the room, nervous apprehension filling her as she waited to see what Anita would do next. Alexander had explained the potential dangers in some detail.

Anita took the steps one at a time, the air around her growing denser as she inched closer to her target, like the molecules were somehow crammed closer together, trying to protect the box that was her goal. She reached out and touched the nondescript, brown object, exhaling sharply when she found that nothing untoward resulted from her touch. She lifted it from the table and turned to look at Cleo, who had moved to the base of the steps, looking expectantly up at Anita, willing her on.

Anita flipped the latch open and swung the lid back on its hinges to reveal a glimmering brass cylinder inside, lying unceremoniously on a bed of hay. She walked down the steps, carrying the box with extreme caution, not wanting to give the cylinder a second chance to escape.

She sat on the bottom step, Cleo joining her. 'What should we do now?' asked Anita. 'Open it and take the risk?'

'I don't know,' replied Cleo, her fear a tangible thing. 'If Alexander's right, it could kill us both if you open it.'

'But if I never open it, we never find out what's inside.'

'True… and time is of the essence.'

'But you're right; it could kill us both, and if it does that, then we die by the riverbank with no explanation and nobody would ever know we found the cylinder.' Determination settled across her shoulders. 'We'll leave it here and come back when we've told the others.'

'Okay,' said Cleo, reluctantly. 'It goes against every fibre of my being, but… okay.'

Anita closed the box and placed it back where she'd found it before pulling them out of the meditation.

They woke to find Thorn dragging a branch roughly six times his own length towards them. They laughed as they got to their feet, Anita calling to Thorn, who grudgingly put down his prize and trotted after them.

'So,' said Anita, meaningfully, as they started on the walk back to Empire, 'you've got some stuff to fill me in on... something about you and someone we know called Henry?'

Cleo laughed, shoving her friend.

'Tell me everything.'

* * * * *

Anita and Cleo met Bass and Anderson on Temple Mews, the sun hanging low in the sky, its rays making the cobbled street shine. The hanging baskets of summer were gone, festoons of autumnal fairy lights hanging in their place.

Temple Mews was beautiful, lined with shops selling things that made you believe you were in a surrealist painting; florists with displays that defied gravity, tea rooms selling cakes so light and fluffy that you might have been eating a cloud, perfumeries, and coffee and chocolate shops evoking daydreams of sailing off into the Wild Lands to explore, and outfitters filled with beautiful swathes of silk, surely meant for a Goddess.

The cold hadn't yet fully set in, but the air had a notable new crispness that made them not want to linger too long outside. They headed for Anita's favourite café, Mungo and Meg, but, as Anita was about to step over the threshold, a cold hand closed around her wrist, tugging her vigorously backwards. She spun around, her energy hostile, ready to fight whatever threat this was, but found herself looking up into a pair of familiar, now smug, electric blue eyes.

'It's rude to sneak up on people,' said Anita, flirtatiously, placing a hand on Alexander's chest, her eyes alight, energy rapidly rising.

'I thought you might be pleased to see me,' he said, a look of mock affront across his face.

'What gave you that impression?' she asked, as he leaned down and gave her a peck on the lips. She pushed him playfully away before heading for the café. 'Come on,' she said, 'someone told me to keep a low profile.'

They entered the café, reaching the table the others had chosen, to find a conversation already in full swing about the meeting in Kingdom and subsequent action to be taken. Alexander and Anita sat on opposite sides of the table at the only two remaining chairs, their eyes meeting at every opportunity. Cleo rolled her eyes, causing Anita's cheeks to blush a deep red, which only spurred Alexander on.

Mungo and Meg looked insignificant from the outside, with only a tiny frontage: a sign, a door, and two small windows crammed full of adventurous treats. However, inside was a space at odds with the unassuming exterior. It was enormous; a cavernous room filled with mismatched sofas, chairs, and tables, home-grown plants in terracotta pots siting on the centre of each.

The back of the building had been extended; an enormous, glass, double height orangery occupying the space where one would expect an ordinary stone wall. As a result, light flooded the cafe.

It was Anita's favourite spot for many reasons: the food changed daily, it was large enough to provide privacy, and it was unexpected; something different on the inside from what it seemed to be. She and Cleo came here a lot, so the waitress simply asked, 'Usual?' when she approached.

'Yes please,' said Anita and Cleo together, Alexander and Bass sending them questioning looks that asked what the 'usual' included.

'We have the soup of the day and a selection of salads from the counter,' said Cleo, pointing to a bar by the door full of platters piled high with a range of bright and interesting offerings.

'I'll have that too,' said Bass.

'And me,' said Alexander.

'Me too,' said Anderson.

The waitress nodded efficiently and left with the order.

'So,' said Anita, 'what happened?'

They all looked at Alexander expectantly, so he started the recount. 'The main meeting was yesterday. The councils had already held a series of smaller meetings over the previous two days, and by the time we got there, the number of protestors outside the temples was overwhelming. They were chanting about how food prices were being manipulated for the Descendants' and councillors' gain. By the end, there were so many of them, we all had to be escorted out of the building.

'Anyway, the chamber was tense, like the councillors were holding their breath, like they were in on something that was about to go down. The energy of the Mind and Body councillors was different to normal. Most of the Minds were excited, the Bodies nervous, but some were openly angry. We took our places and waited.

'They gave several ordinary updates; reports from the Wild Lands about crop yields, trading volumes, all the stuff we normally get. The numbers were down on what we'd usually see, but those giving the reports were tempering the truth, the tone from every single one of them inappropriately upbeat. Someone, presumably Austin, must have got to them. But Bass told the pure, unadulterated truth.'

Pride swelled in Anita's chest as she took in Bass' stony face.

'He reported that the energy remains at dangerously low levels, and that it's still dropping,' said Alexander. 'He said the protestors outside were proof that the situation is bad enough to necessitate action.'

'From there,' said Bass, 'it descended into chaos. The Mind councillors hurled accusations at me, accusing me of inciting riot, of associating with the Institution, of stirring up the masses for my own gain. They called for me to be sacked.'

'What?' said Anita, outraged.

'Then the Body councillors started,' said Alexander. 'They were less offensive, but still bad. They called into question Bass' evidence. They asked if the reading equipment might be malfunctioning, and even suggested it's Bass's research that's causing the downward energy spiral.'

'Wow,' said Anita.

'What about Austin? I'm assuming he was front and centre, throwing abuse?' asked Cleo.

'Austin was unusually quiet. He just sat there and let it all unfold, Peter doing the same.'

'Hardly unusual behaviour for Peter,' said Bass, his hands balled into fists.

'What happened next?' asked Anita. 'Did it descend into a full-on brawl?' She sounded almost hopeful.

'Oh, please tell us that's how it went!' said Cleo. 'The impervious councillors resorting to out-and-out fisticuffs would be too good to be true!'

'I hate to disappoint, but not quite,' laughed Alexander. 'I went to Bass' side, throwing my support behind him, the Spirit councillors broadly following my lead. Some of the Body councillors came around as well, when they saw others willing to support what Bass was saying.'

'That's when Austin got involved,' said Bass. 'Even he could feel the shift in the room. Nobody could deny the protestors outside, nor that they're increasingly militant. Austin took charge before he lost control completely. He gave a speech about riding it out and not doing anything rash.'

'And the notion that things could stay like they've always been struck a chord,' said Alexander, shaking his head. 'As ever, change is too terrifying a prospect for their pea sized brains.'

'The room was swaying back to Austin's command,' said Bass, 'and, recognising his advantage, Austin pushed for more. He suggested I step aside, seeing as, in his view, the responsibility of running the observatory is beyond my capabilities.'

Anita let out a string of expletives.

'Surely the others didn't go along with that?' said Cleo. 'Bass is the most qualified person we have.'

'Qualifications aren't top of Austin's version of the job description,' said Bass. 'He's more concerned with the sheep like qualities and lack of professional backbone exhibited by his councillors.'

'What happened?' asked Anita, eager to hear the rest of the story.

'Austin was about to put it to a vote when the protestors reached the doors of the council chamber. They tried to gain entry, shots were fired, and we were shepherded out through the back tunnels. Nobody inside was hurt, but reports say Austin's guards fired on the protestors. Some are suggesting it was Amber who instigated the whole thing.'

'Do you think that's true?' asked Cleo.

'I honestly don't know, but if it was, she didn't get the timing quite right: Bass is still in charge of the observatory. The protestors have taken up residence in the council chamber, and it's only a matter of time until they discover the tunnels. It's not safe for any of us to go back there. We agreed to reconvene in Empire, as the unrest here hasn't yet boiled over.'

'Until Amber or the Institution stir up bad feeling here too,' said Cleo.

'Why do you think the Institution had anything to do with this?' asked Anderson, defensively.

His tone was a surprise: he was more dedicated to the Institution than Anita had realised. She changed the subject. 'Do you think Austin's behind the protestors' attack?'

'Why would Austin cause riots that contradict his opinion that nothing's wrong?' said Cleo.

'Who knows,' said Alexander, 'but chaos has always been Austin's friend. Maybe he's planning a full takeover; to rule alone. Maybe he'll tell the protestors he's the only one with the power to help them. Maybe the attack had nothing to do with him at all. But if Amber already has a foothold with the protestors, then he's well positioned to use them to his advantage, whatever his purpose. If the prophecy really is over, then there's no reason to continue ruling as we do.'

'This is nothing but speculation,' said Anderson, as the waitress arrived with their food.

'True. Maybe the Institution is behind the protests,' said Bass, pointedly.

Anderson frowned. 'Who knows what they're all really up to and what they really want, but we need to stop Austin from removing Bass from the observatory; we're so close to a breakthrough.'

'Really?' said Anita, both intrigued and feeling a pang of gut-wrenching guilt. She hadn't been to the observatory in days, and she was supposed to work there... 'What have you found?'

'We're not sure yet,' said Anderson, 'but we may have found a way to enhance energy transfer, so it becomes more powerful.

'Powerful enough to move objects large distances,' said Bass, Anita not missing the well-concealed annoyance he was directing at Anderson. Curious...

'Ooh, how exciting! Anita and I made a bit of a breakthrough ourselves,' said Cleo, not giving Anita a chance to stop her. 'We meditated together and...'

'...you meditated with Anita,' Bass interrupted, a hint of jealousy in his tone. 'Why would that help?'

'We found the cylinder!' Cleo's excitement was all-consuming, making her oblivious to their reactions.

Anita was furious. She shot an apologetic look at Alexander, who, although putting on a brave face, was trying to fight his disappointment. Bass's energy was happy, if a little sulky, and Anderson's was intent, eyes fixed on Anita.

'Have you opened it?' Anderson demanded, as the others reeled from the revelation.

'No,' said Anita, firmly.

'Why not?'

'Because we don't know if it's friendly or hostile. We didn't want to open a hostile cylinder, kill ourselves, and no one ever know what happened.'

'Fair point,' he said, backing off a bit. 'When are you going to try? How are you going to do it?'

'No idea,' said Anita. 'Alexander and I need to discuss it before we decide what to do.' Her words were pointed, the discussion closed.

* * * * *

After lunch they went their separate ways, Alexander steering Anita towards the North West of the city, a side she didn't regularly visit. The houses petered out, giving way to rolling fields, and Alexander led her towards the river. He obviously had a destination in mind, but where that was, Anita neither knew nor cared to ask.

'I'm sorry you found out about the cylinder like that,' said Anita, throwing a stone into the water.

Alexander squeezed her hand. 'It's hardly your fault; Cleo just got carried away.'

'It wouldn't surprise me if Anderson tells Helena though, given his reaction when we talked about the Institution.'

'I know. I felt that too, but there's not much we can do about it, and at least it gives us an idea where his allegiance lies.'

They walked for a while in contemplative silence.

'How did you find the new place in your mind?'

'The same way you and I tried. Cleo and I meditated to the boat and searched high and low for anything Mind related. We looked everywhere and found nothing. We were about to give up when Cleo found the anchor, hanging just out of sight.'

'It seems so obvious now you say it. Of course, the anchor.'

Anita felt his disappointment, presumably because he hadn't been the one to help find it, but ignored it. If they wanted to stand a chance in all this, they had to take help from wherever it came. The two of them alone could never hope to have all the answers.

'What was the place like?'

Anita described the throne room with its throws and tapestries, the balcony above, and two ornate seats. She told him about the out-of-place table with the box on top. 'You'll see it for yourself soon.'

'And then what are we going to do?'

'You know what we're going to do… we're going to open it. If it is hostile, it hasn't done much to try to kill me so far. Why would something designed to kill me run away instead of carrying out the task it was made to do?'

'I suppose that's a good point,' replied Alexander, his shoulders tense. 'Helena's story, and your mother's diaries, do imply it contains something of use.'

'So, we have to open it and see what's inside. And at least if we die, we'll die together,' she said flippantly, looking up at him from under her lashes.

He rolled his eyes and didn't reply. Instead, he steered her away from the river and into the woods, heading up a steep bank, following an almost hidden path. They reached the top and burst out into an open field, a beautiful cottage sitting just beyond the tree line.

Alexander pulled Anita around to look back the way they'd come. She beamed when she saw why. They had a panoramic view over the whole of Empire, taking in everything: the town, The Island, the observatory, and even Austin's castle on the other side of the valley.

'Wow,' she said, turning to Alexander, grabbing his arm. 'That view is amazing, but who are we here to see? Who owns the house?'

'We're not here to see anyone,' he replied happily. 'The house is mine.'

Anita raised her eyebrows. 'Really? This is the Spirit Descendant's residence in Empire?'

'Yep,' he nodded, smiling, delighted at her reaction.

'But it's so small and unassuming,' she said, stunned at herself for not wondering before now where the Spirit family stayed when in Empire. The rooms under the Spirit Temple were too small for an entire family.

'You expected something grand and pompous like Austin's castle?' mocked Alexander.

'To be honest, I hadn't even considered that you had a home here, but this is perfect; it's beautiful.'

The cottage was immaculate on the outside, six green-grey sash windows around a heavy wooden front door, four windows on the left and two on the right. Flowerbeds flanked the house and a path leading from the woods to the front door, with no other visible route by which people could come and go.

They entered through the front door into an impeccable little entrance hall, stairs off to the right with a lovely striped carpet runner leading to the top. The windowsills were slate, big and deep enough to sit on, some of them with cushions laid out for exactly that purpose. The fireplaces had wood-burning stoves that sat on stone hearths, the floors flagstone, covered with beautiful exotic rugs that must have come from the Wild Lands. The furniture exuded a smart yet casual feel, like it was fine to put your feet up, but only so long as you didn't leave your shoes lying around when you were done.

The kitchen had a light-filled extension at the back, the same grey-green colour used for the windows at the front continuing through to its wooden frame. An Aga filled a recess where a fireplace had once stood, and a large Belfast sink, set into handsomely crafted cream wooden kitchen units, sat in front of a window that looked out onto the garden beyond.

From what Anita could see, the garden was equally flawless. Raised vegetable beds were visible towards the back of the totally enclosed, walled space. A stately but solitary apple tree occupied a large plot in the corner, and bountiful flower beds filled the remaining space.

'It's breath-taking,' said Anita, moving to stand next to Alexander as he put a kettle on one of the Aga's rings.

'I thought you'd like it,' he said, wrapping his arms around her, kissing her on the lips. 'I'm glad you do.'

'How could anyone not?' she said, burying her head in his chest, running her hands across his muscular lower back.

'Some people prefer the draughty, expansive experience afforded by living in a castle,' he said, breaking away to pull a floral tin out of a cupboard. He opened it to reveal the most delicious looking treats. 'Apple and rhubarb slices,' he said, placing the tin on top of the wooden kitchen table.

'Did you make these?' asked Anita, surprise clear in her voice.

Alexander laughed, pulling out two mugs and a teapot, before taking the boiling water off the stove. 'No. We used to have a full-time cook here when I was younger. The lady who used to cook for us, Mrs Patrick, still lives in Empire. When I'm here, I sometimes ask her to stock the house with food. She loves it; she's always trying to probe me for gossip, and her cooking is spectacular. Next time I'll ask her to make one of her signature quiches. Her pastry is out of this world.

Anita smiled, euphoria squeezing tight in her chest.

They sat at the table, eating cake washed down with breakfast tea, idly chatting about Alexander's trip to Kingdom. Anita was onto her third slice of cake before the conversation turned serious.

'I've been meaning to tell you something,' said Alexander.

'Uh oh; sounds ominous,' said Anita, her tone hiding the sudden heaviness in her stomach.

'When we were in Kingdom, I found a note hidden in my grandfather's study, in a secret compartment under his desk. It was addressed to me, but I don't even begin to understand it. I still can't believe how lucky I was to find it, given how well buried it was.'

'What did it say?' Anita asked impatiently.

'It was odd,' he replied. 'It said:

Remember the lessons from Philip & Fred.
Be a good scholar.
Jeffrey will help you unlock the light.
Destroy this note when you have memorised what I have said.
I have faith in you.'

'Cryptic,' said Anita, loosing a breath as the weight evaporated from her insides. 'Do you understand any of it?'

'I think *the lessons from Philip & Fred* refer to the famous fairy tales written by Oscar and Lewis. My grandfather always called them Philip and Fred: no idea why. His favourite story was about a princess, banished by her father, the King, because he went mad when a group of powerful sorcerers arrived at court. The story was about the princess' quest to retake her rightful position and rid the land of the evil sorcerers.'

Anita nodded. 'I know it well. Cordelia used to read it to me when I was little. But what relevance does that have?'

'I don't know, but there are parallels to your life.'

Anita laughed.

'No, seriously. Think about it. Helena told us the Descendants effectively banished you, like the powerful sorcerers did to the princess. And you're fighting to help send the Relic back, which would end the Descendants' rule. It fits well, and it's perfectly feasible that Philip could have found out the bloodline was still intact.'

'They all thought I was dead.'

'Apart from Christiana. Peter told her you were alive. Maybe Philip got wind that Christiana was trying to find you.'

'Even if we say, for argument's sake, that's the right explanation for the first bit, what about the rest of it?'

'Well, *be a good scholar* was something Grandfather always used to say. He was referring to the fact that "good scholars" question everything, even the things that are taken for granted, that we think we know to be unequivocally true.'

'What does that mean?'

'Who knows? It could relate to anything. It could be another hint the bloodline is still intact, that we should question the identity of the Descendants. And of course, after reading the diary, I think maybe the third part about Jeffrey helping to *unlock the light* is something to do with your mother's husband. I don't know any other Jeffries.'

'And unlocking the light refers to what exactly?'

'I don't know. The only connection I can make is to the inscriptions around the Relic. One of them says, *look to the light,* remember?'

'How could Jeffrey help to illuminate something Spirit related? He was a body.'

'I don't know. Maybe it has something to do with Clarissa, or Jeffrey's Institution missions, or the cylinder in your head. Or maybe it all relates to the secret we already know: that you're the true Body Descendant.'

'Maybe,' said Anita, 'or maybe it's referring to the cylinder in my head. That's something we need to unlock, and we've put it off for long enough; it's the only concrete lead we have.'

Alexander looked serious. 'Are you sure you want to do this? You know what the ramifications might be.'

'As do you if we don't do it,' Anita shot back, angry that Alexander was once again asking her this pointless question. 'Look, Alexander, I know you're trying to be nice, but you know as well as I do, we have to open the cylinder. If someone wants to kill me, there are far more efficient ways of doing it, and it's counterintuitive for something that wants to kill me to be so difficult to find.'

'I know, you're right,' he said, relenting. 'When do you want to do it?'

'No time like the present,' said Anita, getting up and taking Alexander's hand. She pulled him into the sitting room, pushed the ottoman out of the way, and sat down cross-legged on the opulent rug. She sank in a little as she landed, which she very much appreciated. Alexander followed her lead without uttering a word, sitting down and closing his eyes, waiting for her to direct their energy.

Anita pushed them to the boat, then quickly made for the anchor, transporting them to the throne room with only the lightest touch against the unforgiving metal.

Alexander looked around, as though he were trying to notice and catalogue everything in these new surroundings. 'Do you know where we are?' asked Anita, who was already making for the small wooden box in between the thrones.

'No,' he replied slowly. 'It feels almost familiar, but I don't know where we are.'

Anita lifted the box from the table, then walked down the steps to where Alexander waited at the bottom. She held her breath as she opened it, feeling deep relief that the cylinder was exactly as she'd left it, still nestled on a bed of hay.

'How do we open it?' she asked.

Alexander eyed the cylinder suspiciously, as though he suspected it might explode at any second. 'Normally, you just need to touch it and direct your energy towards it, willing it to open. At that point, depending on what's inside, a couple of things could happen. An image might appear, or we might be transported somewhere else and shown a memory, or we could hear a voice, or it could contain a physical note. There's no set way for it to reveal its message, we'll just have to see.'

'Okay,' said Anita, and without hesitating, she reached towards the cylinder, the brass shimmering unnaturally in the candlelight. As her fingers landed on the strangely warm metal, she directed her energy towards it, waiting for... she wasn't sure what. After a few moments of nothing, she looked up at Alexander to find he was nowhere to be seen. Nothing appeared to have happened, and yet she was now on her own, not having witnessed any discernible message. Had she missed it? Was it a fake? What was going on?

She removed her hand from the cylinder and felt a weight lift from her shoulders that she hadn't even noticed had settled. She closed the box, set it back on the little wooden table and forced herself out of the meditation. She snapped awake to find Alexander leaning into her, distraught, hands on her face, shaking her frantically, trying to compel her to wake. His eyes were wide with a terror that was chased away by relief when he realized she was awake. He pulled her to him and held her with such ferocity that Anita wasn't sure he would ever let her go.

'What happened?' he demanded, pulling back a little. 'As soon as you put your hand on the cylinder, it kicked me out of the meditation. I thought it was killing you.'

'Nothing happened. I put my hand on the cylinder, focused all my energy towards it, and absolutely nothing happened. I looked up to see if you'd seen something I missed, but you weren't there. As far as I can tell, that was it; no message of any kind.'

'That's it? Nothing else at all?'

'The metal felt warm when I touched it, and when I took my hand off the cylinder it felt like a weight had been lifted off me. It was weird, because I didn't feel the weight descend. Apart from that, there was nothing at all.'

'Well, congratulations,' he said, unexpectedly, 'you've just completed your first solo meditation. It's much harder than meditating with another person and there aren't many people who can do it.'

Anita smiled, glad to see Alexander had recovered from the scare. 'Why's it harder?'

'You only have the energy of one person at your disposal, so it requires a much bigger individual effort to transport yourself anywhere.'

'In that case, I cheated. You were there when we arrived at the throne room, all I did was pull myself out.'

'It's a first step,' said Alexander, exasperated. 'Will you ever just be able to take a compliment?'

'How did the cylinder kick you out?' she asked, changing the subject.

'I don't know. It must have expelled some kind of energy, directed specifically at me, which pushed me out of your mind. I've never heard of a cylinder doing that.'

'How did it know to boot you out and not me?'

'I don't know. Maybe because you were the one touching the cylinder, or maybe it has a way to recognize your energy.'

'Can a person expel another person from a meditation in the same way?' asked Anita.

'Yes. You need to send a torrent of energy towards the other person, willing them out, and so long as the other person isn't defending themselves, you should be able to eject them. It requires a lot of energy though; you couldn't do it too many times without needing to recuperate.'

'Let's see what happens if you're the one touching the cylinder and see if it tries to boot me out.'

'Even if it did, I'd be kicked out too. Something like that would most likely destroy the whole meditation.'

'You don't know that for certain,' said Anita. 'We should try everything we can, even if it seems unlikely, and we should see what happens if I touch it and you defend yourself. If you're ready for the energy blast, you can repel it and hopefully stay inside my head.'

'Okay,' said Alexander.

'Good, let's go,' she said, eager to see what they could do.

First, they tried Alexander touching the cylinder, but nothing happened. It wasn't even warm when he touched it. No weight settled on him, and nothing happened to Anita.

'Seems like it can recognize you,' said Alexander, looking even more wary of the cylinder as he placed it back in the box.

'Apparently so,' said Anita. 'Are you ready to try repelling the energy?' she asked, her hand hovering over the cylinder. Alexander nodded and Anita lowered her hand. Once again it felt warm to the touch, but this time she was aware of a slight haze that seemed to surround her when her fingers touched the metal.

She looked up again to see if Alexander was still with her, but found only empty space. Anita put the cylinder back and pulled herself out of the meditation. This time, she woke to find Alexander, not nervously hovering over her, but slumped over on his side, eyes closed, not moving.

Anita lunged forward and shook him by the shoulder. 'Alexander?' she said urgently, shaking harder when he didn't respond. 'Alexander,' she said, louder, a hint of panic creeping into her voice. 'Alexander, wake up.'

Alexander moaned and opened his eyes, looking groggily around as he rubbed a hand across his forehead.

Anita stopped shaking and pulled his head into her lap, stroking his hair. 'Thank the Gods,' she said, wishing her heart would stop racing.

Alexander slowly sat up, Anita helping him. 'What happened?' he asked, pushing his hair out of his eyes. 'All I remember was you touching the cylinder. After that, everything went black.'

'Exactly the same as last time,' she said, frustrated. 'I touched the cylinder, it felt warm, and when I looked up, you were gone. The only difference this time is that I noticed a slight haze the moment I touched the cylinder. It lifted, along with the weight, as soon as I removed my hand. What do you think happened to you?'

'The cylinder must have sent a stronger wave of energy at me.'

'How can a cylinder store that much energy? And how did it know to use a stronger burst this time?'

'Maybe the bursts get more intense every time someone tries to stay with you, or maybe it knew what I was trying to do… and I think it's using you as a power source.'

'How could it possibly do that?' asked Anita, queasy at the thought of something leaching off her energy.

'I don't know, but I've never heard of a cylinder that's able to hold that much energy.'

'Urgh,' said Anita, annoyed they had failed to open the cylinder and that they'd uncovered a further mystery. 'I need more tea and cake,' she said, climbing to her feet and helping Alexander to his.

Anita made Alexander sit on a deep, comfortable looking sofa in the kitchen while she made more tea.

'There are cardamom and orange biscuits in the other tin in that cupboard,' said Alexander, 'in case you want something different.'

Anita pulled out another floral container and placed it on the table beside the sofa. She handed Alexander a cup of tea, to which she had added two generous teaspoons of sugar, to combat the shock of being knocked unconscious, and sat down beside him.

'What do we do now?' she asked, munching on a crisp, sweet, delicious biscuit. 'Think it's time we talk to Helena?'

Alexander remained silent for a few moments, thoughtfully sipping his tea. 'I just don't know that we can trust her,' he said, carefully. 'But I'm not sure we have many other options. We could try to do some independent research in the archive? Or find academics to ask?'

'We could,' replied Anita, sceptically, 'but it could take us months to find anything in the archives, especially as we don't really know what we're looking for. And any academics with an interest will probably have links to either Austin, or the Institution.' She racked her brains for any other option. 'I suppose we could go to Elistair and ask him what he thinks… but I don't think he would help us, even if he could. Peter might know something, but he's firmly in Austin's pocket…'

Alexander nodded slowly, selecting a biscuit before replying. 'Then we have to go to Helena,' he said, bitterly.

CHAPTER 7

Austin sat in his dressing room, towel around his neck, the barber he'd used for the last thirty years, closely shaving his face. He looked at his reflection in the mirror, lines visible around his eyes that seemed new, grey hairs around his temples, turning him into someone who looked unnervingly like his father.

'I heard there were demonstrations in Kingdom,' said the barber, conversationally. 'Think they'll amount to much?'

Austin sneered. They'd discussed many a political issue over the years, but a reminder of the sorry situation was unwelcome; he was trying to relax. 'I doubt it,' said Austin. 'Next summer we'll be back to normal. There will be plenty of food, and everyone will forget this ever happened.' He said the words in a way meant to shut down the conversation. Unfortunately, his barber wasn't so easily deterred.

'But next summer is a long way off, and we've got to get through the winter before then.'

'Enough,' said Austin, explosively. 'Just do your job.'

The man took the hint this time, changing the subject to something more light-hearted as he finished. This wasn't the first time Austin had blown up at him, and they both knew it wouldn't be the last. They both acted like it hadn't happened. 'There you go, Sir,' the barber said with a flourish and pat of aftershave. 'Spick and span and ready to take on the world.'

'Thank you,' said Austin. 'Look in on Marcus and see if he wants a shave on your way out, would you?'

The barber passed Amber as he left the room, her face like thunder. 'Peter's here to see you,' she said, darkly. 'He's waiting in your office, muttering something about people refusing to pay taxes. He's on the verge of caving; seems to think now is the time to do something, *before this goes too far.* I tried to send him on his way, but he won't go. Says he won't leave until he's spoken to you.'

'Stupid little spineless worm,' spat Austin, standing up quickly, whipping his towel furiously against the door frame as he stormed out of the room.

Austin marched down the stairs and into his office, not bothering to close the door behind him; this would be a short conversation. 'It seems we have a problem,' he said dryly, coming face to face with an ashen Peter. 'Do we really have to go through this again?'

'Well,' started Peter, looking as though he were mustering all of his limited courage, 'it's just that... well... things have moved on since last we spoke. They're revolting in Kingdom, they've stopped paying taxes, and they say people are *literally* starving. If that's truly the case, we've got to do something.'

'Where did you hear all this?'

'Everywhere. No matter where I go, people ask me what's going on and what we're doing about it. The Institution is gaining momentum again. A little more ammunition and we'll have a full-scale rebellion on our hands.'

'No, we won't,' said Austin, pompously.

'How can you be so sure?'

'Because the Institution can easily be divided if we need to play that card.'

'How?'

'That's none of your concern.'

'So, what am I supposed to do? Nothing?'

'Precisely.' Austin's simmering irritation boiled over. 'I know you're not the sharpest tool, but we've had this conversation before. The same terms apply now as they did then: if you try anything, I'll expose Gwyn as the fraud she is. If you think there are problems out there now, wait and see what would happen to you and your family if they find out Gwyn isn't the true Body Descendant.'

'You have no proof of that; it's your word against mine.'

'You think that matters? All I'd have to do is place a seed of doubt in the minds of a couple of key rebels. You'd be lynched so quickly you wouldn't even realise it was happening, let alone have a chance to protest your innocence.'

'You'd have me and my daughter lynched, just so you don't have to admit we're on the brink of a crisis? You think it'll be as simple as watching from the side lines before emerging king of the castle?'

'Going to risk it all to try and stop me?'

Peter looked Austin in the eye, possibly for the first time in his life, then faltered. 'No,' he said, eventually, 'I suppose not.'

* * * * *

The council chamber erupted. Councillors, who, until now, had remained silent, adding their voices to those opposing Austin's idle stance. Austin had reiterated his position, insisting they need nothing other than patience and time, but all the Spirits, and virtually

119

all the Bodies, opposed him. The Mind councillors backed Austin, along with Peter, but the tide had truly turned.

Alexander took the floor and waited for the room to settle. 'Councillors,' he said loudly, projecting his voice to be heard over the remaining ruckus, 'the majority are in favour of action, however, two Descendants disagree, meaning, under normal circumstances, we cannot proceed. I propose, given the severity of this situation, that we take matters into our own hands. I propose we put in place a food rationing plan, that we instigate controls to curb the soaring food prices, and we put increased resources into finding the cause of this prolonged dip in the energy.'

A roar of support went up for Alexander's plan.

Austin stood, slowly making his way to Alexander's side. The room went quiet. 'Well said,' said Austin, his tone sugary sweet. 'I couldn't agree more that we need to start food rationing. It's essential that all suffer in equal amounts during this unfortunate period. Indeed, those in this room must be included, so we show the people that we're all in the same boat.'

A swell of agreement flowed across the room, although most of the Mind councillors looked as though they'd swallowed a wasp.

'However,' Austin continued, 'I cannot condone diverting precious resources towards the futile task of determining the cause. It's simple. As I've said a hundred times before, we're having a bad year. Next summer this will be behind us and we'll be back to normal.'

Alexander paused before responding. He didn't agree with Austin's view, however, official agreement to rationing was better than doing it without Descendant support, especially as Austin's private army was far larger than anyone else's. Alexander could push for more once rationing was in place. 'Well then, rationing is to be put in place immediately. I'll report back on progress at the next meeting. I think that's all for today,' said Alexander, making for the exit before anyone could jeopardize what they'd agreed.

He could feel Austin's furious energy burning into his back as he turned out of the council chamber. He walked through the Spirit Temple and out into the daylight beyond, preoccupied by Peter's bizarre energy. He had been angry, scared, frustrated, brooding... what did Austin have on Peter? Alexander was so preoccupied that he almost walked straight into Helena, not realising she was there.

'Hi,' she said, tentatively.

'Hi,' he replied.

'What happened?' she asked, trying to sound casual.

'We're putting food rationing in place, but Austin vetoed additional research into the cause of the crisis. Peter was his usual, spineless self; he didn't utter a single word.

'That's not surprising, considering...'

'Considering what?' said Alexander, not even attempting to hide his interest.

'It's obvious, isn't it?'

'What's obvious?'

'Austin is controlling Peter.'

'Of course, that's obvious. But why?'

'I don't know, but if I were to guess, I'd say Austin is using Gwyn as a bargaining chip.'

'What do you mean?'

'Really? After everything you and Anita found out the other day?' She paused, shaking her head. 'If Anita is the Body Descendant, then Gwyn isn't. If Austin were to expose that, Gwyn and Peter would be cast out, not to mention, they'd probably be mobbed.'

'But Austin doesn't know Gwyn isn't the Body Descendant.'

'He might not have any concrete proof, but he knows why Christiana came to Empire, and he knows Anita got away that night in the temple. I doubt, given the public's mood, that anyone would stop to ask for proof if they were told something so sensational, especially if Austin was the one who told them.'

'No, probably not,' said Alexander. It fit perfectly: Peter was protecting Gwyn.

'Anita and I have something we need to talk to you about,' he said, changing the subject.

'Really?' she said. 'What?'

'I'm not telling you without Anita. When can we meet?' Alexander was cold and transactional, remembering with an icy jolt that Helena was responsible for his parents' deaths.

'Why don't you come to the farm for dinner this evening?' she suggested. 'Anderson and Bass are coming to tell us about something they've found. You might be interested in what they say, and afterwards, we can talk about whatever it is you have on your mind.'

'Fine. What time?'

'Eight?'

'Okay,' he said, turning his back and walking away.

* * * * *

Austin and Marcus walked side by side along an unkempt farm track. They were on the outskirts of Empire and everywhere around them were signs of stress: gates with broken hinges, farm machinery lying unmaintained, and empty fields where cows and sheep would usually be grazing. They reached the top of the track and walked toward the farm buildings, Amber following a couple of paces behind, flanked by two of her cronies. There was activity all around them; men dressed in black moving this way and that, unloading sacks of who knew what from large trucks, storing them in one of the barns.

This was Marcus' third such trip, and he looked around expectantly for the farmer. They reached the farmhouse with no sign of him or her, so Austin sauntered up to the front door and knocked loudly, receiving an almost immediate response. A thin-faced, harassed looking woman opened the door, eyeing Austin with distaste as she said, 'Can I help you with something?'

'Come now,' said Austin, cruelly. 'It will be easier for all of us if we don't have to play games. Where is he?'

'My husband?' she asked, acting as though she had no idea why Austin was at her door. 'I don't know. He went out this morning as normal, and I'm sure he'll be back for lunch at one o'clock, as he usually is. You're more than welcome to wait in the yard until he returns.'

Austin was fuming. He was used to a wholly different reception, where the farmer would come out and meet him. They would plead with him to let them keep their farm for just a little longer, coming up with some hare-brained reason how, with just a little more time, they could pay Austin what they owed him.

In the beginning, Austin had often agreed, taking livestock or other produce as immediate payment, stipulating more stringent terms for the next time. They had now reached next time, and there was no benefit to be gained from a delay in payment, so Austin rarely granted one. Now, he was taking control of the farms.

In Austin's view, he was more than reasonable, usually allowing the farmer and their family to stay on, so long as they agreed to work for whoever Austin put in charge. Typically, Austin ensconced a Mind councillor, leaving a number of his soldiers behind to both work the farm and ensure there was no delayed resistance.

Today, gifts, promises and pleas were absent. Indeed, it would seem that this farmer was trying to cause offense, presumably as a last, meagre rebellion before accepting the inevitable.

Austin, Marcus and Amber waited in the yard. Austin and Amber's tempers rose as the minutes ticked by, snapping at soldiers, ordering them to bring more tea, or telling them off for doing some small thing wrong. Marcus found the situation amusing. He'd never seen anyone defy his father, and they all knew an act of defiance was exactly what this was. The soldiers had, after all, arrived before sunrise, before the farmer had left for the day. An impending visit from Austin couldn't have been a surprise.

One o'clock eventually rolled around. Exactly on time, a beaten up old four-by-four pulled into the yard. A medium height, medium built, middle-aged man, with a kind, lined face and greying hair stepping out of one side. A tall, gangly man, who couldn't have been older than seventeen, climbed out of the other. They looked at Austin, then at each other, before walking towards where Marcus, Amber, and Austin sat outside one of the larger barns. Austin shooed away the soldiers and stood.

'Nice of you to finally join us, Matthew,' said Austin, his tone terse.

'Didn't realize you'd be dropping in,' Matthew lied, his tone even, giving nothing away.

'I take it you're ready to pay what you owe me then, seeing as you weren't expecting us?'

'You know I'm not; the same as all the others.'

'Then it won't surprise you, in line with action taken in their cases, that we will be taking over the running of this farm.'

'And in line with what happened in their cases, I'm assuming there is nothing I can do to persuade you to do otherwise?'

'I doubt it.'

'Well, I can't say that surprises me, seeing as your men are already wreaking havoc. It would be a shame to stop them now.' He hid the sarcasm from his voice, but that didn't prevent its presence from being felt.

Austin's hackles rose and Marcus held his breath.

'You would be wise to view this as an opportunity to accept help,' said Austin. 'You should embrace it, not fight it.'

'Is that what you would do?' Matthew asked.

'I don't see that how *I* would act is of any concern here. You're a mere shadow of the man I am; a shadow with different tools, living in a very different world.'

'Oh, I see. How foolish I am,' said Matthew.

Austin's eyes flared dangerously. 'Careful, Matthew, or I'll have no option but to see your behaviour as a sign of disobedience. You may even force me to evict you.'

'I thought our staying here was a term of the *agreement*,' said Matthew. 'I thought our working for free on the farm was to help pay off our debt.'

'My my,' said Austin, 'how you people must talk. You're right though, I do expect you to continue working on the farm. You'll be working under the direction of Francis, one of my trusted Mind councillors, who will, I'm sure, do a better job of running the place than you... not that that would be difficult.'

'He has experience in farming?'

'He learns quickly,' said Austin, smiling. 'Make sure you don't go anywhere; I want a progress report in a week.'

'Not from Francis?' said Matthew.

Marcus had to give it to him; this man was fearless.

'You heard what I said. Unless you're stupid as well as inept, you'll do as I say.'

Austin turned to leave. Marcus averted his eyes, suddenly unable to look at Matthew or his son.

'What's the matter,' said Amber, coming up beside him. 'Don't have the stomach for it?'

* * * * *

The table outside at the farm was full of Institution members, old and new. Although the weather was turning and there was a chill in the air, Helena refused to eat indoors quite yet. Instead, they'd brought heaters out, blankets piled around the place. Bass and Anderson sat near Helena at one end of the table, Melia presiding over the other end, everyone talking animatedly with those around them.

Alexander and Anita approached the table, doing their best to hide their discomfort at coming back to both help and seek help from these people. People who had not only kidnapped them, but also revealed secrets that could never be forgiven. As they came into view of the others, a hushed silence fell over the table. They made their way to Helena's end, where two empty chairs awaited them.

To Anita's surprise, Cleo was also present, sitting next to her father, Draeus, who spent most of his time in the Wild Lands. The others were all people Anita recognized from the barn dance, but since she'd never spoken to any of them, she didn't know their names, what they did, or why they were here.

'Hi,' said Helena, as Anita and Alexander sat down. 'I'm glad you could make it.'

'Hi,' said Anita and Alexander together, both of them reserved.

'Let's eat,' said Helena, gesturing to the enormous, colourful platters of delicious looking food that covered every inch of the table in front of them. No food shortage here, thought Anita.

They tucked in greedily, and the conversation flowed as easily as it had before. Alexander and Anita joined in, being careful to direct their attention towards Bass, Anderson, and Cleo, rather than the other Institution members, and certainly away from Helena.

After the main course had been cleared, three enormous apple and blackberry crumbles were placed on the table, along with clotted and double cream, ice cream, and custard. Anita was considering a second helping when Helena cut across her deliberation. 'Anderson, Bass,' she said, looking at each of them in turn. The rest of the table quietened down to listen, 'I think I speak for us all when I say we're dying to hear about your recent findings.' She looked expectantly at them, waiting for them to begin.

Bass looked at Anderson and took a deep breath. His mouth opened to speak, but before he got a word out, Anderson cut across the silence. 'Well, as you know, I've been researching the Relic for quite some time, and one of my areas of special interest is energy transfer. Since coming to Empire, Bass and I have been working on the theory that there may be a way to use energy transfer to send the Relic back to the Gods.'

'But how would that work?' asked a curvy blond-haired girl sitting half-way down the table.

Anderson looked disdainfully at her before answering. Somebody didn't like to be interrupted, thought Anita.

'We think the only viable way of doing it is to create what is, in effect, an energy slingshot. We would trap strands of energy, pull them back, around the Relic, creating a vast store of potential energy, and then, when we're ready, release the hold. The Relic would be flung upwards, into the sky.'

Anderson looked up to be greeted by a sea of confused faces.

'The reason we think it might work,' interjected Bass, 'is that energy behaves almost as though it's elastic. If you imagine an energy wave travelling through the air,' to illustrate his point, he waved his finger up and down, creating the distinctive wave shape, 'you can pinch a bit of the wave and pull it towards you. When you do that, on one side, the wave keeps travelling in the direction it was going before, stretching the pinched wave out, so it becomes flatter, resulting in an increasing force that tries to pull the wave back to its original course. On the other side of the pinch, the wave bunches up behind where you've pinched it. The force here, trying to push through the blockage, builds as the waves pile up. As you can imagine, the longer you pinch, the greater the force of the wave pinging back to its original course when you let go. Also, the more powerful the energy you pinch, the greater the potential force that can build up, and the smaller the wavelength, the faster the force builds up.'

'How many strands will you pinch?' said the blond.

'We're not sure yet. We need to run more tests,' said Bass.

'And if I understand correctly,' the blond continued, 'the Relic will be like the stone inside a slingshot?'

'Exactly,' said Anderson, sounding exasperated.

'But surely that's going to be dangerous?' she said. 'What if someone got in the way of the energy release?'

'They'd die,' said Anderson, Bass shooting him a disapproving look.

'We have many calculations to work through, to determine the feasibility of this,' said Bass, firmly. 'We need to be extremely precise with our measurements around lengths, types and origins of wave, what we'll use to pinch the energy, what we need to do to ensure the energy wave won't oscillate as it returns to its rightful path... We need more time to work out the details, but it's the best theory we have so far.'

'How do you know that returning the Relic to the Gods means sending it into the sky?' asked Anita, sceptically.

Anderson smiled patronizingly. 'We don't think that sending the Relic into the sky is the same thing as sending it back to the Gods. What we think will happen is that the Relic will go up and then come back down again. The key is to ensure it lands in a location devoid of non-partisan eyes, and more importantly, in a place we can recover it. Once we've created the impression that we've returned the Relic, we can work on how to actually return it to the Gods in slow time, if that's even still possible, given the state of the Body bloodline.'

'You're banking on the fact that, if everyone *thinks* the Relic has been returned, then the energy will return to normal?' asked Anita.

'Yes,' said Bass. 'In the same way that it was only after Austin announced Christiana's death that the energy dropped rapidly, and not when she actually died. We're hoping if people think the Relic has been sent back, the energy will respond, despite the Relic still being with us.'

'You're saying the energy levels are totally subjective?' said a skinny, dark-haired man of about thirty, sitting next to Melia.

'We think so,' said Bass, 'and even if not totally subjective, then at least partially.'

'And entirely dependent on people rather than other natural forces?' the skinny man said.

'People do seem to be the biggest driver from what we know to date,' said Bass, 'although, truthfully, we don't know the extent to which other factors affect the levels. Our logic is that people are subjective and respond to news emotionally, whereas other natural forces don't do this; they can only respond to actual stimuli, like, for example, less energy being available because of the general low mood of our population. As a result, we're in control of our own destiny in a way that the rest of nature is not.'

'But how does our general mood translate into crops dying?' asked a ginger haired girl.

'We don't know exactly,' said Bass. 'All we know is that everything takes energy from the planet to survive, and if there isn't as much energy going around, there isn't as much for the plants to use.'

'Sounds a bit tenuous to me,' said the dark-haired guy.

Bass laughed. 'That's because it is tenuous. In the same way that we don't understand fully how our brains and bodies work, or what goes on in the depths of the oceans, or why we're all here anyway, we don't fully understand how energy moves around and affects everything it touches. All we know, as a fact, is that it does.'

'But we don't even know that for a fact,' countered the dark-haired guy. 'What if Austin's right? Maybe this crisis will blow over. If we don't really understand how energy affects everything, how can you know that it does, in fact, affect everything?'

'Evidence,' said Bass, a little edgily. 'The same way that we know all the other stuff we think we know.'

'So,' said Helena, in a way that said the edge in the air had better disappear, 'your next steps are to test your hypotheses?'

'Exactly,' said Anderson, regaining the attention of the table. 'We're not sure how long it will take, but of course, we'll work as quickly as we can. The tricky bit though will be after we have a technical solution, when we have to get the Descendants to play along and act as though they're sending the Relic back. Good luck getting Austin to agree to that...'

'You leave Austin to me,' said Helena, coolly. 'Once you've got something reliable, I'll make the Descendants play ball.'

Anita inwardly shook her head. How on earth did Helena think she could 'make' Austin and Peter help the Institution?

* * * * *

After dinner, Helena gave everyone apart from Alexander, Anita, Melia, Draeus, Cleo, Bass, and Anderson a very obvious signal that it was time to leave. Anita breathed a sigh of relief when they'd gone; she'd never been comfortable in a crowd.

They sipped coffee and made small talk for a while, until Anita decided to put aside the niceties. 'We found the cylinder,' she said abruptly, cutting across some mundane comment Melia was making.

Helena spun her head, boring into Anita's eyes. 'And?' she asked. 'What was in it?'

'We don't yet know,' said Anita, a warning in her tone. 'We tried to open it, but for some reason, we can't. Also, it kicks Alexander out of the meditation whenever we try to. We came because we wanted to see if you have ideas we haven't tried yet.'

They discussed all the things Alexander and Anita had tried to date and then quickly drew a blank. 'I'm not an expert,' said Helena, 'but I've never heard of a cylinder resisting when someone tried to open it.'

'Me neither,' said Melia, intrigued.

'Nor have I, I'm afraid,' said Draeus. 'It wouldn't be publicly researched either; bit sensitive, I'd say. Maybe the kind of thing they would look into on Cloud Mountain though.'

'True,' said Helena, slowly, 'and Clarissa was given the cylinder at Cloud Mountain, so it would make sense that someone there might be able to help.'

Melia nodded in agreement.

'What goes on at this Cloud Mountain?' asked Cleo.

'It's home to the Spirit Leader and his or her followers,' said Melia. 'Before the Relic and prophecy were discovered, the temples existed, but were run differently. Each temple had a leader, and each leader had followers, much like the Descendants and their councillors today. However, the focus then was learning about the disciplines associated with each temple, rather than the political nonsense that dominates today.'

'What happened to the Body and Mind Leaders?' asked Cleo, not waiting to see if Melia would continue without a prompt.

'The Mind Leader became the Mind Descendant and the Body Leader died in a climbing accident around the same time the Descendants were named. The Body Leader's followers mostly became councillors to the new Body Descendant, not seeing the point in having two separate groups of people representing Bodies. The Spirit Leader, on the other hand, saw merit in maintaining a separate group, for research and development. They've always kept a low profile, and being so out of the way at the Cloud Mountain, they've never been a problem for the Descendants.'

'Or at least, never a big enough problem,' said Helena.

'How exactly were the Descendants chosen?' Cleo probed.

'Nobody's entirely sure,' said Melia. 'If it's recorded anywhere, it'll be in the Descendants'' private vaults. What is public knowledge, is that around the time the Relic was discovered, those who became Descendants were visited by their relevant deity. The Gods told them of the prophecy, and their duty to fulfil it. The evidence of that must have been compelling, given how painlessly they moved from the old structure to the one we have today.'

'But the monks at the Cloud Mountain never share what they find?' asked Anita, incredulous.

'There is some sharing,' said Alexander, 'but it's limited. The good stuff never makes it out without a trade.'

'What about the work the Spirit academics do here and things we learn from the observatory? Do those findings get communicated back to the Cloud Mountain?' asked Anita.

'Yes, generally they do,' said Draeus. 'Certainly, everything that becomes public knowledge, because traders like me take information about new findings into the Wild Lands. The Spirit Leader pays us for knowledge. They also bribe our academics for secrets, and sometimes even go so far as to plant moles.'

'So the academics here could have the key to something they're working on at the Cloud Mountain, or vice versa, and they would never know?' said Cleo.

'Yep,' said Alexander. There's too much distrust to share everything, especially at times like these.

'And there are no Spirit academics in Empire or Kingdom who you think could help us open the cylinder?' asked Anita, not directing the question at anyone in particular.

'No,' said Helena, 'not that I know of, and even if there were, Austin has spies everywhere. The risk of him finding out what we're doing is too great.'

'So, the Cloud Mountain's the only option we have?' said Anita, her voice flat, devoid of emotion.

'That's where the cylinder was given to Clarissa. Not only is it the only option, it's also a good one,' said Helena.

Anita read the energy of everyone around the table. She read nothing other than affirmation, including from Alexander. 'Okay,' she said, 'Alexander and I will go. Do you think anyone else should come too?'

Helena considered the question, her energy tinged with surprise, but before she could reply, Anderson jumped in. 'Yes, I think I should come too,' he said, keenly. 'There may be something we can learn about energy transfer.'

'And I'm happy to escort you,' said Draeus. 'That'll provide you with a cover story for your presence in the Wild Lands: trading trip to assess the current situation first-hand.'

'Sounds good,' said Anita. 'When do we leave?'

'Give me a couple of days to organize everything,' said Draeus. 'I'll be in touch to let you know exactly when. We'll leave at night, always easiest, and you'll need to pack clothes for both hot and cold climates. The Cloud Mountain is about as far as you can get from civilization, so we'll be travelling through a good number of lands on the way. Don't worry about anything else; I'll provide everything we need.'

'Great,' said Anita, despite herself, quite excited at the prospect of an adventure into the wild.

* * * * *

Matthew woke in the middle of the night. It was silent, as he'd expected, having meticulously checked the soldiers' rota. Most of them would be asleep, only two guards on duty, and both positioned near the house, mainly to monitor him. Matthew rolled over and shook his wife, Emily, awake. She came to life quickly, instantly understanding that now was the time they'd been waiting for. She quickly got dressed and, without the aid of lights, silently made her way to their son, Henry's, room. She woke him before making her way downstairs to meet Matthew.

By the time they arrived downstairs, Matthew had already retrieved the food parcel he'd hidden the previous evening, along with packs of clothes and other essential items. He handed packs to Emily and Matthew and then headed for the back door, motioning for them to follow.

Matthew gingerly pulled the door open a crack, praying the oil he'd applied to the hinges the previous day would prevent it from screaming. His prayer was all but answered, the door making the smallest of protests before swinging willingly open. They waited a few moments, listening intently to the noises of the night, heartbeats drumming in their ears. When Mathew was sure the coast was clear (thankfully the guards wore heavy, noisy boots), they creep through the door, noiselessly closing and locking it behind them.

They slunk round the edge of the yard, passing through an open gate into a grass field, following the hedge all the way to the far side, careful to keep in its shadow. They entered the woods that backed onto the field, thankfully having only to cross a small ditch, no hedge to hamper their escape here. They hurried, the goal to get as far away from the farm before dawn as possible, speed more important than silence as they sped through the trees. Apart from the odd look back over their shoulders, they took no precautions to ensure they weren't being followed, assuming, because they hadn't been challenged, that they had got clean away.

But open challenge wasn't always Amber's style. Tonight, she'd chosen stealth, tracking the family through the woods along with four of her most trusted and skilled soldiers. So Amber watched as Matthew, Emily, and Henry made their way to the river. She listened as they met up with two other families from two other farms. Then she followed as they headed in the direction of the Wild Lands, filled with the most delicious sense of apprehension; where were they going, and what secrets would they help her uncover?

CHAPTER 8

The following day, Anita got up and acted as though everything was as it should be. She started her day with yoga in the garden, followed by a breakfast of homemade granola and orange juice with Cordelia, before heading to the observatory to work. Cordelia, never one for small talk, decided breakfast was an ideal time to probe Anita on her current relationship status. When Anita told her that Marcus was no longer on the scene, Cordelia dug for information about what, exactly, had happened.

Anita managed to just about dodge the questions, providing vague and flimsy responses, before deliberately diverting the conversation towards other topics, namely, the weather and what Cordelia was going to make for the rapidly approaching winter festival at the temples.

Anita finished her cereal and escaped the inquisition, thinking about the upcoming trip to the Wild Lands on her walk to the observatory. She realized that other than a few descriptions from people who had been there, she had no idea what to expect from each of the different lands they would travel through; she didn't even know which land was where, and which connected to another. She decided she would hunt out a map and study it before they departed, so as not to look ignorant on the trip.

Anita arrived at the observatory, climbing the stairs to find Bass, Gwyn, and Patrick (Bass' lab assistant), chatting about the winter festival and Gwyn's role as a Descendant. 'I won't be taking the main Body role this year, obviously,' Gwyn said sweetly, lapping up their undivided attention. 'Dad will do that, but I'll still be in the procession, and I'll be wearing a beautiful white silk dress and a spectacular flower wreath in my hair; it's got loads of tiny little white flowers all around…'

'… morning,' said Anita, loudly, purposefully cutting across Gwyn's description.

'Hi,' said Bass and Patrick, clearly surprised to see her.

'Haven't seen you for a while,' said Patrick, in his usual crass way.

Anita ignored his jibe and sat down in her normal spot before saying, 'Anything new with the energy?'

'No,' said Bass, shooting a sideways glance at Gwyn, 'nothing has changed; still on a downward trajectory.'

'No surprise there then,' said Anita, turning her attention to the display in front of her. 'Descendants decided to do anything about the crisis yet?' she asked, looking determinedly at the brass dials, so as not to have to see whatever face Bass was making.

'I… uh,' Gwyn started.

'That's a no then,' said Anita. She didn't know why she was being so unpleasant. It just seemed like the right thing to do, seeing as Peter wouldn't stand up to Austin, and it was all because of Gwyn's real identity… not that Gwyn knew…

'Right,' said Bass, awkwardly. 'Well, I suppose we should get to work, Patrick.'

Everyone recognized that as Gwyn's cue to leave. Instead, she leaned over Bass, stroked his hair, and said in her most sickly voice, 'Will you show me what you're working on?'

Bass looked up at her with wide eyes, like a rabbit caught in particularly bright headlights. Gwyn was giving him pathetic puppy dog eyes, so it was no surprise he agreed.

'We're working on energy transfer,' said Patrick, desperate for Gwyn to turn her attention to him. Anita rolled her eyes. 'We're looking at how we can transfer energy from one object to another.'

'Really?' asked Gwyn, pretending to be fascinated as she followed Patrick to the other side of the room.

Bass made to follow them, and Anita shot him a warning look as he went. 'Careful,' she said, under her breath, so he could barely hear her. 'Given who she is, just... be careful.'

* * * * *

Three days later, the travelling party of Anita, Alexander, Anderson, and Draeus were ready to leave. They met at Cleo's house, Anita feeling harassed because of the argument she'd had with Cordelia before she left. Cordelia had questioned, for the hundredth time, where Anita was going, and what she was doing. Anita had, for the hundredth time, reassured Cordelia that she was going on a trading and research trip, nothing more. Cordelia was paranoid about the reported riots and didn't want her to go.

Anita had almost blurted out that she didn't plan on dying, like Jeffrey's mother had, which would have been difficult to explain... She'd eventually extracted herself, reassuring her fearful grandmother that she would be careful, wouldn't take any risks, and would be back as soon as she could.

They departed Empire in a 4x4 energy vehicle just before midnight, having checked and rechecked their supplies. Draeus had been clear that they should travel light, but as they each had garments suitable for conditions ranging from the scorching deserts of Wild Sands, to the icy roads of Wild Ice, they weren't travelling light at all. Draeus cursed at the fully laden vehicle.

They drove for hours, stopping only when absolutely necessary, the sun high in the sky by the time they approached the edge of Wild Water. It was breath-taking; enormous pools of water everywhere with connecting streams and rivers. Magnificent waterfalls fell from the sky, spray flying up to cover them, lush green grass everywhere the water didn't dominate.

Draeus laughed at Anita's reaction. 'If you think this is good, you should go to the middle of Wild Water; this is only the very edge.'

After another few hours of driving, they approached a massive expanse of water that filled the horizon as far as the eye could see. 'The Salt Sea,' said Draeus, coming to a halt at its shore. 'We're going to camp here tonight.'

'Where are we?' asked Anita, clearly the only one not to know.

'We're on the northern edge of Wild Water,' said Alexander. 'The Salt Sea isn't really a sea; it's an enormous lake, as it's landlocked. Nobody knows why it's salty, but if you go in, you'll float; it's very surreal.'

'Sounds like fun,' said Anita.

They put up the tents and lounged around for the rest of the day, Anita and Alexander going for a swim while Anderson and Draeus went to a local food seller and bought fish, potatoes, and some kind of green vegetable similar to cabbage. Draeus wanted to avoid trading posts, just in case someone recognized Alexander and word got back to Empire or Kingdom.

Draeus cooked the fish over the fire with oil and lemon, boiled the potatoes in a large pot, and steamed the greens in a bamboo steamer over the top. They ate greedily, then retired to their tents before the sun had fully set.

* * * * *

Cleo entered the archive, as she had for the last ten days, descended to the second basement level, and took up her usual seat near the back of the floor. She'd chosen this spot as it was secluded, yet provided a great vantage point to see who was coming and going across the rest of the floor. She was hidden for the most part by the racks of books and manuscripts, but could see out through a couple of helpfully positioned gaps in the artifacts.

So far, the most excitement she'd witnessed was when two volunteer workers had snuck down here to make out. They'd almost been caught by the girl's father, who, it turned out, was one of the senior categorizers. Thanks to Cleo, they'd escaped down a level, Cleo seizing the opportunity to aid a kindred spirit, waylaying the father by asking a pointless question. They'd thanked her later that night at The Island, trying to buy her drinks all evening.

As she'd been doing for the last ten days, Cleo poured over newspaper articles and any other material she could find that referenced the discovery of the Relic. There was something about it that just didn't add up, and she was determined to find out what.

The bright, stark, cold lights of the archive floor were getting to her, not to mention the disappointing lack of a discovery, but she persevered, flicking through an account of the first public announcement of the prophecy. The most interesting part was at the end, where the author had recorded the questions from the audience: Where, exactly, had the Relic been discovered? Why should they believe it was true? Why had the Gods chosen to hide both the Relic and the prophecy for so long?

She was just coming to the end when a movement caught her eye. Other than a brief appearance by a volunteer here and there, she was getting used to being the only person around, so was curious to see who it was venturing into this soulless basement.

Cleo peered around the nearest bookcase to see a medium height man, with a slight build, and dark, wavy, shoulder-length hair walk across the floor, heading for one of the locked doors in the back wall. He moved seamlessly, stride light and graceful, limbs responding effortlessly to his every command, and Cleo sat mesmerized by him, curious.

The man unlocked one of the doors, pausing as he turned the handle, moving his head to look in her direction. He smiled a little as he pushed the door open, disappeared through it, leaving it open behind him.

Cleo paused for a split second, snapping herself out of the trance he had somehow put her in, following him through the door before she'd had time to process what she was doing.

She stopped short as the man looked up from behind a workbench, giving her an encouraging yet questioning look, the shadow of a smile on his lips. She said nothing, so he raised a promising eyebrow.

'Hi,' said Cleo, her usual confidence evading her in the face of a man with such self-assured poise. 'I'm Cleo.' She paused, waiting for his answer, but he didn't oblige, instead, holding her gaze with mesmerizing hazelnut eyes and waiting to see what she would do next.

'I've been working down here for days and have been dying to see what's behind these doors,' she said quickly, hoping vehemently he wouldn't throw her out. 'It's all so mysterious, don't you think? Locked doors, secret artefacts... who knows what scandals hide down here, sheltered from prying eyes.' The words came out in a rush and she silently told herself to *get it together* before taking a step towards him.

The smile that had been threatening since she'd walked in finally fought its way to his lips, lighting up his face as he waited again for Cleo to make the next move. Cleo was getting frustrated; people weren't usually so comfortable with silence. 'What are you working on?' she asked, deciding to give the direct approach a go; it would be rude for him to ignore a direct question. Unless, of course, he couldn't speak... she pulled a nervous expression, suddenly anxious. She was never anxious.

She took a deep breath, clasped her hands, banished the undesirable facial expression in favour of a neutral one, and forced herself to stay silent. She waited for a response, compelling herself to hold his gaze, telling herself that she was calm and composed, despite her racing heart.

* * * * *

The silence stretched, the man taking his time to appraise Cleo, determining who she was and what she was really doing here. There were very few allowed to enter the room in which they were standing. There were those who would literally kill for the opportunity to stand where he had allowed her to. However, he decided his initial impression had been correct; she posed no threat to him or the work he was here to do, so he took a path he had not trodden for some time; the frivolous one.

'These rooms are so bland, don't you think?' he said, taking her by surprise. 'You would have thought that a place such as this, of such import, a place containing the secrets of our past, would have warranted some design consideration. But then, I suppose it's safe to assume those drawn to the noble profession of categorizing and maintaining aren't in possession of the greatest artistic talent.'

'Unlike yourself?' asked Cleo, leaning forward.

'Beauty is in the eye of the beholder; maybe those who built this place think it is beautiful, in its own way.'

'Do you ever respond to a question with a straightforward answer?'

'You're researching the Relic?' he asked.

'Do you think the Gods amuse themselves by toying with us?' said Cleo.

He smiled: she was playing his game. 'Who are we to second guess the pastimes of the Gods? If they want to toy with us, is it not their right?'

'Their rights... but what of their responsibilities? Are the Gods not also burdened with that weight?'

'What's to say a God is not as human as a human? We saddle them with perfection. Do we not expect too much?'

'Do we expect enough? Our expectations couldn't get much lower; we're in the middle of an energy crisis and nobody expects anything of the Gods... But we digress; I'm not concerned with great philosophical questions; let a Spirit tread that unfulfilling path. I care only about facts, specifically, how the Relic was really discovered.'

'Is that not common knowledge, making yours a dreary pastime?'

'What is it you're researching that's so much more tantalising?'

'Who's to say I'm researching anything at all?'

'Isn't that the whole point of this place?' she asked, moving to his side, obviously trying to get a look at what he was doing. 'Unless you're adding new material? That would be even more delicious, given where we're standing...' She looked up at him from under her lashes as she said the word 'delicious'.

'What's your favourite place in the Wild Lands?' he asked, covering the document in front of him (only a page from yesterday's paper), shielding it from her view, knowing she would find this simple secret intolerably frustrating.

Cleo's eyes flicked to the papers. She took a moment before responding. 'That's where you're from?' she asked, her eyes returning to his before she walked deeper into the room. 'You're not from here, that's for sure.'

'I do try to make it obvious,' he said, following her through the shelves of documents, fascinated by this strange girl.

Cleo rounded the end of the nearest set of shelves and spotted a file entitled *Relic Research: Volume One*, on the workbench at the end of the room. Her energy jumped with excited anticipation and she reached out her hand to pick it up.

He quickly stepped up behind her and took hold of the offending hand, spinning her around, away from her prize, a jolt of energy flying through them at the contact.

The man's eyes went wide, and he threw away her hand. He stepped towards her, placing his hands on her arms, Cleo backing up, her way blocked by the workbench she was now leaning back against. He looked deep into her eyes, feeling the energy coursing through them, trying to process just what he'd felt. 'You've been there?' he said, although it wasn't clear if he was asking himself or her.

'Where?' she asked, perplexed. 'The Wild Lands?'

'Or maybe you haven't actually been there, but you've *seen* it.'

'Seen what?' asked Cleo, her energy turning cross, and maybe a little concerned.

He snapped out of it, releasing her arms but staying tantalizingly close, his eyes locked with hers. He looked at her, taking his time to decide, then said slowly, 'The Great Hall of the Magnei.'

He watched for her reaction, but when she gave him nothing but a questioning head shake, he stepped back, putting distance between them.

'It's time for you to go,' he said, his voice even but firm as he marched her towards the door.

'Why?' she asked. He could practically see the cogs turning as she racked her brain for a reason to stay.

He didn't answer, but as they reached the room's threshold, she suddenly became determined, knocking away his hand as she spun to face him. 'The Great Hall of the Magnei?' she asked, shocked. 'That's what it is? It's in the Wild Lands? How could you possibly know about that?'

He held up a hand to halt her questions. 'You've seen it but haven't been there. How?'

'A little meditative practice can yield the most surprising results,' she said.

He nodded, understanding her meaning but not understanding how it was possible. 'You should go,' he said finally, pushing her through the door.

Realizing he wouldn't answer her questions, and thinking it best to leave on good terms, she turned to leave. 'Before I go,' she said, pausing, 'what's your name?' She threw her most seductive look back across her shoulder, but found, to her immense surprise, the man gone and the door closed. She tried the handle but found it locked. She shivered. What had just happened, and who was that enchanting man?

* * * * *

Anita, Alexander, Draeus and Anderson travelled for another six days, weaving their way towards Wild Air. They took an exasperatingly indirect route that avoided both the busiest trading roads and the areas with most reported riots.

They came first to Wild Fire, camping by one of the most remote, yet most beautiful hot springs. Alexander and Anita disappeared to the furthest pool as soon as the tents were up and were playing a spirited game of tag when Draeus and Anderson clattered to a halt beside them, hissing at them to shut up.

Reading from their energy that there was something seriously awry, Alexander and Anita sped to the side of the pool, threw on their clothes, and followed Draeus in silence to find a place to hide nearby. They heard voices approaching, and saw, to their astonishment, a cohort of Mind councillors appear out of the scrub to surround the pool.

All four of them held their breath in anxious anticipation, silently wondering how they could have been so easily followed. It turned out, from what they could overhear, that the councillors were on a tour of the most medicinally beneficial hot pools.

The councillors stripped off and took a dip, made extensive notes both from their own observations and from what their guide was telling them, and then promptly dried off, re-clothed, and went on their way.

With the threat gone, the four of them fell about laughing at how they had so nearly been rumbled by such an unlikely coincidence.

Next, they travelled through Wild Ice, where they stayed in a miniscule trading post surrounded by fir trees and covered in snow. Draeus assured them that very few people travelled this way, so it was worth the risk for a bed and a roof.

Anita wondered how a trading post that was so out of the way could survive, but knew better than to ask Draeus, a private man with secrets even his gossip of a daughter couldn't wheedle out of him. Instead, she was grateful for the roaring fires, mulled wine, and spit roast beef that was lavished upon them in abundant quantities from the moment they stepped through the door. By the time she and Alexander retired to their room and collapsed into their fur lined bed, she was feeling full and more than a little drunk.

The following morning, after a breakfast of venison and juniper berry sausages, Anita discovered first-hand how the trading post survived. She was looking for Draeus, to tell him they were all packed up and ready to leave, when she inadvertently witnessed him making a dubious-looking trade with a dangerous-looking man. The owner of the trading post was also present, both parties handing him a wad of cash when the items, whatever they were, had changed hands. Anita retreated, hoping nobody had noticed her presence.

They made it to Wild Wood that night, this time back in their tents, and by the end of the following day, reached the far side of the region. It was pitch black when they finally stopped, and were about to once again set up the tents, when they saw a strange series of twinkling lights through the trees in front of them. They froze in perfect unison, looking to Draeus for an explanation. He shook his head, raised his shoulders, and put a finger to his lips, then held up his hand, signalling for them to stay put. He crept forward through the trees to investigate.

To his astonishment, from all around him, people were materializing out of the darkness, drawn to the lights like moths. The lights were set up in a clearing around a makeshift wooden stage, and on the stage stood a slight man, dark hair tied back in a ponytail.

The man was back-lit, which gave him a spooky air. Draeus couldn't make out his features, only his outline, an outline focusing intently on the growing crowd, now at least fifty strong, and pressing forward towards the stage. The swarm quickly became larger, thicker, the once open space eaten up by a crush of humanity, the atmosphere becoming heavy, potent.

The movement around Draeus lulled, then stopped abruptly, apprehension palpable as all eyes strained to focus on the stage. Moments later, the back lights cut out. The clearing turned pitch black before Draeus's eyes adjusted, previously unnoticed torches casting a warm, flickering, orange glow upon the man on stage.

'Comrades,' he began, in a revolutionary manner, 'thank you for making the journey. I know, for many of you, it was not only lengthy, but also dangerous. Thank you for being here tonight, at what I know we shall come to think of as *the beginning*.' The man paused, his voice carrying a hypnotic gravitas that was entirely unexpected considering his stature.

'We stand here at a crossroads, the likes of which we have never seen. One road leads to our end, the other, nothing less than our salvation. One route is well travelled, for it represents the status quo, the Descendants and their councils, dictatorship, lies, starvation, whilst the other,' he paused, 'the other, is an opportunity for those who demand more, for those like *us*, who demand freedom, equality, and justice.'

A roar went up from the crowd.

'But,' he continued, when the noise died down, 'to succeed, we must prepare. We must be a step ahead, have a plan. We must map out how we will take the world down the path of enlightenment and freedom. And we must be patient.'

The crowd stayed silent, the mood teetering on a knife's edge. 'I know this will be unpopular with many of you, especially those of you who have already had your property and livelihoods destroyed or stolen. The landscape is shifting: Austin is stepping up his activity, the Institution is swelling its ranks. We need to bide our time. Do not misunderstand me,' he warned the crowd, 'I am here to overthrow the system, to bring about a world led by us, those who have suffered the most. But we have only one chance, one vital opportunity with the element of surprise, and it would be catastrophic if we were to waste this advantage.' He paused again, pacing the stage, making eye contact with as many of the crowd as he could.

'So, we must elect leaders. Those who will work closely with me to infiltrate other rioting factions, to bring them together with us, and then to plan our attack. That is why we are here tonight.' The man let silence settle across the clearing, allowing his words to sink in. 'So, who will stand with me to lead us to revolution?'

The silence continued, awkward shuffling of feet and a couple of stifled coughs all that followed. The man on stage waited, standing absolutely still, scanning the crowd to see who would speak first. What felt like minutes passed, people now looking anywhere but the stage, the silence like a chasm into which their energy was being sucked; everyone willing someone else to say what the rest were thinking.

Draeus couldn't understand what was happening. Moments before, the crowd had roared. They had been behind their leader one hundred percent. The man had given a rousing speech, yet now, at the moment of action, they had deserted him.

More moments passed, seconds creeping by like great gaping minutes, until eventually, Draeus felt something shift, then he saw movement. His eyes found a ripple, moving through the crowd, starting at the back and flowing forwards, fanning out as it went, the sea of bodies parting to help someone pass. The ripple gained momentum, transforming into a wave, a man at its epicentre, hurtling towards the stage. The wave reached its destination and broke, an explosion of force that propelled the man up the steps. He reached the summit and turned towards the audience. A fire raged in his eyes, sparking something in the throng that sent a shiver down Draeus' spine.

* * * * *

Matthew's band of travellers had been walking for days through the Wild Lands, avoiding the busiest trading posts and roads in case Austin had asked his cronies to keep a lookout for them. Matthew's biggest worry had been that Austin would track them down; after all, Austin's resources were far superior to Matthew's own. However, they'd made it without incident and relatively unscathed. Aside from a few blisters, a lack of sleep, and numerous aching muscles, the trip had been surprisingly straightforward. It had, however, taken considerably longer than Matthew expected, the pace far slower than if he'd been travelling alone. They had been so slow, in fact, that they'd only just made it to the meeting on time, arriving at the back just as their leader had begun his address.

Matthew listened in astonishment as the man they knew as Doyen told them they needed to wait before acting. The time was right now; anyone with eyes could see that. If they left it any longer, who knew what damage the Descendants would let happen to the world? If they waited any longer, it could well be too late...

The mood in the crowd had shifted. Minutes earlier, they'd been ready to follow Doyen anywhere he might lead them. Now, Matthew could practically taste the disappointment and disbelief. Matthew looked around as the silence stretched, waiting to see who would put voice to what they were all clearly thinking. He held his breath, along with those around him, willing someone else to take to the stage. As the silence gaped, it was clear that no one would.

Matthew turned to look at his wife, Emily, who read the intention in his eyes and firmly shook her head. He held her gaze; he had to do this. They'd travelled this far, risked everything; it couldn't be for nothing. Emily's firm gaze turned to something softer, a plea, but he'd made up his mind.

Matthew took a deep breath before placing his hands on the shoulders of the men in front of him, gently pushing them out of the way. The movement caught the attention of those around him, who, after breathing a collective sigh of relief, moved aside, clearing a path to the stage.

He moved slowly at first, then more quickly as the whole gathering came to realise what was happening and fell over themselves to let him pass. Matthew reached the front, not really sure how he had got there, and mounted the stage with a confidence he didn't even come close to feeling inside. He averted his eyes from

Doyen, lest his conviction evade him, his feet somehow turning his body to face the crowd. A vague thought registered in the gloomy fog of his mind that he had not a clue what to say, and then, by some miracle, the words flowed.

'A month ago, a friend came to me and told me it was time to act, time for us to escape to the Wild Lands and join the revolution, to make a difference in the world before it was too late. That friend had just had his farm stolen by Austin in an unjust and barbaric act. Not only had he had his land and buildings commandeered to pay Austin's *safety tax*, but Austin forced him to stay on, a prisoner, and work for free to cover his so-called debt.

'My friend watched as Austin put a Mind councillor in charge of his business, the livelihood that had run in his family for generations, which he had inherited from his mother and had intended to pass to his daughter.

'He watched as the Mind councillor stole what little the farm could still produce, to bolster his own personal supplies. My friend put up with the councillor, who made bad planting decision after bad livestock decision. The result of those decisions will, in time, be reduced production, and no doubt further, unreasonable, excessive, and unjust demands from Austin.

'And what did I do when my friend looked to me for help? When he tried to warn me there was nothing we could do as individuals to stop the tidal wave of Austin's forces? When he tried to explain there was only one route open to us: to act, to join those who had suffered in countless other ways and overthrow those who oppress us?

'Well, I am ashamed to say, I did nothing. I told him it would be better to cooperate than to fight someone as powerful and established as Austin. And in truth, I thought it might not happen to me, that I might escape unscathed, and that it would be foolish to defy someone like Austin with no good reason.'

Matthew paused, a heavy silence settling.

'And then, just days ago, Austin paid me a visit, and of course, I, like all of you, did not escape unscathed. Now I have a reason strong enough to drive me to action too. When Austin took my farm, I told my friend I was sorry, that I had been a selfish coward, and that I would stand by his side and join the revolution.

'We gathered our families, who had been enslaved in the houses we used to call our homes, and we fled in the middle of the night, from farms crawling with Austin's private army. We risked our lives to come here, to a place full of hope and promise, to a leader who we were excited to think was about to take action, to do something. But instead, what do we find? Not revolution. Not salvation. Instead, we find more of the same rhetoric we've heard a thousand times before, followed, not by a call to arms, but to *caution*.' He spat the word 'caution' and turned for the first time to look at Doyen, surprised to see him calm and collected, looking almost bored by Matthew's speech.

'Well,' Matthew continued, turning back to the crowd, his resolve renewed, 'I'm not here to sign up to tea round the campfire, wasting weeks as part of a planning committee. I'm here to take the fight back to Kingdom, right to Austin's doorstep, right to the Relic he's supposed to be returning to the Gods... and I'd like to know: who's with me?' A roar went up from the crowd, followed by banging, clapping and stamping as they rallied to this new, uplifting message of war.

Doyen walked towards Matthew, who turned to face him. He forced himself to meet his eyes, emboldened by the hammering of the crowd below them. Doyen took hold of Matthew's hand and shook it, placing his other hand warmly on Matthew's arm.

'The revolution has a new leader,' he said, his tone even and respectful. 'I wish you luck and hope you achieve our dream. I may disagree with your approach, but we want the same thing.'

'Thank you,' said Matthew, surprised by how well he was reacting. Then Doyen's words hit him: he was the revolution's leader. Is that what this meant? Holy Gods. How had this happened?

'I will take my leave,' said Doyen, heading to the steps.

'You're leaving?' said Matthew, an edge of desperation in his voice.

'The last thing you need is me hanging over your shoulder. My being here could divide opinion, and that's the last thing our cause needs now. Good luck,' he said, vacating the stage to another roar from the crowd.

Matthew looked down and took a deep breath, a feeling of deep foreboding eating at his insides. What had he done?

* * * * *

Amber stood back in the shadows and watched as the scene in the clearing unfolded. She and her cronies had followed Matthew's band of travellers all the way from his farm, a feat that had been mind-numbingly simple and certainly not worthy of her skills. But she understood the need; Austin didn't trust anyone else not to screw it up. But really, they hadn't even posted lookouts when they slept, and not once had anyone doubled back to make sure they weren't being followed...

She watched with disbelief as Matthew strode towards the stage and made his pathetic speech. She was gob smacked when the intriguing man on stage stepped down with not so much as a terse word or bitter backward glance. It was all just... too easy... not to mention good news for Austin. If Matthew followed through on his speech, they would act soon, in disorganised fashion, and take the fight to the capitol. Defeating them would be about as much trouble as crushing an army of ants.

She nodded to the men around her; time to report back. She'd been away for an infuriating amount of time already, and who knew what the other idiots Austin kept around had been filling his head with while she'd been away.

* * * * *

Doyen watched as Amber melted into the darkness. 'Run back to your master little messenger,' he said aloud, before slipping away into the woods, a smile on his face. Mission accomplished, he thought, as he too disappeared into the night.

* * * * *

Draeus slipped away, the commotion providing cover for his retreat, and returned to where he had left the others. However, he was greeted, not by three relieved faces, as he'd expected, but by an icy hand of foreboding clenching his insides. The vehicle and all of their supplies remained exactly where he had left them, but Alexander, Anderson, and Anita were nowhere to be seen.

Draeus scanned around for any signs of a struggle, or indeed, any footprints, but there wasn't enough light to see by, and it would have been foolish to draw attention to himself by getting out a torch. Instead, he stalked back into the trees, found a secluded vantage point, and waited for dawn, praying the others were okay.

However, he'd barely settled when he felt a tap on his shoulder and heard the urgent whisper of Alexander's voice, 'It's Alexander, don't scream!'

'Of course I'm not going to scream,' said Draeus indignantly, biting his tongue to stop himself from snapping further. 'What happened? Where are the others?' he asked instead.

'We're here,' said Anita, also appearing out of the foliage. 'Amber almost discovered us, so we hid in the trees.'

'Amber?' exclaimed Draeus, not believing his ears. 'What the hell is she doing here? Was she looking for us? How did you get away without her spotting you?'

'I'm the Spirit Descendant, remember?' said Alexander. 'I'm pretty good at reading energy.'

* * * * *

Alexander kept to himself that it had been Anita who had recognised Amber's hostile force; they had agreed it best not to disclose Anita's ability to read energy.

'When Alexander realised someone was approaching, we retreated into the trees and watched,' said Anita. 'Amber saw the vehicle but paid little attention. She didn't even bother getting her men to search it. It looked like they were following someone, but it wasn't us. She and her men came back past here just before you did. She looked pretty smug.'

'Any idea why?' asked Anderson. 'What was with all the lights?'

'We've stumbled into the heart of the rebellion,' said Draeus. 'They were discussing their next move.

The leader suggested they take time to plan their attack, but the crowd disagreed, and overthrew him.'

'What?' said Anita. 'We only heard cheers; it must have been a quiet takeover!'

'The old leader didn't seem that cut up about it. He just stepped aside when the crowd turned, then disappeared into the trees.'

'Weird,' said Anderson. 'I can't imagine anyone in the Institution doing something like that. Could you imagine Helena just stepping aside?' Anderson laughed at his own joke.

'Did you recognise anyone?' asked Anita, ignoring Anderson. 'The old leader or the new one?'

'No. But the new leader is from Empire. He was a farmer, who, along with many of his peers, has recently had his farm seized by Austin. Austin is effectively keeping the farmers prisoner, forcing them to work for someone Austin puts in charge.'

Anita scowled. 'I knew it.'

'What?' asked Alexander.

'Never mind,' said Anita. They could talk about Marcus' inability to curb Austin's despicable activities later.

Alexander gave her a curious look. 'So the rebellion has a new leader. Did you hear what they're planning to do next?'

'Not exactly, but they overthrew the old leader because he wanted to take his time. The new leader wants to act now, so whatever they do, it's likely to be soon.'

'And Amber knows they're coming,' said Anita.

'It would seem so,' said Draeus. 'They've already lost the element of surprise.'

'It'll be a massacre,' said Alexander. 'Austin's army is enormous, not to mention disciplined. They won't stand a chance.'

'Unless they do something clever,' said Anita, never one to write off the underdog.

'We'll have to find a way to return the Relic before this all gets totally out of hand,' said Anderson, pompously.

Alexander and Anita shared a disdainful look.

'Let's get out of here before we get caught up in anything else,' said Draeus, rallying the group to action. 'We've still got a fair distance to travel.'

They gave up trying to camp and travelled through what was left of the night, reaching Wild Sky as the sun came up. It was nothing short of breath-taking, the sun catching the clouds that billowed and corkscrewed across the great open expanse above them, casting a purple and orange glow over the sweeping plains below.

They travelled at speed across the mostly flat terrain, marvelling as the light transitioned to stark white shards, making the frosty ground sparkle as they raced past. Although Wild Sky was one of the biggest provinces, they took only two days to cross, the going consistently good. Even when they approached Wild Air's mountainous boundary, the ground undulated in pleasant rolling hillocks, rather than becoming treacherous sheer inclines. They camped in a copse of trees both nights, the second night, with the Cloud Mountain looming forebodingly in the distance.

'Another half a day and we'll be at the base of the mountain,' said Draeus, sipping at a cinnamon hot chocolate spiked with hazelnut liqueur; a speciality of the region. The temperature had steadily dropped as they'd travelled, both because of the time of year and their proximity to the mountains, renowned for remaining chilly all year round.

CHAPTER 9

As Draeus had predicted, they reached the base of the Cloud Mountain around lunchtime the following day. They had to ditch the 4x4, which had somehow, miraculously, got them this far, and hired mountain ponies to take them up the single track that wound its way to the top. It took another day for them to scale the mountain, the ponies knowing the way almost too well; they seemed nonchalant about the perilous climb, taking turns at excessive speed.

Anderson suffered where the others were exhilarated, his knuckles white from holding on so hard, face tinged green, eyes averted from the edge. Despite the gruelling pace, Anita found the whole thing really quite elating, although even she was glad to see the ancient shack at the halfway checkpoint, after a full day's ride.

They stayed at *The Lodge* for the evening, gratefully accepting delicious roast chicken with fennel and clementines that the nondescript monks had rustled up. Evidently supplies up here weren't scarce. They made small talk, the monks never once probing for the reason they were here, Anita wondering how they didn't freeze to death in the thin, flesh-exposing robes they wore.

They slept on hard beds with thin sheets covering them, Alexander and Anita wearing their warmest clothing and huddling together to try and keep from contracting frostbite. Draeus told them it would be rude to get out the sleeping bags. Anita wondered if it wouldn't have been better to seek shelter in some secluded corner somewhere outside. The Lodge seemed to almost purposefully channel icy drafts through every room, gaps of several centimetres around the windows and under the doors.

The following morning, they got up early, all red-eyed and shivering, except for Draeus, who somehow appeared at breakfast refreshed and rejuvenated. Draeus rolled his eyes at the others. They ate a breakfast of boiled eggs and toast before thanking the monks for their hospitality and continuing up the mountain. They left the ponies behind, picking their way up the narrow path, all that remained between them and the Spirit Leader.

The path took another two hours to ascend, Anderson frustrating Anita no end by insisting on a slow pace and frequent stops. She could read from his energy that he was terrified, but selfishly, she didn't care. The path wasn't entirely treacherous, and she was impatient to find out what was lurking inside her mind.

They finally made it to the summit, where the gradient flattened out into a small, enclosed courtyard. The other side of the courtyard stood a large, wooden, arched door, which opened as they approached. A short, medium built man, with thick, wavy, sandy coloured hair appeared. He stood in the centre of an entrance hall that seemed to be made entirely of white marble, the whole place gleaming in the sunlight.

The entrance hall, although not excessively sized, had ornate columns at the four corners, an imposing, round, marble table in the centre, complete with a shiny silver bowl of dead still water sunken into its middle. Shafts of light streamed down from the ceiling, hitting the water, although it wasn't apparent from where these came.

The hall had only two openings: the one they had just come through, and a similar door on the other side, through which Anita assumed they would soon walk. This made the room oppressive, a bit like a prison cell. Anita hoped she would never find herself in there with both sets of doors closed.

A powerful, penetrating voice that didn't at all fit the man in front of them interrupted Anita's thoughts. 'Welcome to Cloud Mountain,' he said. 'It's a pleasure to welcome you to our temple.'

Draeus and Anderson bowed before the man, Alexander remaining resolutely upright, Anita a little confused as to what was going on.

'Spirit Leader,' said Anderson, in a gushy voice that surprised Anita, 'the pleasure is all ours.'

The Spirit Leader ignored Anderson, reaching past him to take Draeus' hand, pulling him to his feet. 'Draeus, it's been too long,' he said, with a warm smile, pausing a moment to study Draeus' face before turning his attention to Alexander and Anita. 'Alexander, I don't believe we've had the pleasure of your company since you were... what... ten?' He said the words in an overly familiar way, as though Alexander were a fond relative, the Spirit Leader a mildly patronizing uncle.

'That's correct, Timi,' said Alexander, his energy neutral, but a warning edge to his voice, 'it's been a long time.'

Timi, of all names! It seemed to both suit his intimidating self and diminish his authority.

'And you must be Anita,' said the Spirit Leader, taking Anita's hand and lifting it to his lips. 'I've heard a great deal about you.'

162

This caught Anita off guard, not just because of the strange, old-fashioned greeting, but because he knew who she was; knew things about her. She recovered enough composure to say, 'Lovely to meet you, but I'm afraid until a few days ago, I didn't know your existence.' She smiled sweetly, not meaning for the words to sound so aggressive, wondering how hostility had crept in. She pushed aside the thought, resolving to be nicer; she had, after all, come here to ask for his help with the cylinder.

The Spirit Leader turned, and they followed him out of the entrance hall into a snowy, cobbled, circular courtyard beyond, a grey stone fountain still trickling water, despite the cold. There were buildings on all sides that had the look of squat, miniature castles, each building turret-like, with a conical shaped roof perched on top. The buildings were connected by grey stone corridors with sloping tiled roofs. Glassless windows allowed glimpses of the burning torches that adorned the walls inside.

They followed Timi across the courtyard, through an empty archway, to a stone staircase containing an endless number of steps. The staircase was completely open on one side, nothing but air standing between them and a deadly drop off the mountain. Anita smiled cruelly at Anderson's energy, which was going crazy at the threat. They climbed them, emerging in a flat, open area at the top.

The drop was now on two sides, and Timi lingered for a moment before leading them to a stone table and chairs, sheltered only by a few pieces of fabric that ballooned in the wind. Timi motioned for them to sit and help themselves to the steaming tea, laid out on a tray on the table. Draeus helped himself, leaning back in his chair and savouring its warmth, but the others refused. Anderson's hands were shaking too wildly, and

Anita and Alexander were more concerned with the conversation that must inevitably follow.

Timi helped himself to tea, then turned to face Anita directly. 'Very well,' he said, making no effort to hide his irritation at their refusal of his hospitality, 'you've come to discuss the cylinder, I presume?'

Anita inhaled sharply. 'How could you possibly know that?' she asked, shock and confusion filling her energy.

'There's very little I don't find out, one way or another,' he said.

'Very well,' she said, echoing his words, the hostile edge she had resolved to banish returning in full force, 'are you able to help us open it?'

'You've finally found it.'

'Your information isn't up to date?'

'I didn't say I know everything, Anita.'

'But you're involved with the Institution? That's the only way you could know.'

'Yes, I'm involved with the Institution. That's why Helena was happy for you to seek my help.'

Anita inwardly rolled her eyes. 'We've found it, but we can't open it. Alexander gets thrown out of the meditation when we try, and nothing we can think of will work.'

'What have you tried so far?'

Anita ran through everything: mentally willing it to open, physically trying to pry it open, dropping it, twisting it, examining it for a secret mechanism, rolling it around on the floor in the vain hope it would spontaneously reveal its secrets...

Timi laughed. 'Have you tried meditating with anyone other than Alexander?'

'No,' she said. 'It seemed unlikely that anyone we can trust would be a better bet.'

'Hmm,' said Timi. 'The first step is for us to meditate together. I need to understand exactly what we're dealing with. We can do it this evening, after dinner, which, of course, you are all invited to have with me, in my private quarters.'

Anita read Alexander's energy to see what he thought of this suggestion, but it was resolutely stable. This meant he was either fine with it, or was purposefully covering up his feelings in front of Timi. The latter seemed to Anita the more likely of the two scenarios.

'Fine,' she said, 'after dinner. But what about your research, or records relating to the old Spirit Leader? The one who gave the cylinder to Clarissa? It may be helpful to work our way through those as well, to see if there are any clues.'

'I'll do that only if I deem it necessary,' said Timi, firmly. 'Only the current Spirit Leader may access those records, and we may be able to open the cylinder without needing to.'

Anita knew it was futile to protest, so didn't bother, but this seemed stupid to her. There was likely something in those records that could help them...

At that moment, a monk at least twice the age of Timi appeared at the top of the stairs. His robes were dishevelled, white, wispy hair blowing around in the breeze, back a little stooped.

'Ah, Jonathan, perfect timing as usual,' said Timi, motioning to Jonathan to come closer. 'Jonathan will show you to your quarters, where lunch has been laid out for you. Then, if you would like, he will show you around. Dinner will be at seven o'clock; Jonathan will show you the way.'

They nodded and got up to follow the old monk back down the torturous staircase, Timi putting a hand on Draeus' arm to stop him from leaving. 'Stay a while longer,' said Timi, warmly. 'I'd like to talk to you about supplies; there are a few things we need.'

* * * * *

Jonathan showed them to their quarters, which were in one of the turret-like buildings they'd seen earlier. The accommodation was spread over three floors. The top floor had a large double bedroom and bathroom, the middle floor had two single bedrooms and a bathroom, and the ground floor had a large seating area, dining area, and a small kitchenette off to one side.

It was pleasant enough, although the décor was mismatched and old, most of the furniture missing slats, holes from years of wear apparent in the seat covers. The beds were made from spindly brass frames with mattresses that had seen better days, sinking in the middle, ready to give anyone who ventured into them back ache come the morning.

The rooms had odd layouts, a result of most of the walls being curved. Pieces of furniture stuck out at jaunty angles, baths and beds sat in the middle of the rooms, the other furniture squeezed haphazardly into the spaces left over.

The curtains were thin and had been patched many times. Light came only from flickering flame torches, and the stairs groaned nervously with every step. The place had a homely, cosy feel, in a rough-around-the-edges sort of way. The windows, thankfully, had glass in them, and a roaring fire on the ground floor somehow kept all the rooms, if not toasty, at least not cold.

Anita and Alexander took the top floor room, dumping their belongings unceremoniously on the floor, washing the travel dirt from their hands and faces before racing back downstairs. By the time they returned, Anderson was already tucking into the bread, meats, cheeses, and pickles that had been laid out for them. Anita accepted a bowl of pumpkin and goat cheese soup from Anderson, ripped off a hunk of bread, and tucked in greedily. She relished the warmth of the food as it slowly crept down her throat and into her ravenous stomach.

They ate everything the monks provided, then leaned back in their chairs, stuffed full. Anita was contemplating a nap when Jonathan returned to invite them on a tour. She wondered how he'd turned up so exactly on cue, considering briefly the disturbing possibility that they were being spied on…

They followed Jonathan out of the turret, the monk moving with surprising speed as he weaved through the maze of corridors, the three of them having to stride out to keep up. He showed them rooms for every purpose: large dormitories for sleeping, an eating hall with long tables and benches, spa-like communal wash rooms complete with steam rooms and saunas, reading rooms, lecture theatres, research labs with all manner of interesting looking brass measuring devices, and most fascinating of all, rooms dedicated to meditating.

The meditation rooms were located all over the temple, each with unique characteristics. Jonathan explained they had each been designed to have a different impact on one's energy, but every one contained a bowl of still water in the middle.

'What's the bowl of water for?' asked Anita, curious. Alexander had never suggested they use one when meditating.

'They focus the energy in the room,' said Jonathan, 'sucking up any background energy noise. It reduces distraction and creates a purer experience.'

'A bit like at the observatory?' said Anita.

'Yes,' said Jonathan, 'exactly.

'They're only used by an adept few,' said Alexander. 'The ability to discern small outside energy shifts when in a meditation is extremely advanced.'

'Indeed,' said Jonathan, 'although, even those less experienced can benefit from a pool, especially when performing a solo meditation. Distraction is more of an issue in that case, so it's even more helpful.'

'Why do people meditate on their own?' she asked, curious. Although she had technically done it, she didn't know the benefits.

Jonathan smiled indulgently. 'For several reasons: to find the solution to a problem that's been vexing them; to understand themselves better; to develop skills. Not only are you in a highly focused state, but you talk directly to levels of yourself that you can't ordinarily access. Some claim they've accessed their own subconscious, not that there's much proof to support those claims. I've certainly met no one convincing in that regard, and we're at the cutting edge of research in that space.'

'Fascinating. What other research takes place here?' said Anita, as they passed a lab packed full of exciting instruments and boring monks.

'Oh, a number of things,' he said. 'The effects of energy on crop production. The interaction between personal energy and energy in the immediate vicinity. Energy interruption and transfer…'

'Energy transfer?' asked Anita and Alexander together.

'Well, yes, of course. We've made some really interesting progress recently,' said Jonathan, looking at Anderson. Anderson's energy spiked, although it was gone before Anita could fully make out the emotion.

'Yes, we have,' said a second voice, cutting icily across the corridor. 'Some of our research the Spirit

Leader will tell you about later, I'm sure, and some, we would rather keep to ourselves.'

Jonathan's energy, which had been static until now, flickered with something... fear, perhaps? Anita tried to get a look at the new monk, but he was hidden in the shadows, turning to leave before she could make out his features. Who was that, and what was he trying to hide?

* * * * *

They returned to their turret for the rest of the afternoon. Anita took a long bath, followed by a nap, Jonathan turning up at five minutes to seven to escort them to dinner. To her surprise, they retraced their earlier steps, up the staircase to where they'd had tea when they'd arrived.

Anita gave Alexander a questioning look; surely Timi wasn't expecting them to eat dinner outside, in the freezing cold? Alexander smiled and shook his head, Anita intrigued to see where they'd end up.

Jonathan led them past the table, through the billowing fabric at the back of the structure, and down a short flight of shallow stone steps the other side. Here, they stooped to enter a cave hollowed out of the rock, following a low corridor into a small room beyond.

The corridor and the room, like everywhere else, were lit by torches, the orange glow giving the place an enigmatic feel. The room, like their turret, contained mismatched furniture at odd angles, although none of it looked nearly as comfortable as the items in their own quarters.

Timi, who, along with Draeus, was sitting at a circular, wooden table in the centre of the room, greeted them. A decanter of a deep-red wine was between them. Other than that, the room held only three pieces of furniture: a messy desk, covered in sheets of paper and brass instruments, and two wooden benches, each with a couple of cushions, which did nothing to make them look comfortable.

Rugs covered the floor, which gave the room some semblance of warmth, but they were threadbare, the summers of their lives long gone. Vicious drafts whistled through the glassless slit windows, their fur coverings failing to keep the wind at bay.

In the far corner, three or four rugs had been piled on top of each other, with a single blanket over the top. Anita assumed this must be where Timi slept. She couldn't think of anything more miserable, but he seemed in good enough spirits as he stood to greet them, opening his arms in welcome.

'Good evening,' he said enthusiastically. 'I hope you're rested after your journey?'

'Yes, thank you,' said Anderson, speaking for all of them as they took their seats at the table.

'Lucky you,' said Draeus, 'some of us have been holed up here all afternoon, talking trade.' He nudged Timi's arm good-humouredly.

'I trust it has been productive for us both,' said Timi.

'Most productive,' replied Draeus, as several monks appeared, placing steaming dishes of food on the table.

The food looked bland and boring. It was vegetarian, mainly lentils, beans and pulses, but when she tucked in, Anita was surprised to find that it had been skilfully flavoured with herbs and spices that caused explosions of flavour with every bite.

The conversation over dinner was superficial, the topic of energy pointedly avoided, along with talk of the Institution or the state of the political world. The mood was light as a result, the only blip when Timi asked Anderson where his wife, Bella, was. It was unusual for them to be separated for so long.

Anderson's energy turned reticent as he explained, over a dessert of soft fruit and yoghurt, that she was with her sick mother in Kingdom. The prognosis wasn't good, and Bella was distraught.

Timi expressed an appropriate amount of regret, then steered them to light-hearted territory. By the time they were sipping herbal teas and eating dark chocolate gingers, they were all laughing, Anita feeling less than sober.

'My dear friends,' said Timi, when a lull in the conversation presented itself, 'much as I could continue with this merriment all evening, Anita and I have work to do.'

'Of course,' said Draeus, looking relieved at an opportunity to escape. Draeus and Anderson stood to leave, but Alexander stayed put, his energy undecided. He looked at Anita, who sent a reassuring nudge to the edge of his energy field. He got up and followed the others, neither saying a word nor trying to hide his energy, sending a clear warning to Timi that he had better not hurt Anita.

As the others vacated the room, Timi moved to sit cross-legged on one of the worn rugs on the icy floor. He motioned for Anita to join him. 'Don't look so nervous,' he said, in what he obviously thought was a reassuring tone. 'I'll follow your lead. Just take me to the cylinder and we'll go from there.'

'Okay,' Anita nodded, settling herself down on the floor in front of him. She closed her eyes and focused on the boat, pushing all her energy towards that place in her mind. The last thing she wanted was for Timi to see her centre, and she wasn't confident that she could go straight to the throne room, so this seemed like the best bet.

To her relief, Anita opened her eyes and found herself sitting next to Timi in the stern. The meditation felt strange, the air around her almost buzzing with energy, the experience less intense than with Alexander, but the atmosphere closer, like everything had been condensed.

She pushed the thought aside, making her way to the bow before Timi had a chance to say anything. She reached for the anchor, feeling the familiar shock of cold metal, which, to her relief, had the desired effect, transporting them to the throne room.

So far so good, thought Anita, as she strode quickly to the box sitting in between the thrones. She picked it up and took it to where Timi was standing at the back of the room, handing the whole thing to him, so he could examine the package in its entirety. She realized she wasn't breathing, her body forcing her to take a deep, restorative breath.

'This is it?' Timi asked, cautiously.

'Yep,' said Anita, trying to hide her eagerness.

Timi inhaled, examining the box carefully, taking in every aspect before turning it over in his hands. When he had gleaned everything he could from the outside, he gingerly pulled open the lid, peering cautiously inside to see what he would find. He took in every detail before reaching out confidently and touching the cylinder itself.

'Interesting,' he said, after a minute of touching it with closed eyes.

'What?' asked Anita, impatient for information.

'Nothing,' he said, wonder in his voice. 'Absolutely nothing at all.'

Anita exhaled sharply, frustrated. 'What did you do? Did you try to open it?'

Timi laughed. 'No, not yet. Patience, Anita.'

The words were pointed, and a look of annoyance crossed her features.

'I tried to read the energy contained within, but it's giving nothing away at all.' He picked up the cylinder, putting the box down on the floor, and held it out in front of him, one hand either end. 'Now I'm going to try and open it.'

He focused on the cylinder for a few moments, Anita hoping for at least some small reaction, but, again, nothing happened. Timi closed his eyes, a furrow of irritation appearing on his brow. He stayed like that for what must have been a full minute before reopening his eyes. 'Absolutely nothing,' he said, clearly aggravated, 'it's like there's nothing in there at all.'

'You don't have to take my word for it,' she said, petulantly pleased that opening the cylinder wasn't straightforward for the almighty Spirit Leader either. 'I'll show you.' Anita reached forwards.

'Wait,' said Timi, urgently. 'Before you touch it, you said Alexander was expelled when you touched the cylinder?'

'Yes,' she said.

'I'll try to keep myself in the meditation,' he said. 'Was he forced out gradually, or as soon as you touched it?'

'Immediately, I think.'

'Okay, go ahead.'

Anita reached out and took the cylinder from Timi, the brass warm, as it had been before. He instantly disappeared, the now familiar haze enclosing around Anita, making it seem as though her eyes were out of focus.

She reached down and placed the cylinder back in the box, the weight lifting as she let go. She left the meditation and woke up to find Timi pacing in front of her, deep in thought. 'It expelled you too?' said Anita, doing nothing to hide her smug satisfaction.

'Yes, and when I tried to get back in, it wouldn't let me. It was like a brick wall surrounded your mind.'

'Interesting,' said Anita, 'Alexander never tried to get back into the meditation, I didn't even know that was possible.'

'It is if you know what you're doing, but it's much more difficult than jointly meditating from the beginning, as you're essentially trying to force your way into a solo mediation. It requires an extremely deep level of concentration. Let's try again. Now I know what to expect I should be better at defending against it.'

'Okay,' said Anita, 'but you should know, the second time it expelled Alexander, it knocked him out. It seems like the force gets stronger each time.'

'Interesting,' said Timi. 'Okay, I'll be ready.'

They re-entered the meditation and Anita crouched down to open the box, which was, she was glad to see, in the same place she had left it. 'Ready?' she asked.

'Yes, go ahead,' said Timi, visibly steeling himself.

Anita placed her hand on the metal, keeping her eyes on Timi, expecting him to disappear as he had before. To her surprise, he didn't, or at least, not fully. His form was still there, but it was outside the haze surrounding her and looked as though the lower half of him was being sucked towards the back of the throne room. His arms were stretched out in front of him, like his hands were desperately holding onto something, keeping him inside.

Unlike all the other times she'd touched the cylinder, this time, Anita felt the weight press down on her, but also, unlike usual, it got heavier and heavier, seeming to force her into the floor. The weight came in from the sides too, compressing her body, the pressure on her chest making it difficult to breathe, her brain crushed under the immense burden. The edges of her vision blurred, the air shook, electricity everywhere, sparking as it came into contact with her skin. Darkness clouded her eyes, her pulse thundering in her ears until she could withstand it no longer, her body collapsing, lifeless, to the floor.

Anita woke to see Alexander's face immediately above her, a look of terror contorting his features. 'Anita?' he said, as she opened her eyes. 'Are you okay?'

'I think so,' she said, taking long, deep breaths, testing her limbs to see if they still functioned. She blinked a few times until her eyes properly focused, wondering vaguely how Alexander was here. She tried to sit up, hands rasping strangely against the rough fabric beneath her, but her head spun with such force that she slumped back to the floor, fearful she would black out again. 'Might be best if I stay down here for a while,' she said, smiling up at Alexander's worried face. 'What happened?'

'Quite,' said Alexander, venomously. 'What exactly happened, Timi, that resulted in your being absolutely fine, with Anita blacked out on the floor?'

Anita hadn't noticed Timi, who she now saw was sitting casually on one of the uncomfortable looking wooden benches.

'Well, Anita told me about the increase in force used to expel you the second time, so I knew I'd have to try something different to remain in her head. Instead of trying to fight the force of the cylinder pushing me out, I anchored myself to Anita's mind, holding onto her, pulling myself in.'

'You used Anita's own mind to try and overcome the force of the cylinder?'

'I suppose you could put it like that,' he said, nonchalantly. 'It seemed likely that if anyone could overcome the power of the cylinder, it would be its host.'

'You could have killed her,' spat Alexander, looking as though he might pin Timi against the wall by his throat.

'Only a slim possibility at most,' said Timi, as though he were objectively weighing the probabilities of an experiment's likely outcomes. 'It seemed an acceptable risk to take given the circumstances.'

Alexander couldn't contain himself, standing violently and striding to where Timi sat. 'Anita is not a lab rat for you to play with,' he hissed, his face inches from Timi's.

'What did you see?' asked Anita, pushing herself up on her elbows, cutting through the strained atmosphere, refocusing them on the matter at hand.

'Unfortunately, not a great deal,' he replied. 'I saw you looking in my direction, although it looked as though you were on the other side of a protective shield. I felt the force trying to expel me, the strength of which increased as the seconds ticked by, and then you blacked out, and I was expelled from your mind. What did you experience?'

'It was like usual, but this time I could feel the weight before letting go of the cylinder, getting stronger and stronger. It pressed me down, crushing my lungs, compressing my head, and then I blacked out.'

'The head compression was probably because Timi was holding on to your mind,' said Alexander, bitterly, back at Anita's side.

'And we're no further forward,' said Anita, dejectedly. 'What do you suggest we do now?'

Timi contemplated his answer. 'I don't know,' he replied. 'I've never seen anything like this. I'll consult the works of the Spirit Leader who placed the cylinder in your mother's mind. Other than that, I'd suggest solo meditation. You should see how long you can stay touching the cylinder, see if anything else happens the longer you're in there. Try the different meditation rooms; you may find one that helps.'

'Are you researching anything relevant?' asked Alexander.

'No,' said Timi, 'as I said, I've never come across anything like this before.'

'What about your research into brass cylinders, or energy transfer? Can we speak to the monks leading the research to see if they have any ideas?'

'No. We don't share our research with outsiders; it's a non-negotiable rule. I will, however, have a conversation with the monks researching those areas, and let you know if there is anything that may help us.'

'Why all the secrecy?' asked Anita, hotly. 'What have you got to hide?'

Much to Anita's annoyance, Timi ignored the question, saying, 'You need rest, Anita; it'll take you a while to recover. I'll consult our records and speak to the other monks. Let me know if you find anything through solo meditation.'

Anita was furious, but knew there was no point in arguing. Timi's mind was made up and nothing she could do or say was going to make any difference. She looked at Alexander, shaking her head in frustration, as if her energy wasn't speaking loudly enough. He helped her up, Anita leaning heavily on him as they made for the exit.

'Sleep well,' said Timi, to their backs. 'See you tomorrow.'

They didn't reply, Alexander muttering, 'Idiot,' under his breath as they stepped out into the freezing night air.

CHAPTER 10

They stayed at the Cloud Mountain for another three days; it took that long for Anita to get back to full strength. She completed a number of solo meditations in that time, in different meditation rooms, as Timi had suggested. The results had been the same as before. The only difference was that she felt more tired after each session, proving what Alexander had said, that solo meditation took more energy than when meditating with someone else.

Timi's research had been similarly disappointing. He had scoured through the records of the Spirit Leaders, including the one Clarissa had meditated with, and found nothing of any use. There had been some reference to brass cylinders, all of it now general knowledge, and certainly nothing sounding similar to the cylinder in Anita's head. Timi had also spoken to the monks leading current research, but they couldn't think of anything that would help. In short, the visit had been a complete waste of time.

Alexander, Anita and Draeus left the mountain in the morning. They left Anderson behind to participate in some top secret experiment the rest of them were 'not authorized' to know about. Anita was irritated at not being allowed to know the details, but was happy to see the back of Anderson. She didn't know why Bass and Alexander liked him.

They thanked Timi for his hospitality, animosity still evident between him and Alexander. Timi played the courteous host and wished them a good journey, inviting them back at any time, should they need him.

They travelled at a pace, making it to the bottom of the mountain by the end of the day. Each of them breathed a sigh of relief as they reached the mountain's foot, by that time, the moon the only light to guide them.

They retrieved their tents from the 4x4 and put them up a good distance from the trading post that sat at the mountain's base. They ate a dinner of chicken pie and salad that Draeus had bought from the trading post, washed down by a decent quantity of wine. They were more relaxed than they had been in days, like they'd escaped the clutches of an oppressive parent.

'Strange visit,' said Draeus. 'They're up to something. Need to find out what.'

Alexander nodded. 'Definitely something strange going on. Now we're back down here, it feels like the energy is… different… less heightened?' He looked at Anita for confirmation.

'I know what you mean,' she replied, ignoring the surprised look on Draeus' face. 'It feels less concentrated, and less positive. You would have thought something like that would be impossible to sustain.'

'Well, I found it bloody tiring,' said Draeus. 'You don't need to be a reader to know something weird is going on.'

'You're right,' said Alexander, 'it was surprisingly tiring considering the energy was so intensely upbeat.'

'Maybe it's just that: the intensity,' said Anita, pondering. 'Dealing with so much of it... it's tiring to have anything coming at you all the time.'

'I suppose so,' said Alexander, 'and all those doors we weren't allowed to go through and labs we weren't allowed in. It's all so unnecessarily secretive; you'd think that would breed negativity.'

'Maybe all the monks have access... and now, so does Anderson,' said Anita, bitterness tinging her tone. 'What do you think they want him for?'

'Who knows,' said Draeus, 'but I'd imagine it's on Institution orders. Timi's a member. He too must answer to those further up the hierarchy.'

'But Anderson didn't seem involved in the research when we were there,' said Anita. 'Did he mention to you he was going to stay before this morning?'

'No,' said Draeus. 'I was as surprised as you; had no idea.'

'What did Timi want from you on the first night?' asked Anita, realizing he hadn't told them the specifics.

'He wants regular supplies for the mountain; inordinate amounts. He wants herbs, spices, cocoa, metals, energy meters, chemicals, loads of things he's never asked for before. I suppose they're for all the experiments they're running up there.'

'You're going to do it?' said Alexander.

'Of course,' said Draeus, with a rueful smile. 'I'm a trader, and Timi pays good prices for me to be discrete. He pays upfront, and he gets monks to take the supplies to the top of the mountain, so I only have to deliver to the trading post. He's a dream client.'

'I don't trust him though,' sniped Alexander.

'I wouldn't trust him in anything but trade either,' said Draeus. 'What he did to Anita...'

'It's like he didn't care if she died,' said Alexander. 'It was careless, like testing his abilities was more important than Anita's life, regardless that if she died, the cylinder and its contents would be gone forever.'

'Well, I'm still here,' said Anita, not appreciating being spoken about as though she wasn't. 'There's no way we're telling him if we open it.'

'The Institution will do that for us,' said Alexander, dryly.

'Only if we tell them,' said Anita, sending a wary glance in Draeus' direction.

'Keep me out of this,' said Draeus. 'I support the Institution's aim of energy stability. I'm a member and I follow my orders, but when it comes down to it, I'm a trader. I make a living through buying and selling things, and the Institution has never asked me to do anything other than gather information and carry messages.

'I don't want to know what's in that damned cylinder; it would put me in an awkward situation. Cleo would kill me if I ever betrayed your confidence, Anita, so do me a favour and keep me out of it.'

'Fair enough,' said Anita, glad that Draeus had laid his cards on the table. 'We won't tell you if we find anything.'

'Thank you. Now, we're taking a different route back. I want to get to the coast before dawn, so it's going to be an early morning. Time for bed.'

* * * * *

It felt like they'd only been asleep for minutes when Draeus shook Alexander and Anita awake. They quickly packed up their kit, piled most of it into the 4x4, then climbed onto horses Draeus had somehow made appear overnight. Neither of them asked where they had come from, knowing he preferred it when they didn't ask questions. Instead, they mounted up and plodded along after Draeus, eating delicious apple flapjack that had, happily, appeared along with their steeds.

They made it to their destination, the coast, specifically, Sky Dock, just as the sun was coming up, golden rays piercing the reddish orange horizon. Only one large trading vessel was currently at dock, however, you wouldn't have known it from the level of activity. A swarm of people scurried this way and that, moving crates from land to boat with startling efficiency.

'Leave the horses here,' said Draeus, dismounting and handing his reins to a young boy with scruffy hair. Alexander and Anita followed suit, trailing after Draeus as he climbed the ramp from dock to ship. They narrowly avoided being flattened by the crates being bundled aboard, those manoeuvring the cargo seeming to have a callous disregard for the safety of all involved.

The boat, made of steel, must have been a hundred feet long. Its hull was black with round white railings, three dumpy chimneys sticking up into the air at intervals down the centre of the deck. An energy store, similar to those used in cars and trains, powered the boat, the chimneys allowing steam from the cooling system to escape.

A row of perfectly round portholes punctuated the hull, indicating cabins below deck. Five minutes later, Draeus ushered them into one of them. It was the Captain's cabin in the stern, and they tucked into bacon sandwiches and steaming mugs of tea, while Draeus explained to them, in no uncertain terms, what would happen next.

'I'll take you as far as Wild Flower,' said Draeus. 'It's only a few hours from here, so we should be there by mid-afternoon. That's where we'll part ways, and you'll make your way back to Empire alone.'

'Wild Flower?' Anita asked. She'd never heard of Wild Flower, nor was she clear why they were splitting up now.

'Wild Flower is a tiny part of the Wild Lands that was taken over by a group of enterprising Spirits decades back,' said Alexander. 'The ruling Spirit Descendant was in on the deal. He founded a sort of safe haven for leading Spirits when they needed a place to escape. Over time, the most prominent Spirit families built houses there. They established a lucrative business, harvesting the flowers that grow in abundance, turning them into perfume, and selling it across the world. It'll provide us with a cover story for where we've been all this time, and it will protect Draeus.'

'Indeed, not that I'm going back to Empire just yet,' said Draeus. 'I'm heading for Kingdom, putting even more distance between you two and me.'

'I see,' said Anita. 'How will we travel back to Empire?'

'You'll take one of the sailing boats from Wild Flower,' said Draeus. 'They're always going backwards and forwards, carrying Spirits to and from Kingdom and Empire. It's a pleasant trip, but it'll take a couple of weeks.'

'And this ship is yours, Draeus?' asked Anita, sinking back into a well-padded armchair, cradling the tea in her hands.

Draeus nodded. 'Yes. I've got several boats that transport cargo, and seeing as this one was scheduled to be here anyway, it worked out well. I'll come ashore and trade a crate of alpine flowers from the Cloud Mountain when I drop you off, so there'll be a legitimate reason for me to be there.'

Anita nodded, a little uncomfortable that events were so out of her hands, although she had no choice but to go along with it.

'You two make yourselves at home in here,' said Draeus. 'I'm going to check we're ready to leave. It would be better if you stayed down here until we get to Wild Flower.' His words sounded like a suggestion, but they all knew it was an order. Draeus had easily transitioned into the role of Captain aboard his ship. 'As I said, it shouldn't be long.'

* * * * *

The journey was as smooth as it could have been, the sea flat calm, the sky a vibrant blue, with not a cloud to be seen. They arrived in Wild Flower just after lunch, making excellent time, and waited for Draeus to go ashore and trade before they disembarked.

It was a beautiful place, delighting all the senses: pristine, whitewashed beach houses spread along the shore. Wooden slatted walkways that *thunked* with every step, sprinkled with a light dusting of sand, surrounded by rustling grass dunes. Warehouses and perfume factories seemed to melt into the background, looking more like beach huts than industrial buildings, and an enticing floral aroma danced lightly on the breeze.

Alexander led Anita along the beach, away from the most densely populated area. He took her towards a large, fairy-tale beach house sitting in complete seclusion just around the nearest headland. Anita couldn't help but smile. 'I take it that one is yours?' she said happily.

Alexander smiled back, lifting her hand to his lips, placing a light kiss on her skin.

They reached the front of the house, Alexander unceremoniously dumping their bags by the door before pulling Anita towards him, kissing her lips. He pulled back, and, grinning devilishly, kicked off his shoes and socks, stripped down to his underwear, and ran for the water. Anita laughed, following suit, her energy soaring at the prospect of icy water against her skin. Gooseflesh erupted across her body as she dived under, gasping at the shock of the cold as she emerged.

Alexander was twenty feet out by the time Anita reached the sea. She swam after him, invigorated by their sudden and unexpected freedom from others. He swam to meet her, and when they met, she grabbed his shoulders, wrapping her arms around his neck, revelling in the feel of his bare skin against hers. She flashed him a mischievous smile before dunking him under, freeing herself from his grasp, gaining an advantage in the race back to shore.

Anita reached the beach first, splashing mercilessly as Alexander came within range. He reached the sand, scrambled to his feet, and chased her back towards the house. They tumbled to the sand together when he caught her, Anita landing with the advantage, which she used to pin his arms above his head.

Alexander looked up at her, still for a moment, before launching a full force retaliation, throwing her sideways and rolling on top. Never one to give up, Anita moved her hands to his sides and tickled his bare flesh, Alexander wincing and squirming hysterically, trying to get away from her offending fingers. He finally got hold of her hands, and pushed them outwards, Anita laughing so hard there was nothing she could do to stop him.

His eyes flicked to her mouth as her laughing subsided, then back to her eyes. He bent his head and kissed her with his sea salt lips, his body warm and inviting against hers. He broke the kiss and pulled her to her feet, draping a casual arm around her shoulders as they walked back to the house.

Alexander showed Anita around, each of them dripping water all over the wooden floors, until they reached a bathroom and wrapped themselves in fluffy white towels. He took her upstairs first, showing her four, big, airy, perfect seaside bedrooms, each with its own walk-in wardrobe and immaculate white bathroom.

Each room had a different feel, largely because of the hard-wearing fabric curtains and upholstered furniture. One was whitewashed and floaty, one had blue and white stripes, one had large, contemporary, statement floral prints, and the fourth was also floral, the flowers smaller, giving it a cosier, cottage-like feel.

Anita and Alexander took the whitewashed room, changing quickly into linen clothes and flip-flops they found in the wardrobe. The clothes were too big for Anita, so she wore a shirt long enough to pass for a dress, with a belt wrapped around her middle.

They returned downstairs, Alexander giving her a quick tour of the mainly open plan layout. The kitchen and dining area were set slightly off to one side from the large sitting room. Enormous windows occupied most of the wall space around the ground floor, giving panoramic views of the beach and sea beyond. A wood-burning stove sat at the edge of the sitting room, which Anita imagined would make for a heavenly setting if a winter storm raged outside. The large, squishy sofas were neutral tones with slate grey cushions, the tables made of driftwood, flowers dotted here and there, making the house smell fresh and pure.

Although a house keeper came once a week to clean and ensure everything was in order, Alexander kept no full-time staff. This meant they would need to fend for themselves, and Anita would, for the first time, be treated to the delights of Alexander's cooking.

They headed into town to buy groceries, leaving the house by the back door. They made their way along one of the slatted walkways before climbing a flight of steps to the top of the small cliff behind the house. To

Anita's surprise, halfway up, they came out onto a terrace sporting a tiled swimming pool. Several four-poster beds sat around the pool, the fabric at their corners floating lightly in the breeze.

'It's a bit much, isn't it!' laughed Alexander, seeing Anita's reaction.

'No, it's beautiful,' she said, turning around to take in the astonishing view out to sea, 'just... unexpected.'

'You have no idea how much hassle building that pool caused,' he joked. 'Philip decided he wanted it, but it took five years to get it operational. It was Philip's favourite topic of conversation for the best part of a decade!'

Anita laughed. 'It was worth it; it's amazing.'

They continued up the steps to the top, then walked the short distance along the cliffs into the centre of town, not that you could really call it a town. There were five shops on the main street: a butcher, a grocer, a fishmonger, a baker, and a hardware store. Apparently these five shops provided sufficient supplies for all who came to stay.

They went from shop to shop, picking up enough food for a couple of days, joking with the shopkeepers as they went. They entered the hardware store, not because they needed anything, but because Anita was curious to see what they had for sale. They'd been browsing for a few moments when she heard her name, and stopped in her tracks.

'... Anita. I can't believe that dear Alexander would stoop so low,' said a high, prim voice.

Anita pictured a mid-fifties busybody. Plump. No. Painfully skinny with spikey collar bones.

'Of course, he *should* be married by now, but to someone from a nice Spirit family. With no one left to guide his choice of wife, it's no surprise he's been led astray by an avid social climber.'

187

'Quite,' said a more softly spoken women. 'Moving from Marcus to Alexander so quickly... it's indecent.'

'The poor boy dodged a bullet if you ask me.'

'Dear Alexander doesn't have a father to protect him. Now she's got her claws in, he might never escape...'

'And at a time like this, when we need the Descendants to work together, not to be pulled apart by a divisive little hussy like her.'

Alexander heard every word, and, deciding they'd listened to enough, put his hand on the small of Anita's back and steered her out of the shop. They made their way, in silence, back along the cliffs to the house. Anita's energy was despondent, Alexander's brooding.

* * * * *

They reached the safety of the beach house, and Alexander breathed a sigh of relief. He dumped the bags in the kitchen, then followed Anita to the sitting room, where she was staring out of a window.

He walked up behind her, wrapped his arms around her, and pulled her to him. He bowed his head and kissed her hair, willing her to relax into him, wishing her energy would respond. After a few moments, it did, just not in the way he'd hoped. He felt anger build within her, boiling up until she tore his hands from her waist and whirled away, putting space between them.

'Anita,' he said, undeterred by the desolate look on her face, 'you've got to ignore them. This stuff comes with being part of my life. People have always gossiped about me and what I should or shouldn't be doing. If we're going to be together, this is going to happen all the time.'

'They think I'm some kind of social climbing slut,' she exclaimed. 'Too lowly for the likes of you.'

'Because they probably want me to marry one of their daughters,' he said, the half laugh on his lips a dreadful mistake.

'You think this is funny?'

'No, of course not. I couldn't care less what they think. That they even stopped to talk about us says more about them than it does about us.'

'But people think I'm only with you because I want to marry a Descendant. Do you know how that feels?'

'Anita, *you* are a Descendant.'

'So? They don't know that.'

'Who cares what they think? They don't know who you are any more than they know who I am. They think they have some right over me and my life because I take part in parades and sit in council meetings, but they don't. They're jealous of you, because they think they're the kind of people who should be my life, and they're not. They're stuck up and entitled, and there's nothing we can do but ignore them.'

Anita turned from him and left the house, heading back up the cliff. Alexander let her go; she needed time to calm down. With a deep exhale, he turned to the food. At least now he would have time to prepare their meal without Anita looking over his shoulder.

An hour later, with lamb cutlets marinating, chocolate mousse setting, and salad made, Alexander selected a bottle of sparkling wine from the cellar, a variety made from grapes and not ginger. He picked up two glasses and headed back up the cliff, hoping Anita hadn't gone far.

She hadn't. He found her sitting on a daybed by the swimming pool, looking out to sea, watching the setting sun. Shiny sweat covered her skin, face red, hair dishevelled. 'Been running?' he asked, handing her a glass of wine.

'Yes,' she said, looking up at him as she accepted it. 'Exercise helps clear my head.'

'And?'

'You're right, I know you are. What gets me is that I can't do anything to influence what people say, I'm powerless.'

'Even if you could show them who you really are, show them the true nature of our relationship, you'd never be able to get everyone on side. It would drive you mad if you tried. Whatever you do will be wrong in the eyes of somebody. Take it from me, I've been living with it my entire life.'

'I know. People have whispered about me and how odd I am for my whole life too. I've been winning Body challenges for years, but that's always been about me and something I've chosen to do. I learnt to deal with it. I don't like being someone who's only noteworthy in relation to someone else. They were only talking about me because of my relationships with you and Marcus; I could be anyone at all and they would have said exactly the same things.'

'Doesn't that make it more palatable? That it's fiction?'

'I'm not interested in being noteworthy only because of who my boyfriend is.'

'But that has nothing to do with this. You were noteworthy after you won the Chase, which had nothing to do with me or Marcus. They've just moved on to gossip about something else. Next time you win a challenge, they'll talk about that.'

'It would be easier if you found a girl from a prominent Spirit family.'

Alexander laughed, a little off balance from Anita's sudden change of direction. 'People like those women have been trying to make that happen for long enough. Yes, it would be easier, but it would be my idea of hell... and would end in divorce.'

Anita shoved him as he sat down next to her. 'Who said anything about marriage?'

'I was talking about Perfect Spirit Girl, not you.'

Anita leaned across, grasped handfuls of his shirt, and pulled him towards her. His face split into a broad smile as he complied with her touch, bending forwards, placing his hands either side of her face.

He rested his forehead against hers, breathing deeply, enjoying her familiar Jasmine scent. He closed his eyes, savouring the moment before touching his lips to hers, kissing her with a gentle, demanding intensity. Her lips responded, softly at first, then more urgently as she moved her hands from his chest to his shoulders, pulling herself on top of him.

'Do you have herbs?' she asked, her lips brushing his jaw. 'Contraceptive blends?'

'This is Wild Flower,' he said, nipping her earlobe. She shivered. 'We have herbs for everything.'

She grabbed handfuls of his hair, tipping her head back, giving him access to her neck. He kissed, and sucked, and nipped, then moved his hands to her waist, unbuckling the belt holding her shirt in place. Their kisses reached fever pitch, hands roaming, bodies pressed together. He swung her around, pushing her back onto the bed.

He pulled the shirt over her head, discarding it as he positioned himself above her, removing his own shirt. She looked up as he hovered over her, moving so he was just out of her reach any time she tried to touch him. He forced her to wait, anticipation rising, as he studied every inch of her toned body, Anita doing the same to his chest.

He leaned forward slowly, reaching down to kiss the middle of her chest, shivers of energy radiating out from the spot. Her back arched, sparks shooting between them. He dwelled there, the buzz of their mingling energy pulsing where they touched. He moved to the swell of breast visible at the top of her bra, biting the skin there, Anita gasping, hands going to his neck.

Taking advantage of her arched back, he unclipped her bra, sliding it off her arms. He kissed his way to her other breast, taking the nipple between his lips, playing with his tongue as she grabbed handfuls of his hair.

He released her slowly, kissing his way down her ribcage, across her stomach, reaching the tantalising dip away from her hip bone. He blew gently on the sensitive skin, delighting in the gooseflesh that formed, then kissed it away with light touches of his lips. His hands grasped her writhing hips, holding them still.

He removed her underwear, kissing his way slowly down her inner thigh before working his way at leisurely speed back up the other, her energy coursing ever more powerfully as he grew closer. His lips reached her, and her energy exploded, powerful convulsions racking through her, Alexander smiling in triumph.

She relaxed back onto the bed, her energy subsiding as Alexander removed his remaining clothes, then covered her with his body. She kissed his lips as he pushed inside her, exhaling reverently.

He moved above her, sliding an arm under her hips, pulling her to him, her legs wrapping tightly around him. She pushed him sideways, and he rolled them until Anita was astride him, moving slowly. He grabbed her hips, and she moved faster, their energy combining as it pulsed and snaked between them, heightening the ever-increasing tension that consumed them.

They climaxed together, a sudden surge of energy, electricity radiating out from everywhere they touched. Anita folded forwards, lying on Alexander, her face resting on his chest. He wrapped his arms tightly around her, a contented lull settling on them both.

CHAPTER 11

Draeus walked into Monty's back room. It had been a while since the Institution had used it for meetings, but they were running out of safe locations in Kingdom; the demonstrations had stepped up a gear. Austin had doubled the size of his personal army, and it now outnumbered the official police force three to one. The capital usually had so little crime that there wasn't a need for a big force.

Amber, having assumed the role of Austin's Commander-in-Chief, was hoarding, preparing for battle. She was raiding warehouses by the docks, stealing food, and forcing farmers to sell what little produce they had directly to Austin. This meant that Austin both had ample food to feed his growing militia, and could control food prices. Worse still, they were capturing and interrogating suspected rebellion and Institution members. Fear was spreading through the people like wildfire; fear that they would be the next wrongly accused.

Amber had paid Helena a visit, to warn her she was being watched, and to tell her, should she put a single foot out of line, that 'justice' would be served.

'How did it go?' demanded Helena, as Draeus crossed the threshold, greeted by the expectant, impatient faces of Helena, Rose, Melia, Bass, and Gwyn.

'Not as well as we'd hoped,' said Draeus, taking a seat. 'Timi couldn't work out a way to open the cylinder. He stayed in Anita's head longer than Alexander, but he did that by anchoring to Anita's mind, and she passed out under the strain.'

'Alexander must have loved that,' said Melia.

'It didn't go down overly well.'

'Is she alright?' asked Bass, Gwyn shooting him a sideways glance.

'She's fine. No damage done. She's more annoyed that we went all that way and got no further forward.'

'Where are they now?' asked Rose, Bass' mother. 'Marcus has been putting out feelers for their whereabouts ever since they left Empire... he's embarrassed...'

'... my son is not embarrassed,' snapped Melia. 'He's glad to be rid of her, after the way she treated him.'

'Not what I heard,' said Gwyn. 'I heard he's a wreck.'

Melia was gearing up for battle, but Helena cut across them. 'Enough,' she barked. 'We're not here for petty gossip. Where are Anita and Alexander now?'

'At Wild Flower, as we planned,' said Draeus. 'They'll return to Empire soon and tell everyone that they were spending time at Alexander's beach house.'

'Good,' said Helena, some of the tension leaving her features. 'The question now is what we do next? We've got to get that cylinder open, one way or another.'

'But we can't wait for that to happen before we act,' said Rose, her no nonsense tone not inviting disagreement. 'Tensions are rising; it's like a tinder box out there. It won't be long before Austin lights a match.'

'She's right,' said Draeus, 'we came across a meeting of the rebels in the Wild. They elected a new, more impatient leader. He wants to strike soon.'

'And the energy's still dropping,' added Bass. 'If we don't do something soon, we'll have to ration transportation as well as food, and next year's crop yields are going to be even worse than this year's...'

'So what do you suggest?' asked Helena.

'We send the Relic back,' he replied evenly.

Melia and Gwyn sniggered.

'How do you intend to do that, given that generations of Descendants have failed?' asked Melia, her tone reminiscent of her former husband, Austin's, patronizing put downs.

'Well, aside from the obvious, that Descendants haven't failed for any reason other than that they haven't tried, I'm not talking about actually sending it back to the Gods; I don't know how to do that. I do know how to *appear* to send the Relic back.'

'What good would that do?' asked Gwyn, predictably resistant to anyone other than a Descendant having a say about returning the Relic.

'I hope it would follow the same pattern we observed after the last Body Descendant's death,' said Bass. Gwyn looked blank, so he kept going. 'Christiana died several days before Austin announced her death. The energy didn't react until after the announcement, meaning it was people's reaction to her death and not her actual death that made the difference to the energy. I'm hoping the same thing will hold true for the Relic; all we have to do is make people think we've returned the Relic to the Gods. This should cause a surge in the energy, and we can figure out how to actually return it later.'

'You don't think the prophecy is true?' asked Gwyn.

'I believe in the prophecy, but I also believe in what we observed after Christiana's death. There's a very real possibility this won't work, or that the Gods will send us some other punishment for trying it. I don't think it'll work as a long-term measure. Lies have a certain negativity about them, which gets out and spreads. But I think it could help us preserve order in the short-term.'

'Last time you told us about this, you still had work to do,' said Rose, eying her son with a reserved look. 'Have you figured it out?'

'I think so, yes,' said Bass, 'although, obviously we can't have a trial run, so it's not without risk.'

'How could you have figured it out?' asked Melia, her scepticism palpable. 'Anderson has been away for weeks.'

Bass's usual even-headedness wavered. 'Anderson had little to do with the idea, and I certainly didn't need him to test my hypotheses. He's more of a book-based academic, rather than a practical one.'

'Where is Anderson anyway?' asked Helena, realizing she'd heard nothing of him since he'd left for the Wild Lands with Draeus, Alexander, and Anita.

'He stayed at the Cloud Mountain,' said Draeus, quietly.

'Why?' asked Helena.

'Don't know, I'm afraid. Said he wanted to stay and help with some research. I saw no reason to object.'

'When's he coming back?' Helena asked, riled, given she was Anderson's handler within the Institution, and knew nothing of his intention to stay in the Wild.

'No idea,' said Draeus, 'but I'll be returning to the Cloud Mountain shortly, so I can ask him when I get there.'

Helena gave a frustrated shrug; there was little else she could do. 'Bass' idea is the only one we have, and I think it could work. What do you need us to do to help?' she asked.

'The most important thing we lack is the support of the ruling Descendants,' said Bass, pointedly. 'I can get the technical side set up in a few weeks, but if the Descendants aren't there to put on a show, the plan falls apart.'

'Alexander will help us,' said Helena, confidently, 'and Gwyn, I think we should have you there and not Peter; the Body bloodline travels down through female heirs, after all.'

Every face turned to Gwyn, who shook her head in disbelief. 'I can't believe I let you talk me into coming here,' she said to Bass, then got up and left the room. Bass shot Helena a dirty look, then went after her.

'It's down to you to sway her, Bass,' said Helena, making his shoulders stiffen.

'What do we do about Austin?' asked Melia.

'What do you suggest?' asked Rose, jumping in before Helena could respond.

'The only way to get to Austin is via my son,' said Melia, coolly, 'even though Helena will no-doubt try one of her midnight encounters with my ex-husband.'

Helena looked ready to punch Melia. Rose intervened again. 'Do you think you can get Marcus on side?'

The enormity of the task wasn't lost on any of them.

'I don't know, but I suppose I'll have to try.' Melia got up and made for the door. 'I'll be in touch when I have news,' she said, closing the door behind her.

Draeus, Helena, and Rose sat back in their chairs. Rose looked ragged, and Helena knew she did too.

'The trials of leadership,' said Draeus, as he poured them all strong, black coffee from the pot in the middle of the table.

'Don't mock,' said Helena, but the warning had little venom.

'All we can do now is wait,' said Rose, sipping tentatively at her coffee before adding liberal quantities of sugar and cream.

'I suppose so,' said Helena. 'Why are you going back to the Cloud Mountain so soon?' she asked Draeus. He usually steered clear of the place, preferring those who worked for him to make the trips on his behalf.

'Timi wants a large shipment, and insisted I personally oversee it.'

'What does he want?' asked Helena. Timi was always looking to fortify his precious mountain retreat, so the news was no particular surprise.

'Everything and anything: metals, rare dried flowers, seeds and bulbs, building supplies. You name it, he probably wants some of it.'

'Why?' asked Rose.

'No idea, but he's paying handsomely and wants the utmost discretion, so I take it I can trust you two not to go gossiping?'

'Not really our style,' said Rose, dryly.

'In which case, I have some buying to do. If you'll excuse me...'

'Be careful of Timi,' said Helena, before he made it out of earshot, 'he's the most devious person I know.'

* * * * *

Bass and Gwyn sat on the top floor of the observatory, legs dangling over the side as they looked out over Empire. It was odd for it not to be Anita sitting by his side.

'I'm just not convinced this is the only way,' said Gwyn. 'Austin keeps saying he has a better plan, another way to tackle the situation.'

'Refreshing he's finally acknowledging that we have *a situation*,' replied Bass, doing nothing to hide the hostility he felt.

'He can hardly deny it; there are protesters outside his houses and at all the temples.'

'That's just a symptom. What about the cause?'

'He's doing what he thinks is right,' said Gwyn, defensively.

'So he says. But he's wrong and following his advice means scores of people will die, either at the hands of his burgeoning army, or because they don't have enough food to eat.'

'He says he has a plan.'

'Really? What is it?'

'I don't know; obviously he won't tell me.'

'And let's assume, for just a moment, that his plan fails? Or that he doesn't really have a plan, seeing as he's not keen on sharing it? Or that his plan is to use his army to take over and try to lead by himself?'

'He wouldn't do that.'

'Really? Give me one convincing reason why you think that.'

'Because he swore an oath.'

'Like all ruling Descendants do? To send the Relic back? Fat lot of good that does anyone.'

'How dare you? You have no idea what goes on behind the closed doors of our residences.'

'You're telling me it's research into how to send the Relic back?' he laughed.

Anger burned hot on Gwyn's face. 'Gods, Bass, how can you mock me, when all you do is sit here, looking at declining energy readings, pining for Anita, who has never been and will never be interested in you.'

Bass' face tumbled, pain contorting his features, his energy choked up inside. He struggled to clear the fuzz of shock, searching for something to say. But he couldn't think of anything to respond to her vicious, personal attack. Instead, he met Gwyn's eyes, let her see his hurt and confusion, then got up and left her. He needed, more than anything else, to be on his own, craving the rush of the river as company, rather than this spiteful girl, who he thought he'd been falling in love with.

'Bass,' she called after him, as he ducked through the window and hurtled down the stairs, almost knocking Patrick over as he whistled passed. 'Bass, come back,' she pleaded, but he was gone, and even if he had heard her, his brain would have blocked out her words.

*   *   *   *   *

Gwyn's words didn't go unanswered. 'Are you alright?' asked Patrick, gently, making his way out onto the roof, perching on a pipe.

'Do I look alright?' Gwyn snapped, wanting this little runt of a man to disappear.

'Not really, no,' he replied frankly. 'You look like you've been caught up in Bass' obsession with Anita.'

Gwyn looked around, shocked at his words. 'What do you mean?' she demanded.

'Sorry, but I couldn't help overhearing. It seems to me, everything he's doing—all the stuff with the Institution—he's only doing it for Anita. He's been looking for a way to impress her for as long as I can remember, and if he saves the day, it's safe to assume he'd achieve that.' Patrick paused, the air pregnant with implication.

'You don't think he believes in what he's doing?'

'Now, I didn't say that, not exactly. Who knows what's going on in the inner workings of his mind, or what he really thinks? It just seems a bit rash to resort to a fake return of the Relic, when we've tried nothing else. What if Austin's right? What if there is another way? What if the Gods punish us, and especially the Descendants, for going along with a lie of such enormous magnitude?'

'You think they would? Punish us, I mean? Even if we were only trying to do what was best for the people?'

'How do you know this is what's best for the people, when you haven't heard Austin's plan yet? What if Bass' plan isn't the only way?'

'That's what I tried to tell Bass, but he wouldn't listen.'

'Because, if Austin's plan is the one to succeed, then Anita will have no reason to reconsider her decision about Bass.'

'What should we do? You think we should try to stop him?' Maybe she'd underestimated Patrick; his words made such sense.

'We don't have the power to do that, even if we wanted to,' said Patrick, 'but there are others who have the power.'

'Austin,' she said.

'He certainly would.'

'You think we should tell Austin about the plan?'

'I don't know,' he said. 'I don't know him at all... but you know him well. What do you think?'

'What would he do to Bass? I don't want him to get hurt.'

'He'll only get hurt if Austin thinks Bass is the instigator…'

'Then who?'

'Bass' tormentor.'

'Anita?' Would that work? Would Austin believe it was Anita's plan?

Patrick shrugged innocently. 'Austin already hates Anita for what she did to Marcus, and he hasn't tried to exact revenge for that. I'm sure Anita would be perfectly safe, whereas, if he found out Bass was involved… he's an easy target.'

'He might just rough her up a bit, like before. And it would be for the good of us all… We don't want to anger the Gods,' said Gwyn.

'Anita could lie low for a while; go back to the Wild Lands and leave Bass in peace.'

'Will you come with me?' she asked, her mind made up. It was her duty to inform Austin of the plan, but she wasn't quite confident enough to go through with it on her own.

Patrick hesitated, and Gwyn frowned. 'Of course,' came his resolute reply.

* * * * *

Alexander and Anita had arrived back from Wild Flower earlier in the day. They sat in Cleo's apartment, recounting the story of their journey through the Wild, drinking fruit smoothies spiked with rum.

'I wish Dad would tell me what he gets up to in the Wild Lands,' said Cleo, longingly. 'I'm sure he must have been in some terrifying scrapes.'

'He certainly seems to have friends everywhere,' said Anita. 'No matter where we went, he knew everyone.'

'Typical Dad,' she said, rolling her eyes. 'I can't go anywhere without someone recognizing me as his daughter and asking after him. One day, I'm going to insist he takes me with him. Just think of all the gossip to be found.'

Anita laughed. 'Glad to see you want to go to broaden your horizons.'

'I'd like to dig further into my latest archive discoveries, actually,' she said, with mock offense.

'Oh yes?' said Anita. 'You're a proper little academic these days?'

'Yes, actually. I've been looking into a couple of things. Firstly, how the Relic was discovered and by whom; there's definitely something fishy about it...'

'... why?' asked Alexander.

'Well, there are hardly any records relating to it, and for such a momentous moment in our history, you would think there would be stacks of stuff written. But also, because, from the little there is, it seems like it all happened so quickly. A group of academics were out in the Wild Lands, they stumbled across the Relic, and hey presto, the prophecy was found.'

'How else would it happen?' asked Anita, not sure what Cleo was getting at.

'It just doesn't feel right; there's something the archive isn't telling me.'

'I'll take your word for it,' said Anita, thinking the rum may have gone to Cleo's head. 'The second thing?'

'Ah, yes,' said Cleo, taking her time to build the usual suspense before sharing a secret. 'I was in the archive, the place devoid of life, as usual, when this man came in and entered one of the locked rooms at the back of the floor.'

Alexander raised an eyebrow. 'I can count on my hands the number of people allowed in those rooms,' he said, surprised, 'and they rarely go into them.'

'He was in there filing a document, I think, and he left the door open behind him. Naturally, I had a look around. At first, he was panicky, telling me I had to leave the room, or he might get into trouble.' Anita read from Cleo's energy that this wasn't exactly how it had happened, but she let it slide. 'I calmed him down and asked him what he was doing. He wouldn't give much away, but it was to do with something called *The Great Hall of the Magnei.*'

'The what?' asked Anita.

'According to the research I've done since, they're an elusive group of individuals who live in some secret location in the Wild Lands. No one is really sure who they are or what they do. Every now and again one pops up somewhere to run an errand, usually demonstrating a crazy skill in the process.'

Cleo and Anita both looked at Alexander, questions in their eyes.

He paused before responding. 'I've heard stories about them, but I thought it was just rumour. You wouldn't believe some of the stuff they make up about the Descendants, so why not about another group? Anyway, the rumour I heard is that there's a group of people, people with significant Mind, Body and Spirit skills, who live out in the Wild, and meddle in our affairs. I'm not sure how they're supposed to meddle, as I've seen no evidence of it, and neither have the other Descendants, as far as I'm aware. I never paid much attention; never had reason to, so that's all I know.'

'But they're powerful,' said Cleo.

'Apparently,' he replied.

'What could they possibly be up to?' asked Cleo.

'Nothing, probably,' said Alexander. 'People love to make up stories about things they don't understand. They're probably just a group of hermits who turn up at trading posts occasionally. They probably look a bit different, so people make up stories.'

'Hmm,' said Cleo, sceptically. 'There's no smoke without fire.'

'How many of those have you had to drink?' teased Anita, motioning towards her friend's empty glass before refilling it from a pitcher.

'Not nearly enough,' said Cleo, taking a large gulp from her full glass. 'Anyway, I think the guy from the archive might live in the Wild Lands too. I think he might even be one of them, but I found a document that suggested they're all mad, like it's a kind of asylum. He didn't seem mad... just a little strange... intense.'

'And at that point, you've got to question some of the documents in the archive,' laughed Alexander, brushing aside the conspiracy. 'Given the kind of people allowed in those rooms, the man was most likely an extremely senior academic, who the Descendants have rigorously vetted.'

'I'm not so sure,' said Cleo. 'There's got to be something to it, don't you think? People don't make things up with no reason, and there's something else I haven't told you... The reason he told me about the Magnei was because he touched me and knew I'd seen the Great Hall.'

'What do you mean?' said Anita.

'I mean, the Great Hall of the Magnei is the hall in your head, the one where the cylinder is.'

'You told him about the place in my head?'

'No, of course not! He touched me, then went all weird. He knew I'd seen it but hadn't actually been there, and he asked me how. I didn't even know what he was talking about until I realised the hall in your head was the only place it could be. I told him it was via a meditation and it was like he immediately understood.'

'What did he tell you about it?'

'Absolutely nothing. He freaked out. He pretty much pushed me out of the room and then just disappeared.'

'What did he look like?' asked Alexander, foreboding settling across his energy.

'Medium height, quite slim, dark hair tied back in a ponytail.'

'And his name?'

'He disappeared before I could find it out.'

'And you haven't seen him anywhere since?'

'No.'

'Sound like anyone you know?' asked Anita.

'No, but only a handful of people are allowed in there, so I can see if that description matches anyone on the list.'

Cleo's eyes came alive. 'You have access to those rooms?' she asked excitedly, continuing before giving him a chance to answer. 'Because I saw a book in there about the Relic and how it was discovered, but didn't have time to look through it. If you could get me in, I might find out something meaningful.'

'Sorry, no can do. The Descendants aren't allowed in. A few decades back, Austin's father got especially power hungry, and started doctoring records. The other Descendants put a stop to it, and they all agreed to only access stuff they really needed, and only with two, impartial academics present. But I can get a list of who's allowed in, so at least that gives us something.'

'I suppose so,' said Cleo, disappointed.

'Can you find anything else out about the Great Hall of the Magnei?' Anita asked Alexander. 'It might help us with the cylinder.'

'I can try, but it sounds like Cleo's already looked into all the publicly available stuff, and I can't get into any of the private rooms without drawing attention to the reason.'

'Do you know anyone who's researched the Magnei, or who might know something helpful?'

Alexander shook his head. 'As I said, even the existence of the Magnei is considered a fairy tale; no self-respecting academic would ever research them.'

'That'll have to be the purpose of my first trip into the Wild then,' said Cleo, frivolously. 'To find the lost asylum of the Magnei and expose their secrets to the world.'

'Careful,' said Anita, 'they might lock you up and never let you go. You are kind of crazy after all.'

* * * * *

Alexander and Anita left Cleo's as the sun was going down. Cordelia was visiting a friend in Kingdom, so Anita had to take Thorn for a walk, and Alexander needed to run a few errands. 'I'll come over later?' he asked, kissing her goodbye.

She nodded. 'Perfect. I'm sure Cordelia's left something delicious to eat, so you won't get to sample the delights of my cooking,' she said, playfully, giving him another quick kiss on the lips, savouring the feel of his hands in her hair.

'I sampled quite enough in Wild Flower,' he teased. She glared at him, her eyebrow arching aggressively. 'And it was all utterly delicious.'

He gave her a last quick peck on the lips before they parted ways, elated by Cleo's outlandish theories and too much rum. Neither of them noticed Marcus watch them go.

CHAPTER 12

Gwyn and Patrick arrived at the castle, the door opening before they reached the top of the steps, Amber providing a hostile greeting. 'What are you doing here?' she said, intrigued both by Gwyn's nervous body language and the weak little man accompanying her. He seemed to be doing his very best to melt into Gwyn's shadow.

'I… um… I need to talk to Austin,' said Gwyn, feebly, looking anywhere but into Amber's eyes.

'I see,' said Amber, at a leisurely pace. Most people she would send away, tell them to make an appointment, but Gwyn had never turned up unannounced, asking to see him before. And Amber had never seen Gwyn looking so uncertain… it was worth the risk. 'In here,' she said, herding them into Austin's study. 'Sit on a sofa and touch nothing. I'll let Austin know you're here.'

* * * * *

A few minutes later, Austin entered the room, surveying the scene, his lip twitching as he tried to hide his smile. Gwyn's appearance was exactly as Amber had described it; this had all the hallmarks of something entertaining. He sat purposefully on one of the leather sofas, looking at each of them in turn, increasing their discomfort. He finally asked, 'How is it I can help, Gwyneth?'

'Well, um, you see, um…'

'… Anita's found a way to make it look like the Relic has been returned to the Gods. She's working with the Institution to go through with it,' said Patrick, in a rush, sending an apologetic look at Gwyn.

Austin raised his eyebrows, now fully amused. 'These are very serious accusations, ah… what was your name?'

'Patrick,' he said, shrinking under the weight of Austin's stare.

'Patrick. How could you possibly know about such a plan?'

'I work at the observatory, as does Anita. I overheard her talking about it,' he said too quickly.

'I see. And what does this plan entail?'

Patrick shrank further, Austin surprised that was possible. He looked like a rodent, paralysed by fear, searching for a way out. He looked pleadingly at Gwyn, who averted her gaze; her support only went so far, it would seem.

'She wants to send the Relic back using a kind of energy slingshot. It will send the Relic into the sky and appear to all who watch that it has been returned to the Gods. In fact, it will be thrown to another location, where someone will be on hand to pick it up. The world will think the Relic had been returned, which will lift the energy in the short-term, buying the Institution time to work out how to truly return it to the Gods.'

Austin's mouth tightened into a thin line. 'But this plan could only hope to succeed with the help of the Descendants. They would need credible witnesses.'

'The Institution are going to try and convince the Descendants to take part.'

Austin turned his gaze to Gwyn. 'Which is where you come in, I suppose?'

She nodded. 'But I know you have a plan. I don't want to go behind your back, not when you have a way to get things under control.'

Austin softened. 'You were right to come to me,' he said, reassuringly. 'Thank you, both of you, for bringing this to my attention. I'll investigate further at once.'

'What will you do to Anita?' asked Gwyn, her hands trembling in her lap.

'That will depend on what I find. As you know, my son is fond of Anita. She will come to no harm.'

* * * * *

Austin's words did nothing to reassure Gwyn. His eyes were steely, devoid of emotion, and dread ate away at her stomach.

Gwyn and Patrick left the castle and parted ways. Patrick sickened her; he was over the moon at the evening's events.

She went directly to the Body Temple, to pray to the Goddess, hoping against hope that she hadn't made a terrible mistake.

* * * * *

A guard greeted Marcus when he arrived home. 'You're wanted in the study,' he said.

'Thank you,' said Marcus, entering the study to find Austin and Amber sitting by the fire. He joined them, helping himself to a tumbler of whiskey first.

Austin told Marcus about Anita's plan, then, sipping whisky from his own crystal glass, waited patiently for his son's reaction.

'What are you going to do?' Marcus eventually asked, trying to tread lightly, not sure what his father wanted from him.

'What do you think we should do?' said Austin, Marcus not missing the use of the word 'we'; apparently, he was now a part of this.

'Find out more about the allegations to see if they have any truth in them?'

Austin sneered. 'After everything that girl has put you through, you still think she could be innocent? What a fool you are.'

'I'm no fool,' said Marcus, slamming down his glass, 'but nor am I so intent on revenge that I'm willing to act entirely on the say so of Gwyn and some unknown.'

'Do you know where she's been these last few weeks?' he asked, cruelly.

'With Alexander in Wild Flower,' said Marcus, looking his father in the eye, taking satisfaction from not giving him the reaction he sought. 'Do you know where she'll be tonight?' He continued without waiting for an answer. 'Having a romantic dinner with Alexander at Cordelia's cottage. Some things you just have to live with.'

'Not in my world you don't.'

'So you'll do what? Torture her again? Kill her? Regardless of the truth? You've wanted to do it for a while, so I suppose any excuse will do…'

'Fine, you're right,' said Austin, unexpectedly changing tack. 'We should investigate further. You find Alexander and see if you can glean any information from him. Gwyn said she's been approached by the Institution. They asked for her help with their plan, so it makes sense that they would approach Alexander too. Go to him and see what you can find out. Say you want to help them but need to know what's going on first. I'm confident he'll confirm Gwyn's story, and we can decide what to do from there.'

Marcus was taken aback. 'You trust me to go?'

'Of course. Alexander won't see you as a threat, and you sought his help before, so why not again now? If Alexander thinks you're trying to help his beloved Anita, he'll fall over himself to work with you.'

'Okay,' said Marcus, 'I'll find him tomorrow.'

'No. Go tonight. Who knows what the Institution is up to; we can't afford to waste any time.'

'Fine, I'll go now,' said Marcus, happy to play such an important part in his father's plan. 'Hopefully I'll be able to catch him before he goes to Anita's, otherwise, the conversation will have to wait until the morning.'

* * * * *

Bass arrived at Anita's just as she was returning from walking Thorn, which had been more of a run, and somewhere muddy. He crouched down to pet Thorn, wiping his hands on the back of Anita's already filthy t-shirt when he was done.

'Just passing by?' asked Anita, stretching.

Bass sat on the old, rickety swing. 'Not exactly,' he said. 'I think I've got a way to make the slingshot work.'

'Really?' she said quickly, breaking her stretch. 'How can you be sure?'

'I can't. But I've made the concept work on other things, large rocks and so forth. I've been sending them increasing distances using the same method. Dad's been helping me, actually.'

'What?' asked Anita, surprised. 'He hates anything to do with the Institution. How did you change his mind?'

'I didn't. I told him about the concept of an energy slingshot and asked for his help. He jumped at the chance to spend time with me. I think he's found it therapeutic to use his brain for something other than arguing politics, which is all he seems to do these days.'

'So, it's ready to go?'

'Almost. It'll take another couple of weeks to perfect, but it's almost there. But we need the Descendants, and Gwyn's not keen to help. Do you think Alexander will?'

'I should think so; I'll talk to him about it. The Gods only know what Helena's planning to do to get Austin to help... but we didn't get anywhere with the cylinder, so I'm not sure what else we can do.'

They sat in silence for a moment, watching Thorn roll on the lawn.

'I'm worried though,' said Anita. 'What if the Institution puts in place a system that's even worse than the one we have now? We don't even know who their leader is, yet we're all dancing to their tune.'

'Do we have any choice?' he replied. 'Unless someone can come up with a better idea, and soon, this seems to be the only way forward.'

'What about Gwyn? How are you going to get her to persuade Peter?'

'Helena thinks we should skip Peter and get Gwyn to take part instead. She is, after all, the only remaining female member of her line.' He looked embarrassed. 'I mean, of course, that's fake too; you should really be the one to do it... but, well, you know why we can't bring that into the open. At least we won't have a problem persuading you to help when we really send it back.'

Anita smiled sympathetically. 'Do you think Gwyn will do it?'

'I'm honestly not sure. We had an argument about it. Hopefully she'll come round.'

'Sorry to hear that,' said Anita, pulling a final stretch. 'Cordelia left some pecan and maple cake. Want some?'

'Do I want some?' Bass joked.

Anita laughed. 'Come on then,' she said, heading inside. 'Any ideas for how we actually return the Relic yet?'

'No; one step at a time! But I'm worried about what could happen when we try. The Relic's a powerful object, and we have such a rudimentary understanding of it.'

'What do you mean?'

'Anita! Watch out!' shouted Bass, as they entered the kitchen, Bass throwing Anita to the side. Anita looked up and took in two things simultaneously. First, she saw Bass's body on the floor, a kitchen knife sticking out of his ribs, blood leaking from him. Second, she saw Austin's cold eyes gleam from across the room, moving menacingly towards her.

Without thinking, she grabbed the knife from Bass' chest, pulled it out, and sent it flying towards their attacker. The knife easily found Austin's heart, hours of Body practice saving her life, Austin collapsing to the floor.

Disbelief and anger filled his energy. Even when faced with imminent death, he couldn't help but think of himself as superior. For a moment, she thought he was going to get up and come after her, but the life went out of him; a sudden rush of energy that seemed to surge from the room, before a weaker, secondary energy left him, fluttering into extinction, dissipating into the air.

Anita crashed to the floor beside Bass, frantically trying to stem the bleeding. 'I'm so sorry. Bass, I'm so sorry. He was here for me, not for you.'

Bass' eyes flickered open, focusing on Anita's distraught face. 'Not your fault,' he whispered, as Anita stroked his hair with her free hand.

'It's going to be okay,' she said, tears flowing freely from her eyes. 'I'll get help.'

'No. Stay,' he said, the words barely audible as Anita leaned down and placed her face against his. 'I've always loved you,' he whispered into her ear. His eyes closed for the last time, life slowly drifting from him.

'I love you too,' she whispered, feeling his familiar energy slip away, scattering outwards. Anita longed to chase it, to catch it, force it back into his body. She strained to feel the final, helpless traces of her friend as they disappeared into the surrounding air, treasuring the last imprint of his vibrant life force, a force that she would never feel again.

Anita sat there, silent and still, blood from Bass and Austin mingling with her tears, forming pools around them. She cradled Bass' head, willing him to wake up, then willing herself to wake up from what must be a terrible, terrible dream.

Hours later, strong hands reached for her, pulling her away, drawing her upwards into a safe, warm embrace. She buried her face in Alexander's chest, still praying to the Gods that this was some horrible joke, when she felt Marcus' familiar energy coming down the corridor. He entered the kitchen with a muted cry of alarm. The air compressed as the shock thundered into him, paralysing them all for several never-ending heartbeats. Then, just as suddenly, reality sprang back and hit them, the room too loud in the silence.

Marcus turned and fled.

CHAPTER 13

Austin's funeral took place a week later in Kingdom, the full pomp and ceremony laid on, as was befitting a man of his status. Alexander and Helena had to go, of course, but Elistair was notably absent, as was Anita. The man had killed Bass, tried to kill her, and she could feel nothing about Austin, other than to be content that he was gone.

Not only did she grieve Bass, she was distraught that he'd taken a knife meant for her. How had she not seen it coming? What good was being a reader if she couldn't detect a threat right under her nose?

'Why didn't I feel his energy?' she'd asked Alexander, as he'd tried to console her in the terrible hours that followed. 'How did I not see him there? How was it that Bass, who wasn't a reader, reacted before me? How did he push me out of the way, when I had no idea there was a threat?'

Alexander had had no explanations, and nor did anyone else.

That night, Alexander had called Elistair and Amber to the scene, along with an undertaker, who had removed the two bodies and cleaned up the blood. Amber left quickly, but Elistair stayed until he could bear Anita's apologies no longer.

'Anita, it wasn't your fault,' he said, tears in his eyes, holding Anita at arm's length by her shoulders. 'Bass would have done anything for you, and there's nothing we can do now to change what's done. You put an end to Austin's reign, so something good may yet come from this horrible mess.'

He'd hugged her and left, leaving Alexander with the futile task of trying to console her.

Cordelia had arrived home the following day. She cleaned the kitchen twelve times before realizing it would do nothing to bring Bass back, nor wash away what had taken place in her kitchen. After that, she'd joined Anita in silent mourning, taking Thorn for long walks, or sitting quietly in the garden, wrapped up against the winter chill.

Bass' funeral took place a week after Austin's, in the Body Temple, in Empire. Elistair refused to let the councillors and remaining Descendants process behind the coffin. He told them they could sit with the rest of the congregation, as would have been his son's wishes.

The funeral was low key. Bass' favourite, rousing classical music accompanied his coffin both into and out of the temple. Elistair, Rose, Anita, Alexander, Cleo, and a member of Bass' band carried the coffin, all clad in full length black robes with hoods. The coffin and temple were abundantly decorated with Bass' favourite wild flowers; purples, whites, and greens covering every surface.

The funeral was short. Rose read a poem and Elistair gave a moving eulogy. Not only did he praise his son's work at the observatory, but also his steel and determination in sticking up for what was right, especially at council meetings. He told them that Bass would want everyone to continue his fight. Nothing had been more important to his son than stabilizing the energy, the cause for which he had ultimately laid down his life.

They processed out, not a dry eye in the temple, and Anita saw Gwyn slip out the back. She felt sorry for her. Bass had never introduced Gwyn to Elistair or Rose as his girlfriend, although they had known something was going on. How difficult it must be, to have been so close to Bass in his last few weeks of life, and now find herself excluded. But then again, Gwyn hadn't been to see Elistair or Rose since Bass's death. Maybe she didn't want to impose, or maybe she was the stuck-up bitch Anita had always thought her to be.

Bass' body was cremated, in accordance with his wishes, his ashes scattered from the roof of the observatory. Elistair, Rose, and Anita did it together, a respectful silence falling over them as what remained of him fluttered away on the breeze. Rose left as soon as it was done; she had never much liked the observatory. 'See you at the wake,' she'd said, the death of their son having done nothing to bring Elistair and Rose closer together. Instead, something akin to hatred bubbled just under the surface.

'Anita, there's something I need to tell you,' said Elistair, turning to face her as the last of the ashes disappeared. Anita was glad to see that the wind was taking him to the river.

'What is it?'

'There's no easy way to say this,' he said, his tone business-like, efficient, 'so I'll just tell you, and you can ask me whatever questions you like.'

'Okay,' she replied, puzzled.

'You're the Body Descendant, not Gwyn.'

Anita took a deep breath and turned awkwardly away from him. 'I know,' she replied. 'Helena told me. She told me the whole story of my parents. How they met in the Wild Lands when Jeffrey was there on

Institution business. How Peter and my mother were swapped at birth. How my mother wanted to swap Gwyn and I, but Peter refused. And about how Helena betrayed my parents, which led to the fire at the temple, where they died.'

'Why?' he asked simply, his energy betraying his surprise.

'Because she wants my help, and it was the only way for her to regain some of my trust.'

'You can't possibly be planning to help her, after all she's done?'

'I don't think there's much option,' said Anita, turning back to look Elistair in the eye.

'Now that Austin's gone, we'll persuade Marcus to help you, Alexander, and I find a way to return the Relic.'

'What if we can't do that in time?'

'We will.'

'You and I both know that's unlikely, and anyway, I've already agreed to help her, and...,' Anita paused, knowing what she was about to say was crossing a line.

'And what?' His eyes bore into hers with increasing intensity. 'Anita? And what?'

'And you've already been helping too,' she said with a sigh. 'Bass became a member of the Institution a while ago, and he and Anderson were working on sending the Relic back. They couldn't find anything that would send it back for real, so Bass wanted to fake it.'

'The energy slingshot?' he asked, realization dawning. Anita nodded. 'I don't believe you. Bass would never have got involved with the Institution; he knew how much I hate them.'

'He thought it was the only way, and he was enjoying the excuse to spend some time with, working on his theory. He thought you enjoyed it too, especially with everything going on.'

'I did enjoy it, but if I'd known what it was for, I would have put an end to it. You've got to leave the Institution, Anita, we'll find another way.'

'I'm sorry, I can't. This is what Bass wanted. After what he did for me... I owe it to him to see this through.'

'Then I'm afraid this is where we part ways. I'm sorry to say it, but you'll have to learn the hard way what those people are really like.'

Elistair left, leaving Anita to contemplate his words, but nothing he could say would change her mind. Bass had been committed to the energy slingshot; she had no choice but to see it through.

* * * * *

Bass' wake was held that night at The Island, and it got more than a bit out of hand. Bass' band played, Cleo provided copious quantities of free alcohol, each batch of punch more lethal than the last, and the butcher from Temple Mews provided a hog roast for what seemed to be the entire population of Empire. It wasn't surprising, given that food was so scarce.

Anita avoided Rose, Gwyn, and Elistair. She sat on the deck out the back for most of the evening, with Cleo and Alexander. She refused to go inside, even though they were in the grip of winter, and it was freezing.

Helena arrived late, never one to enjoy social occasions where she might get stuck with people who possessed only half a brain cell. She spoke briefly with Rose, then Elistair, who quickly made it plain she wasn't welcome. Mercifully, she spotted Timi, on route to the exit. She followed him out, happy that she'd done the dutiful thing, and that she had found a swift escape.

'Didn't think a wake would be your kind of social occasion,' she said to Timi's back, as the bar door slammed closed behind her.

'Right back at you,' came his patronizing drawl.

'How long are you here for?'

'I haven't decided. I'll attend the Crowning and the Chase, assuming they have one, and after that, it all depends.'

'Oh? On what?'

'On how your plans go to return the Relic.'

'I see,' said Helena, smiling. 'So you know about that.'

'You thought I wouldn't find out? I'm your handler, not to mention the Spirit Leader. Of course I know.'

'I knew someone would tell you, eventually.'

'Yet you tried to hide it from me anyway.'

'I'm not the only one hiding things, am I?'

'Really? How delightful. Who else has a secret?' Timi's eyes were alight with the pleasure of his game.

'Don't toy with me, Timi. The rest of the world is on the brink of starvation, yet you're stockpiling resources and have not once complained of a lack of food. In fact, all the monks you brought with you look positively chubby.'

'I'll make a mental note to put them on a diet.'

'What are you up to? How come you have enough food to go around, when the rest of us barely know where our next meal is coming from?'

'I have money.'

'So do I, but money isn't enough, and there's something different about you... something's changed.'

'It's a case of survival of the fittest. Those who can fend for themselves will find life not too challenging. Those who can't, will have to tell a different story.'

'You're stockpiling resources that belong to everyone; they're not yours to hoard.'

'Says who? I say they should go to those daring enough to take what they want.'

'We won't let you fatten yourselves on Cloud Mountain while the rest of us go hungry.'

'Fighting talk, Helena. Firstly, we're not doing anything wrong. We're simply making the most of our resources. We're doing that better than the rest of you, but then, we don't have to deal with the petty politics of the Descendants. Secondly, I'd be happy to show you around the mountain, to give you some ideas as to how you can better manage your own affairs. Thirdly, who's going to stop us? You have limited resources, which are better utilized elsewhere.'

'I can put barriers in the way of your shipments.'

'No, you can't. Traders follow money, not politics, and you have bigger things to worry about. Goodnight Helena; a pleasure, as always.'

* * * * *

'Marcus, I can only keep the business going for so long without your help. You're the Descendant, not me. Your father wanted you to take over, that's what he was training you for.'

'So you keep telling me,' said Marcus, enjoying the turned tables; Amber now having to wait for him to call the shots.

'And we need to define our strategy. It's only a matter of time before the rebels I saw in the Wild Lands attack; we have to be ready with a show of strength.'

'Of course,' he said, pausing, pretending to be fascinated by a painting behind his father's desk. No, his desk. 'They may decide not to attack, given my father is dead; Anita accomplished their aim for them.'

223

'Don't be naïve. They want change, and Austin's death alone won't give them that. They want to overthrow the entire system as we know it.'

'You say that like it would be the end of the world,' said Marcus, less because that's actually what he thought, and more because it was a sure-fire way to wind up Amber. 'And Amber, never call me naïve again.' His eyes flashed a warning that made her hesitate.

'Of course, it's your decision; I'm just advising you as I did your father. If you want to keep your position, you need to do something. There are farms to run, taxes to collect, an army to feed and pay. Not to mention the Institution and the rebels. Have you heard anything more about the Institution's plan to stage a return of the Relic?'

'Not yet,' he said, bored of Amber's broken record, 'but I'm sure it's only a matter of time.'

'And? What will you do?'

Marcus fixed her with unamused eyes. 'You'll have to wait and see. In the meantime, concentrate on running everything as you did before.'

CHAPTER 14

They congregated in the valley where the ball was to be held several nights later. Steep hills on either side hemmed them in, and an angry young river wove its way through the middle, white froth bursting upwards as it hit rocks with mighty force. The valley was thirty-five miles outside of Kingdom, slopes that in the summer were lush and green, now frost-covered. The contestants shivered, huddling around, waiting for the Descendants to arrive.

Alexander had suggested that Anita arrive with him, but she'd refused. She couldn't think of anything worse than providing more gossip fodder to the crowd.

Last time, she'd stood with Bass before the Chase. Now, she stood by herself, isolated from the other contestants, trying to ignore that they were, without exception, sneaking looks at her when they thought she wasn't looking.

The Descendants eventually arrived, robed and chaperoned by a gaggle of councillors. As was tradition, Alexander and Peter would not compete, their status as ruling Descendants affording them the luxury of adjudicating, rather than the pressure of competing. Gwyn and Marcus, by the same force of tradition, were compelled to participate. More than that, they carried the weight of expectation that they would come in, if not first, then very near the top of the pack.

Anita shot Alexander a protracted look as he removed his hood, the crowd and contestants falling silent. Alexander didn't give Peter the opportunity to lead proceedings, and, as expected, Peter didn't put up a fight.

'Descendants, councillors, contestants, children of the Temples of the Mind, Body and Spirit. I welcome you here today to the Chase that commemorates and celebrates the life of the Mind Descendant, Austin.' Alexander's tone was business-like; he was not solemn, nor did he engage in the usual pomp that went along with an event such as this. The circumstances around Austin's death had, thank the Gods, not made it into the public domain, but that didn't mean that Alexander had to be nice about the man.

Alexander had told Anita about Austin's infuriating funeral, where compliments had abounded. Alexander wouldn't stand by and let that happen again. The man had been nothing short of evil, and even if he couldn't tell the people this, he wouldn't lie to them.

'Today, the challenge is for our contestants to be the first to either catch the runner who set off from here thirty minutes ago,' he said, gaze lingering on Anita as he scanned the participants, his energy jumping as he took in her battle ready stance. 'Or, if no one should succeed in this, then to be the first contestant to make it back to the Relic. The runner has taken the quickest route, so it would be prudent to track him, if you are able.'

A murmur went up from the crowd at the new format. They whispered, 'I hope no one catches him,' and, 'Not sure about this'.

Anita rolled her eyes. Why were people so resistant to change?

'Contestants, please take your positions,' said Alexander, several councillors stepping forward. Two went to Marcus and Gwyn, taking their robes, Marcus looking gaunt and tired. Several others ushered the contestants to the start line, lining them up so Gwyn and Marcus had the best spots, right at the front.

'You should follow the riverbank downstream until you come across two paths leaving the river's edge. At that point, you must choose your route.' Then, abruptly, not allowing anyone time to prepare, he said, 'I declare this Chase, open.' He bellowed the word 'open' and the contestants jolted into motion. Anita sprinted off behind Gwyn, who had shamelessly jumped the gun.

They followed the river downstream for a couple of hundred meters before two paths split off. One gained a little ground, but broadly appearing to follow the river, the other took a more severe path up the incline, disappearing over the top of the hill to their left. Gwyn slowed as she surveyed the options, but Anita needed no such indulgence, spotting dents in the ground and patches of frost-free bracken on the higher path. Anita raced past Gwyn, easily dealing with the incline, putting her head down, focusing on placing one foot in front of the other.

The others all followed her, so even if she was wrong, so was everyone else. The thought gave her a brief moment of smugness as she reached the summit, to face another choice of paths. It went on like that for miles: inclines, steep declines, and forks with two, three, or sometimes even four paths. Several of these had dummy trails to throw the contestants off.

Several exhausting hours later, they were nearing Kingdom, the spires and walls clearly visible. Only Anita, Marcus, Gwyn, and a couple of young councillors remained in the leading pack, when they caught sight of their prey. The man was running in a straight line for the city, across the flat open fields that surrounded the capital. No more twists and turns, it was a straight shoot to the finish.

Anita upped her pace, wanting to get this over with, and to put as much distance between herself and Marcus as she could. Since Austin's death, Marcus had barely been seen in public. The venom in his energy, venom directed at her, had the effect of sapping her energy, leaving her emotionally drained, lifeless. She wanted to scream at him that it had been Austin's fault. He'd tried to kill her, had killed Bass... but she could barely bring herself to look at him, let alone speak.

She was pulled back from her thoughts by a cry from behind, and the sound of a body tumbling to the ground. She slowed and turned her head, but as she did, a force thumped into her back, sending her, and whoever it belonged to, careering forwards. She landed hard on her side, the full weight of a councillor on top of her, a shocking pain piercing her stomach as someone's foot connected with her flesh.

She looked up, dazed, to see Gwyn and Marcus standing over her, hatred seeping out of them like a toxic smoke. The councillor rolled off her and climbed to his feet, continuing towards Kingdom, leaving the three of them without so much as a backward glance. Anita tried to get up, but a foot connected with her lower back, another shot of pain searing through her.

'What are you doing?' she spluttered, her brain fogged by shock and confusion.

'What are we doing?' Gwyn said, mocking Anita with every part of her being; her eyes, her tone, her foot, as she swung another kick into Anita's stomach. 'Don't you think the question is more, what are *you* doing?'

Anita curled over, grasping her stomach, gasping for air, waiting for the pain to subside at least a little before replying. 'What do you mean?' She could only manage a whisper, as she contemplated the best way to gain an advantage over her attackers.

'Don't be coy,' said Gwyn, reaching down to grab a handful of Anita's hair, twisting. Marcus placed his foot on her side, applying enough pressure to the injury there to make her realise she'd be foolish to retaliate. 'You murdered the ruling Mind Descendant and you have the gall to show up at his Chase? You thought we'd just sit back and let you win?'

'Austin killed Bass,' said Anita, slowly, as though this might be a simple misunderstanding, where they didn't know the truth. 'He was trying to kill me. Was I supposed to let him?' Her confusion was fast turning to raging anger; it took all her self-control not to fight back. The Institution needed Gwyn and Marcus to cooperate if they were to stand any chance of carrying out Bass' experiment. She couldn't give them more reason not to help.

'Liar,' said Marcus, increasing the pressure through his foot.

Anita cried out in pain, turning her head to look at Marcus, his chocolate eyes so beautiful, vulnerable, and... hesitant; this wasn't his idea.

'You know I'm not lying,' Anita said softly, refusing to remove her eyes from his. 'You know what your father and Amber are capable of. You saw what they did to me. You rescued me from them.'

Gwyn slapped her hand hard across Anita's face before springing to her feet, taking several erratic paces away. 'You expect us to believe your bullshit?' she spat, turning back to Anita, kicking her brutally on the shoulder.

Anita cried out again, and Marcus removed his foot. She curled herself further into the foetal position, to protect her stomach, and clutched her shoulder.

Uncertainly crept into Marcus' energy. This was Gwyn's plan, and his resolve was wavering.

'You can believe what you want,' jeered Anita, clenching her teeth against the pain, 'but I killed Austin in self-defence, because he had just killed the man who was supposed to be your boyfriend.' Anita couldn't help herself; she might not be able to defend herself physically, but that didn't mean Gwyn deserved to get off scot free.

'Shut up,' hissed Gwyn, giving her another kick, this one to her back, forcing her to arch against the agony. 'It's all your fault. You're the reason Bass is dead, the reason Austin is dead. Make sure I never see you again, or the consequences will be severe.'

The threat almost made Anita laugh, but she kept a straight face, not wanting to encourage further violence.

'We need to go,' said Marcus. 'The others are catching up.' He pointed to a group cresting the hill a few hundred metres behind them. 'One of us needs to win.'

'You need to win,' she said, to Anita's surprise. 'Fine, let's go.' She made to kick Anita one last time, but Marcus stood in the way.

'We've made our point,' he said, looking down at Anita's battered body. Gwyn, seeing the group behind them rapidly closing, didn't argue. Instead, she threw Anita a bitter look, before launching into a run towards Kingdom. Marcus refused to meet her eyes as he too ran away.

Anita struggled to her feet, pain shooting through her torso, face stinging from the contact of Gwyn's hand. She was furious. She'd resolved not to go to the ball, but after that little encounter, she wouldn't miss it for the world.

* * * * *

Gwyn and Marcus arrived back at the Relic first. The councillor they'd recruited to help bring down Anita had waited obediently at the edge of Kingdom, letting them overtake. Nobody had caught the runner they'd been tracking. The crowds couldn't have been happier, as this meant they got to see a race for the line. They cheered vehemently as the two Descendants came into view. As planned, Marcus reached out and touched the Relic first, and as he did it, the crowd gave a roar.

Gwyn clapped Marcus on the back, ensuring she was the first to congratulate him. He smiled ecstatically up at her, but Alexander could read the trepidation and regret in his energy. That, coupled with Anita's non-appearance, filled him with fear.

Alexander approached his fellow Descendants, warmly congratulating Marcus, pulling him into a celebratory embrace. But as he held Marcus to him, he whispered threateningly in his ear, 'Where is she and what have you done to her?'

Marcus tried to pull back, but Alexander held him firmly in place. Marcus said nothing, and Alexander had to release him so as not to raise suspicions. As he did, he whispered, 'I hope for your sake she's alright.'

Alexander turned to congratulate Gwyn on coming second. Marcus tried to regain his composure as others bustled around him, offering him congratulations and refreshment, a councillor handing him his cloak. Gwyn shot Marcus a puzzled look, not the only one to have noticed his subdued demeanour. Marcus looked away, sick to the stomach, Alexander, reading his energy, full of dread.

* * * * *

Alexander conducted the prize giving as the stragglers crossed the line, presenting Marcus with an engraved brass plate. It was nowhere near as extravagant as the energy metre Anita had won as victor of the last Chase. Alexander considered this a more fitting prize, given the problems the world faced.

Tension filled the air, like dry kindling on a scorching hot day, which, at any moment might spark alight. What might set this gathering on fire, Alexander had no wish to find out, so he quickly concluded the presentation and encouraged the crowd to disperse. He quietly instructed the Descendants and councillors to leave.

They got away without incident, but Alexander knew it had been a close-run thing. Since Austin's death, there had been a lull in the demonstrations and direct action, but Alexander could sense it was only a matter of time before it kicked off again. And, without Austin's army as a deterrent, it would be worse than it had been before.

As they were dispersing, Alexander asked a few of the other contestants if they'd seen what happened to Anita. Most feigned ignorance or shrugged their shoulders, but one Spirit councillor told him he'd seen Anita limping away, in the general direction of Alexander's residence. Alexander returned home as quickly as he could, hoping he would find Anita there, praying she was alright.

His car pulled up at the front steps and he threw the door open before his driver had fully stopped. He brushed past Mrs Hudson, who had somehow got the front door open before Alexander reached it. 'Is she here?' he demanded, throwing his cloak onto a nearby chair.

'She's upstairs, resting,' replied Mrs Hudson, carefully, 'she wouldn't let us do anything or give her anything to help. She said she wanted to be alone.'

Without another word, Alexander raced towards the stairs, taking them two at a time as he hurtled towards the top. He ran to his bedroom and flung open the door, no idea what he would find on the other side. He entered the room to find a small, curled up figure on the bed, a blanket hiding her from view.

Alexander moved to her bedside and gently sat down, placing a hand on her shoulder. 'What happened?' he asked, feeling her wince at his touch.

Anita rolled over, moving gingerly, gasping involuntarily against the pain. 'Gwyn and Marcus happened,' she said, shaking her head, 'and if we didn't need them to help us send back the Relic, they wouldn't be looking so good themselves right now.'

'What happened?' Alexander repeated, relieved that Anita's spirits were high enough for fighting talk.

Anita recounted the story, finishing by saying, 'To add insult to literal injury, I didn't even win the Chase. So I've decided that I will attend the ball, and I've got a good mind to come to the Crowning as well, just to wind them up.'

Alexander laughed. 'What about needing their help to send the Relic back?'

Anita rolled her eyes. 'Fine. I won't come to the Crowning, but I'm definitely coming to the ball.'

'Okay,' said Alexander, 'but first, I'm calling my doctor to have a look at your injuries. I doubt you'll be able to dance.'

'I'll be fine,' snapped Anita. 'The ball's a week away, and I don't think they've broken anything; I'll just have to find a dress that covers up the bruising.'

* * * * *

Despite her vehement protests, Alexander got Anita in front of a doctor. He confirmed she had no broken bones or internal bleeding, concluding that, aside from some serious bruising, she was fine. Alexander still insisted she rest for a couple of days to make sure she properly recovered. Anita reluctantly agreed, mostly because Alexander promised to stay with her, and Anita had nothing else to do anyway.

After two days of lazing around, eating, reading, playing cards, and chatting, Anita was itching to get out and do something. She was ecstatic when Alexander told her, over a breakfast of muesli muffins, that he had something he wanted to show her.

After breakfast, wrapped up against the driving rain, they bundled themselves into Alexander's town car. The driver whisked them into Kingdom, to an area on the outskirts of town that Anita had never previously visited. They pulled up outside an inconspicuous townhouse, and as the car came to a halt, Cleo threw open the front door. She rushed over and sped Anita inside.

'You have *got* to see this,' Cleo squealed, literally pulling Anita through the entrance.

'See what?!' she asked, laughing, and throwing an interrogative look back over her shoulder. Alexander, amused, shrugged his shoulders as though he had not a clue what was going on.

'Words cannot describe,' said Cleo, breathlessly. 'See for yourself.'

Anita followed Cleo across a black-and-white marble floor, past an impressive flower display on an imposing circular table, and up three flights of winding stairs. The stairs ended in a room that looked like a high-end boutique. Rails of clothes adorned every wall, the windows swathed with tulle, opulent sofas strategically placed in the middle of the room. There was even a plush, curtained-off changing area with an impressive array of full-length mirrors.

'What is this?' asked Anita, looking around.

'My mother's wardrobe,' said Alexander, quietly. She hadn't even realized he'd followed them up the stairs.

'She had quite a collection,' said Anita, 'but, why are we here?'

'You need a dress for the ball, now you've decided to come. I thought you might like to borrow one of these,' he said, waving his hand around the room. 'I'm sure you'll find something to hide the bruises, and if anything doesn't fit, Fernandez will alter it before next week.' As he said *Fernandez*, a short, flamboyantly dressed man with round glasses entered the room, flashing Anita a dazzling smile.

'Of course,' said Fernandez, confirming Alexander's statement.

'And I'm here to help you choose, obviously,' said Cleo, leafing her way through the dresses. 'I've already put a couple of options in the changing room. You should start with those.'

Fernandez raised an eyebrow, clearly unimpressed with Cleo treading on his toes. He not-so-subtly made his way into the changing room to inspect her choices. He came out a minute later with a reluctant smile. 'Your choices are excellent,' he said, genuinely, then to Anita, 'you should try them on.'

CHAPTER 15

On the morning of the ball, Helena called Melia, Rose, Cleo, Alexander and Anita to a meeting at Monty's. The Descendants had all but disappeared from public life since Austin and Bass' deaths, so the ball was an unmissable opportunity to get them onside.

Given recent happenings, everyone acknowledged that this would be no straightforward task. 'What about Peter?' asked Cleo. 'Can't we try to get him to convince Gwyn?'

'She's never respected her father,' said Helena. 'He's a source of constant embarrassment to her, not least because he was the one to break the female line.'

'That wasn't exactly his fault,' muttered Cleo, under her breath.

'Alexander could try?' suggested Melia. 'One ruling Descendant to another?'

'Seeing as Gwyn blames me for Bass' death,' said Anita, 'and Alexander is my boyfriend, I think, if anything, that would push her further in the wrong direction.'

'It's best coming from me,' said Rose, heavily. 'Bass was my son; she should at least do me the courtesy of hearing me out.'

'Okay,' said Helena, 'but what about Marcus? Amber will be there watching his every move.'

'I'll try first,' said Melia. 'He's my son, after all. I'll talk to him before the ball. If that doesn't work, someone else can approach him at the party.'

'Who though?' mused Helena.

'Anita,' said Alexander, to the surprise of everyone present.

'What?' choked Anita, not quite believing his words. 'How can you think that would be a good idea?'

'You killed Austin,' he said simply, 'and Marcus will want to know more about what happened. You're the only one who can give him that.'

'He beat me up less than a week ago,' said Anita, indignantly.

'Yes, but he still has feelings for you, any reader can see that.'

Anita flushed, not believing Alexander was saying these things in public. 'That doesn't mean he's willing to even speak to me, let alone trust me enough to buy into the plan.'

'Alexander makes a good point,' said Helena 'The heart makes people do crazy things... it's got to be worth a go.'

'Did it ever work for you?' said Anita, wishing as soon as the words had escaped her lips that she could claw them back.

A shadow passed behind Helena's eyes. 'No,' she breathed, 'but I never stopped trying.'

A heavy pause filled the air, the entire room looking expectantly at Anita. She took several deep breaths, reading Alexander's disappointed energy as she considered her reply. 'Fine,' she said, eventually. 'I'll do it, but don't be surprised if it backfires.'

* * * * *

A knock rang through Cordelia's suite, and she hurried to answer the door. 'Yes?' she said, swinging the door open, surprised to find Melia on the other side. She hadn't expected a visitor, let alone the mother of a Descendant.

Cordelia had come to Kingdom when she'd heard what had happened to Anita during the Chase. She hadn't realized anyone even knew she was there.

'Ah,' said Melia, taken aback by Cordelia's frosty greeting, 'is Anita here? Alexander thought she might be.'

'Yes,' said Cordelia, making no move to invite Melia in.

'May I please speak with her?' Melia's tone took on a heated edge.

'Can I ask what it's regarding?'

'No,' replied Melia, visibly bristling.

Cordelia appraised the woman before stepping back and inviting her in. 'Please take a seat,' she said, motioning towards one of the pristine armchairs, just as Anita entered the room.

'Melia, hi,' said Anita.

'Hi,' Melia replied, her eyes flicking to Cordelia; what she had to say wasn't for Cordelia's ears.

'Let's go for a walk,' said Anita, ushering her back towards the door. 'See you in a bit,' she said to Cordelia, whose energy was furious.

They got out into the fresh air, and Melia visibly relaxed. 'What was up with her?' she asked.

'Absolutely no idea,' said Anita, truthfully. 'I've never seen her react like that to anyone. Normally she'd sit you down and have you eating cake and drinking tea before you knew what was happening.'

Melia laughed. 'It must be me then!'

'She's been a bit off recently; ever since she found out about the two dead bodies on her kitchen floor. Let's just put it down to that.'

Melia didn't reply.

'Sorry, I didn't mean for that to sound so flippant.'

'No, it's not that. It's just so hard to believe it really happened, that's all.'

They walked in silence to the park at the end of the road and sat on a bench. They watched as two naughty children hid from their exasperated mother.

'How can I help?' said Anita.

'I spoke to Marcus.'

'And it didn't go well?'

'It didn't go badly,' she said, a little defensively, 'but he wasn't ready to sign up to the cause when I left him. Amber's sinking her claws in. He said he's continuing Austin's work, which I know from first-hand experience, isn't savoury. He's confused. He thinks he has to honour Austin's legacy, but knows, deep down, he doesn't agree with it. Amber's playing on his uncertainty.'

'So what do you think we should do?'

'You should speak to him. Make him see that Austin had come to kill you, and for Gods' sake, make him see there's a different way.'

'You know he probably won't even talk to me.'

'I think he will,' she said, turning to look at Anita, 'and you won't know until you try.'

'I said I'll try; I'm just not convinced it'll work.'

'One more thing,' said Melia, hesitantly. 'I wouldn't go to the procession and dinner; Gwyn doesn't want you there. She'll use it as another opportunity to manipulate Marcus. She'll tell him you're throwing Austin's death in his face...'

Anita stiffened, livid at the idea of not being able to do something because of Gwyn, but she knew she had to be pragmatic. 'Fine. If you think that's more likely to work, I'll stay out of the public bits.'

Melia nodded as she got up to leave. 'Good luck,' she said. 'He's stubborn, so you're going to need it.'

* * * * *

Anita and Cleo got ready for the ball as planned, with the help, or maybe hindrance, of Fernandez and his three assistants. After hugging Anita excessively, Cleo departed in time for the procession and dinner, leaving Anita behind.

Anita retreated downstairs to a large drawing room. She picked up a magazine to help her kill the time it would take for the others to eat dinner.

When it was finally time for her to leave, Fernandez miraculously appeared to touch up her makeup, before escorting her down the remaining flight of stairs. Alexander's driver was waiting for her at the front door. 'Have a wonderful evening,' said Fernandez, kindly. 'You look spectacular.'

Fernandez and Cleo had selected a modestly cut, but form fitting yellow silk number that hugged Anita's body to the knees, then kicked out extravagantly with swathes of flowing fabric. The dress had elegant drape sleeves, which not only hid the ugly marks Gwyn and Marcus had left on her arms, but also softened the ensemble, giving the impression that she was in some way docile.

'Thank you, Fernandez,' she said, slipping into the back of the car, her guts flipping as the driver sped off towards the valley where the Chase had begun.

She was blown away when they arrived, looking down from the hillside at a hub of twinkling lights and beautifully dressed people, mingling to the sounds of mellow jazz. Miraculously, the councillors had managed to put an enormous marquee over the middle of the valley, including over the river that ran through its centre. The sides of the marquee were mostly open, a see-through dance floor hovering above the river below. Anita couldn't wait to dance on it.

Outside the tent were a number of seating areas, trees alive with fairy lights, providing a gentle glow over the soft seating below. Well concealed heaters were dotted here and there to keep away the cold. Winter flowers blossomed everywhere, in the joins of branches, across and around the marquee, and lining the makeshift paths constructed for the evening.

By the time Anita had descended the side of the valley, passed the security guards who recognized her immediately, and reached the entrance, the first dance was in full swing. Marcus and Gwyn whirled across the floor; only right for them to open the dancing together, seeing as they'd come first and second in the Chase.

They danced demurely, all eyes fixed on them, until the tempo of the music changed, the first communal dance about to commence. Anita watched as Marcus slipped away from the growing crowd, leaving through an exit at the side of the marquee. Gwyn, not ready to stop dancing, replaced him by stealing some other girl's partner, the girl relegated to the side lines, nothing she could do but watch with furious eyes.

Realising she wouldn't get a better chance, everyone else distracted by the opening dances, Anita skirted around the outside of the tent in search of Marcus. She found him sitting on a sofa underneath one of the decorated trees, his back to her, shoulders hunched despondently forward, obviously trying to shut out the world.

She paused a few paces back, neither wanting to interrupt him, nor knowing what to say. He's heard her footsteps crunching on the frosted ground and turned to see who was there. His face remained passive as he took her in, but his energy leapt, casting aside any doubts about his feelings for her.

'Hi,' she said, breaking the still spell that had settled around them.

Marcus said nothing, getting to his feet with the obvious intention of leaving. Anita stepped into his path and placed a hand on his chest, a movement that stopped him dead. 'Please,' she said quietly, 'I just want to talk to you.'

He looked down and closed his eyes, his energy escalating as her fingers lingered, moments flitting by. He finally raised his head, Anita shocked to find the eyes of a lost, exhausted man, no trace of the arrogant stranger who'd pursued her only weeks before. Without thinking, she dropped her hand and pulled him into an embrace. He wrapped his arms around her, burying his head in her neck. She forgot, for a blissful instant, everything that had happened, although it soon flooded his energy, and he pulled away. He sat back down on the sofa.

'What do you want, Anita?'

'I want to talk to you about what happened. I want you to know what happened.'

'Why? You can't change it now.'

'But I can put a stop to the conflict inside your head.'

'Dad tried to kill you and you defended yourself,' he said, 'and Bass must have got caught in the crossfire.'

Anita's eyes went wide with surprise.

'Any conflict I have isn't to do with what happened that night.'

'Oh?' said Anita, trying to refocus. 'Then what is it to do with?'

'Isn't it obvious?'

'Not to me,' she said, paused, 'but I suppose...
perhaps... you don't know whether to follow in
Austin's footsteps? Evicting helpless people from their
farms and businesses? Or whether you should choose a
new path of your own?'

'And what would that entail?' he said, energy
turning hostile.

'Only you can say.'

He sprang to his feet. 'I know what my father did
was wrong,' he practically shouted. 'Of course, I know.
You think I'm some idiot? You think I don't know what
he was like? What Amber's like?'

'Marcus...'

He paced away, then spun back to face her. 'Like
my mother, the only reason you're here, is because you
want something from me.'

'I'm not here to convince you to help the
Institution. I'd be lying if I said I didn't think it's the
only option we have, and as a Descendant, that should
matter to you...'

'... easy for you to say.'

'Not really, no.'

'What does that mean?'

'Do you know the reason Austin was trying to kill
me?'

'He got wind of Bass' plan, but thought you were
the one behind it, so he came after you.'

Anita was, again, taken aback. 'He knew about the
plan?'

Marcus exhaled. 'Yes.'

'Why did he think it was my idea? It had nothing to
do with me.'

'That doesn't matter.' He turned away, dragged a
hand through his hair. 'Why did you think he came after
you?'

Anita paused, then threw caution to the wind. 'Because I'm the real Body Descendant, not Gwyn.'

Marcus laughed, almost cruelly. 'That's impossible.'

Anita raised an offended eyebrow. 'No, it's not. It's a long story, but Peter isn't the real Body Descendant either; my mother, Clarissa, was. Christiana swapped her with Peter at birth, because the Descendants wanted to put an end to the prophecy.'

'Why?'

'For personal gain. If there's no risk of anyone fulfilling the prophecy, the Descendants rule forever.'

'So, why not just come out and tell everyone?'

'Because that would lead to further instability. We need to stabilize the energy, not provide another reason for it to plummet. And anyway, people might not believe it, and we don't have the luxury of time. We've got to do something now, before the army of rebels does.'

'Careful, you sound like Amber.'

'She's right; I saw them myself, in the Wild Lands. They're hungry for action. Even their leaders are struggling to control them.'

'In which case, we should meet force with force.'

'I know you don't mean that.'

Marcus turned away.

'Marcus, we need to give people something to believe in. If we can bring the energy back up, the rebels will lose support; we can go back to normal. If we fight them, things will never be the same.'

'What if it's already too late?'

'Start praying to the Gods,' she said harshly, willing him to snap out of it. She'd pushed him as far as he would go, so she got up to leave. 'At least think about it,' she said, heading back towards the tent.

* * * * *

Marcus exhaled, slumped back on the sofa, and held his head in his hands.

'What did she want?' hissed a hostile voice, seconds later, making Marcus jump. Amber positioned herself right in front of him, giving him nowhere to look but at her.

'What do you think?'

'I don't know; spell it out for me.'

'She wants me to help the Institution with their plan to send back the Relic.'

'And?'

'And what?'

'What did you say?'

'What do you think I said?'

'Don't play with me.'

'Or what?'

'Your father would turn in his grave.'

Marcus jumped to his feet, towering over her, grabbing her neck with one hand, pushing her back against the tree. 'Don't ever speak to me like that again, and do not presume to lecture me about what my father would have wanted.'

Amber raised a slow, seductive eyebrow. 'Finally,' she said. 'Some fight; I knew it was in there somewhere.' She pulled his hand from her neck, then reached up to play with his bow tie. He pushed himself away, turning to leave.

'You're fired,' he said, over his shoulder. 'You can collect your things tonight, before I get home. Anything left after that will be disposed of.'

'Oh, you silly boy,' she said, not quite loud enough for Marcus to hear.

* * * * *

Anita entered the tent as an upbeat number drew to a close, a slower melody filling the air. Alexander felt her presence before he saw her, turning his head away from the councillor he was talking to, rising to his feet when his eyes met hers. He was on a raised platform at the far end of the marquee, where the Descendants had eaten dinner, allowing everyone to get a good look at them. He moved to the steps, seeming to float down them, a path clearing for him as he reached the dance floor at their base.

He melted through the crowd, people opening before and closing behind him, not a single dancing form knocking into him, his energy forming a protective, repellent shield. He reached her, and took her hand, lifting it to his lips. Neither spoke, Anita's energy spiking, his dinner jacket enhancing his already divine form.

He led her silently to the dance floor, pulled her into a firm hold, circled them around the floor, careful to trace the river's course, its wild energy floating up to meet them, pushing their spirits higher.

'You're beautiful,' Alexander purred, spinning her under his arm.

'Such a cliché,' she said, looking encouragingly up into his electric blue eyes.

'You're impossible,' he said, pulling her close, kissing her lips.

She broke away. 'Everyone's looking at us,' she whispered, trying to ignore the sea of gossiping faces. She buried her red face in his shoulder, inhaling his citrus scent.

'Cleo isn't,' he replied, in a tone that could have come from Cleo's mouth.

Anita's head snapped round, her eyes seeking what Alexander's had seen. She quickly located her friend, clad in a racy, low-cut, high-slitted, black dress. And she was looking, intently, into the eyes of a man.

'Indeed, she isn't,' said Anita. 'Let's get closer.'

'No,' he said, firmly. 'Leave her alone.'

Anita shook her head. 'You're no fun,' she said, giving him a peck on the lips before putting her head back on his shoulder, watching faces of the crowd forgotten.

* * * * *

Cleo had been dancing with some councillor or other. He wasn't very good looking, and she couldn't remember his name, but she'd felt obliged to say yes, when he'd asked her to dance. He'd stepped on her toes and his hands had been limp against her skin, so she'd led for the most part, willing the band to bring the song to an end, so she could make her escape.

Eventually, they obliged. Cleo sighed with relief as she pulled back, searching for words that would enable her to get away. However, before she needed them, another figure appeared, and tapped on her partner's shoulder. 'You wouldn't mind if I cut in?' he said.

Before waiting for an answer, her saviour swept her into a tight hold, and spun her away. The band played a slow song, Cleo taking full advantage of the change in tempo, pressing herself against him.

'The disappearing man,' she said, her tone distant, but her body inviting. 'I almost thought I'd imagined you.' His wavy hair was as unkempt as it had been when they'd first met.

His lips twitched into a smile. 'How can I ever make it up to you?' he said, running his hand deliciously down her back to the base of her spine. She arched into him.

'You know you make your dinner jacket look scruffy?'

'How terrible,' he said, eyes smouldering, 'maybe they'll throw me out.'

'Planning your exit so soon?'

'Not if I can help it,' he whispered in her ear, nipping it between his teeth.

She squirmed at the sensation, then squealed at the tight, fast turn he put her through. 'Why are you here?' she said, breathless, and not because of the dancing. 'You live in the Wild Lands... don't you?'

'Do I?'

'The Great Hall of the Magnei; it's in the Wild Lands.'

'Is it?' he said, rolling her out to arm's length, then pulling her firmly back into his hold.

'I'm sure of it, and I'm sure that's where you call home. You're... different.'

'I'm hurt.'

'Oh stop,' she said, playfully. 'Tell me. Is that where you're from?'

'I am from the Wild.'

'Where?'

His head suddenly snapped up, as though he were a wild animal that had caught the scent of a hunter. 'Look for me and you'll find me. I know you will,' he said in a rush, leaning down, kissing her, hands holding her neck. He pulled back, eyes alight. 'Come and find me,' he said, letting her go, disappearing into the crowd.

'Who was that?' asked Anita, suggestively, as she and Alexander approached.

Cleo resisted the petulant urge to stamp her foot. 'I don't know his name.'

'But you've met before?'

'Yes,' she said. 'He's the one who told me about the Magnei.'

'What?' said Alexander, scanning the room for him, but finding no trace. 'His energy was really weird.'

'How do you mean?' asked Cleo.

'Potent. He's a very strong Spirit; probably the strongest I've ever felt, but there was something about it that was strange.'

'Strange how?'

'I don't know…'

'He's probably a Magnei. Maybe they're all like that?' said Cleo.

'Maybe, I suppose, but it's still weird,' said Anita. 'What did he want?'

'Nothing, as far as I could make out. He told me to come and find him in the Wild Lands.'

'Peculiar,' said Alexander.

'What's that supposed to mean?' said Cleo, edgily.

'Come on, Cleo,' said Anita. 'You don't even know his name.'

'That's not the point,' she said, turning away with an exasperated flick of her hair, heading towards the bar.

'Going after her?' said Alexander.

'No,' said Anita, 'she's just frustrated. It's the mystery: for her it's torture.'

* * * * *

Cleo shouldered past several people to reach the bar, not caring whose dress she stepped on, or whose dinner jacket she ruffled. She reached the front of the queue, Timi and Helena her only remaining obstacles, and pushed her way clean in between them, putting an end to their intent discussion.

'Cleo,' said Helena, 'everything alright?'

'Just peachy, thanks,' she said, leaning over the bar and directing all attention towards attracting the bar tender.

'Glad to hear it,' said Helena, raising her eyebrows as she took Timi's arm, steering him away, towards the edge of the marquee.

'What was that about?' said Timi.

'Gods only know,' said Helena. 'Cleo can be... volatile sometimes. As I was saying, our support's dwindling. Followers in the Wild are defecting to join the rebels, and it's draining our resources. The rebels are calling for immediate action. Draeus says even their leaders are struggling to maintain control.'

'And what do you suggest I do about it?' said Timi.

'You're a key member of the Institution,' said Helena, tersely. 'I expect you to take more than a passing interest in a group that's threatening to ruin everything. I suggest you take the message back to the leadership and seek support. And, whilst you're at it, I'd appreciate your help with our plan to send the Relic back.'

'I thought you were against what we're doing at the Cloud Mountain, whatever it is you think we're doing. I rather got the impression you intended to turn yourself into my enemy?'

'Don't be ridiculous,' said Helena, regretting her earlier outburst. 'If you're hoarding resources, then yes, I think you should stop, but the immediate battle is to stabilize the energy. Surely that aligns with your goals also?'

'Of course,' he said, 'how can I help?'

'Help us convince the Descendants to take part in the plan.'

'Why would I be the right person for that job? The Spirit Descendant's already on your side, and I have only limited dealings with Peter, Gwyn and Marcus.'

'Okay, fine, well… at least be there when we send the Relic back; it'll add additional weight to the occasion.'

'Of course. Now, if you'll excuse me,' he said, slipping away without a backward glance.

Helena watched him disappear into the crowd. There was something different about him, but she couldn't for the life of her pin down what it was. *What are you up to, Timi?*

* * * * *

Timi left the tent, making his way to a circle of large boulders with a bonfire in the centre. A group splashed in a shallow section of the river nearby. It mostly involved aggressive flirting; boys threatening to push girls into the river, girls holding on tightly, coquettishly begging them not to.

Timi sat on one of the smaller boulders, pretending to concentrate on the fire. 'How can I help you?' he asked, after a few moments of silence. 'You followed me here for a reason, so I suggest you save us both some trouble and come straight to the point.'

Amber stepped out of the shadows, into the firelight. She sat opposite the Spirit Leader, taking her time, demonstrating that she was not intimidated, nor would she be rushed. 'I have a proposition for you,' she said.

'Oh yes?' he replied, flicking his eyes up from the fire, looking her up and down.

'I've heard rumours…'

'… oh dear.'

'About the Cloud Mountain…'

'… scandalous.'

'About what's going on up there.'

'I'm afraid you're going to have to be a little more specific.' He was doing his best to rile her, but, to his disappointment, she didn't rise.

'I can supply you with an army of trained soldiers. We could come to the Cloud Mountain and protect your cause, whatever that is, although I think I have a pretty good idea.'

'I see. What makes you think I need an army?'

'Who doesn't, in times like these?'

Timi looked squarely at her. 'What's in it for you?'

Amber looked back at him, her eyes reflecting the dance of the fire. 'Austin's dead, and Marcus fired me. I need a cause, and yours is the obvious fit for someone like me. You have monks with great skill and power, but you lack combat experience and physical protection. The time is coming when you're going to need those things.'

'What makes you so sure?'

She shrugged. 'Tensions are rising everywhere. There's a growing army of rebels in the Wild Lands who won't stay passive forever. All the Institution can bring to the table is some crazy scheme to send the Relic back, which will never work. When it fails, it will be an obvious cue for the rebels to seize power. That's what I'd do, if I were them. If you have no army to protect the Cloud Mountain, you'll be easy pickings when they decide to come for everything you've got stashed up there.'

'The Cloud Mountain is impenetrable.'

'Supposedly. But how long can it withstand a siege?'

'Longer than you might think.'

'Wouldn't it be better to have options? So you never have to go through that inconvenience? So, when chaos erupts, you'll have the upper hand… could even seize control yourself?'

Timi briefly considered Amber's proposition. He concluded from her energy that she was speaking the truth, or at least what she believed to be so. And there was no harm in having an army... he had plenty of space, not to mention more food than he knew what to do with. An army wouldn't be too much of a burden... 'How many people are in this army?' he said.

'I don't know, but at least half of Austin's force are loyal to me, I'm sure of it.'

'Fine. Bring those you can to the Cloud Mountain, but make sure nobody knows where you're going. I'll be staying in Kingdom a while longer, supporting the attempt to send the Relic back. After that, I'll meet you at the mountain.'

Amber nodded, got up to leave.

'Just remember, very carefully, this means you work for me,' said Timi, quietly, 'and unlike your last boss, I'm a reader.'

* * * * *

Gwyn had had quite an evening. She'd been fully capitalizing on her status as Chase (almost) Champion, and between that and her position as a Descendant, she'd had no shortage of suitors. Not that she was interested... Bass... an iron hand gripped her insides. She couldn't think about him here... she... oh, Gods... no. Snap out of it.

She excused herself from the company of one of the many men and made her way towards the bacon sandwiches being handed out by the bar. It had been a long, alcohol-fuelled night. That's all she needed; food to soak up the poison. She salivated at the smell of bacon.

Gwyn picked up two rolls and headed out of the marquee, into the chill of the winter air beyond.

'It's great to see you having such a good time,' said Rose, coming up behind her, startling her.

'Rose,' said Gwyn, whirling round, surprised that Bass' mother, who had never spoken to her before, had sought her out.

'Bass would have wanted to see you enjoying yourself.'

'I… um… nothing's happened with any of them.'

'Hush,' said Rose. 'It's nothing to do with me, even if it had, and Bass would have wanted you to be happy.'

'Oh… um…,' said Gwyn, begging her brain to come up with a way to escape this crippling awkwardness.

'Although, he would also want to see his final project completed,' Rose said, wistfully, looking back towards the river. 'He was so passionate about it.'

'Of course,' said Gwyn, everything falling into place, 'but what does that have to do with me?'

'You know exactly what it has to do with you,' said Rose, holding Gwyn's hardening gaze. 'Bass told you all about his research, about energy stability, about the energy slingshot to send the Relic back. You must have also discussed your vital role.'

'That as may be,' she replied coolly, 'I'm not convinced Bass' theory is correct. Austin's view of events was more compelling. Anyway, Bass' plan will never work without Marcus on side, and he would never betray Austin's memory like that.'

'Betray Austin's memory? How would stabilizing the energy and ensuring reliable food supplies be a betrayal of Austin's memory?'

'It flies in the face of what Austin wanted.'

'Didn't Austin want what's best for the world and its people? Isn't that what his role as Descendant bound him to seek?'

'Of course,' she said defensively, wanting to bat Rose back, to get some space. 'Maybe we just disagree on how to achieve it.

Peter and Elistair, unfortunately, chose that moment to leave the marquee, and Peter stopped to talk to Gwyn. The newcomers sensed the tension in the air.

'Everything okay?' asked Elistair, pinning his ex-wife with an accusatory stare.

'We were discussing Bass' research,' said Rose.

'Oh?' said Peter. 'What's that got to do with Gwyn?'

'Bass was working on a way to send the Relic back just before he died,' said Rose. 'It's a kind of energy slingshot. It would only appear to return the Relic to the Gods, the hope being that this would stimulate an energy rise. However, for it to work, and for the people to believe we have fulfilled the prophecy, the Descendants need to be present.'

'Why Gwyn, not me?' asked Peter.

'You know why,' said Elistair, his tone firm but gentle. 'But will Gwyn agree to help?'

Peter and Elistair rounded on Gwyn. The blood drained from her face.

'We were just getting to that bit,' said Rose

Everyone waited expectantly for Gwyn's response.

'No. I will not,' she said sharply, shrugging her shoulders a little to add weight to her point.

'Why not?' asked Elistair. 'I think we've given it enough time to know waiting it out, as Austin suggested, isn't working. The rebels in the Wild Lands are moving to strike. The Gods only know what's going on with Marcus and Amber, and need I remind you, that everywhere around us, people are surviving a winter on food rations.'

'I said *no*,' said Gwyn, shrinking back a little under their scrutiny.

'Well, if you won't help, we'll have to make public the truth about your line,' said Elistair.

Gwyn was suddenly unsure, taken aback by Elistair's words. 'What are you talking about?' She looked to Peter for an explanation, but he kept his eyes on the ground, refusing to look at her.

'I'm talking about the fact that neither you, nor your father, are legitimate Descendants.'

'Don't be ridiculous,' said Gwyn, more assuredly than she felt. 'Even if that were true, nobody would believe you.'

'Want to put that to the test?' said Rose, obviously enjoying herself.

Gwyn once again looked to her father, but, as usual, he provided no support.

'Just help them,' said Peter. 'It will be much easier if you do.'

'You're lying,' she said, 'and you're spineless.' She searched wildly for a way out. They'd backed her into a corner, and even her own father, pathetic as he was, was doing nothing to help. 'Who would replace me?' she said, buying herself time to think, not for a minute expecting them to have an answer.

Elistair and Rose looked back at her with hard eyes, giving nothing away. 'You can help us, or you can find out the answer to that question at the same time as everyone else,' said Elistair.

He wasn't bluffing, she could see that. She was a mere inconvenience and they would shove her aside.

Gwyn looked away, her eyes straying, settling on Anita and Alexander, laughing and joking with someone at the bar. Rage erupted inside her, blood rushing through her veins, hatred clouding her mind. This was all Anita's fault, all of it, and someone had to teach her a lesson.

Gwyn spun back towards the detestable group. 'Fine, I'll help you,' she said, 'but only if Anita has nothing to do with it. She can't be involved, and she certainly can't be there when we go through with it. She can't even know what's going on.'

Rose turned to follow Gwyn's enraged stare, just as Alexander and Anita looked up. Rose's eyes met Anita's. 'Fine,' she said, 'that's a small price to pay.'

* * * * *

Gwyn stormed off and Alexander and Anita walked over to join Rose, Elistair, and Peter. 'What happened?' asked Anita, feeling a strange array of emotions from their energy.

'She agreed to help us,' said Elistair, 'but I had to tell her she's not really a Descendant.'

Anita froze, turning her head towards Peter, expecting him to say something. He didn't, so she continued. 'Does she know the Body line actually runs through me?'

'No,' said Elistair, 'and it would be wise not to tell her. She would only agree to help if you're kept out of it. She doesn't want you there when the Relic's returned.'

The news hit Anita like a punch in the face. She wouldn't be there to see Bass' work come to fruition. Gwyn had taken it away, through nothing more than childish spite.

Her energy plummeted, and Alexander put a hand on her back.

'If that's how it has to be,' said Anita, 'then so be it.' She resolved herself to her fate, still waiting for Peter to say something, to acknowledge her as his daughter. However, true to form, he said not a word, opting instead to follow his other daughter back inside.

* * * * *

Three days later, Helena pulled up at a large farm outside of Kingdom, as Marcus had instructed. She parked her car and entered a yard bursting with humanity; so many people standing in ranks that she briefly wondered if she were delusional. Marcus stood on a makeshift stage in front of one of the barns; he cut a lonely figure, dressed like his troops, all in black, nothing but a microphone stand to keep him company as he addressed the army before him.

'Soldiers,' he began, his voice ringing confidently across the yard. Reminiscent of his father, his shoulders were set square, as though he were entirely assured that these men would follow his commands. 'At least, that was what my father and Amber have always called you. But I think of you as something altogether different, something better than mere soldiers doing the bidding of another. I think of you as people with a choice, a crucial choice at a pivotal moment in our history, that you alone can make.

'You can choose to continue the work you've been doing; to evict poor, helpless people from their businesses and livelihoods, to subjugate those who have no way of fighting back, to continue eating like Gods when the rest of the world starves.' He let his unlikely words sink in. 'Or, you can choose to help solve the problems we face, to help me and the Institution find a way to stabilize the energy, to rebuild our food economy, and to restore faith in the system that has given us prosperity for so long.'

He paused again, and a screeching filled the air, another car hurtling to a standstill at the side of the yard. Four burly men, clad in black, clambered out and escorted Amber to the stage, where she stepped up alone, positioning herself aggressively at Marcus' side. 'What's going on here?' she demanded, raising her voice so the microphone would pick up her words.

'Amber.' Marcus addressed her like an inferior. 'So good of you to join us, and just on cue.' He turned back to address his army. 'The choice you have today is simple; choose to stay with me and help send the Relic back, and work with all groups to forge a new society when that's done. Or, if you'd rather cross your fingers and hope for the best, then stick with Amber.' He turned to face her. 'Presumably, that's what you want?'

She nodded, so he continued. 'Now is the time to make your choice. Consider carefully, as your place in our future depends on it. Those choosing to side with me, please come forward to the stage, those siding with Amber, move to the back. Please make your choice now.'

Helena couldn't believe what she was witnessing. Marcus was helping the Institution to send the Relic back, and then afterwards, he wanted to help build a better world. She held her breath as she watched the mass of people jostle around, unable to make out from the blur which way the majority were headed. A minute or so later, silence fell over the yard, and Marcus addressed his audience once more.

'Those at the back, please leave now with Amber. I wish you all well. Those who have chosen to stay with me,' a good sixty to seventy percent of the force, from what Helena could see, 'please reconvene here in an hour. I thank you for your loyalty.'

As Marcus left the stage, a roar of voices erupted, shattering the shocked silence. Evidently the soldiers were as surprised as Helena at this strange turn of events.

Amber's cronies barked orders at those who'd sided with her, eventually marching them out of the yard, to who knew where, and to do who knew what… Helena had no doubt they would cause trouble before too long…

The yard slowly emptied, Marcus issuing orders to his loyal Lieutenants. Helena hung around, waiting to speak to Marcus, still struggling to get her head around what she'd just witnessed. 'That was quite some speech,' she said, full of admiration, when Marcus had finally finished organising their immediate next steps.

'Thanks. It wasn't a foregone conclusion that any great number would side with me. I invited the key leaders to dinner last night, so I knew I could rely on them, but we've kept more than I could have hoped for.'

'So, what happens next?' Helena asked.

'We're still working that out,' he said, 'but for a start, we're going to stop evicting people from their farms. Then we're going to do everything we can to support the preservation of the livestock we have left. And we're going to try everything we can think of to encourage decent crop yields again next year. And, of course, we send back the Relic. I heard Gwyn has agreed to help too?'

'Yes, she was under duress, but she's agreed to help us. It's going to take a couple of weeks for us to finalise everything. Bass laid most of the groundwork, but there are a few outstanding things to do. Elistair needs to get fully up to speed if we're to have the best possible chance of success.'

'Elistair's agreed to help the Institution? How did you pull that off?'

'We didn't. He decided to join us. He wants to see Bass' final work brought to life.'

'Lucky for us; it's not like we have other options.'

'True.'

'But as I understand it, Bass' plan won't actually return the Relic to the Gods, it will just move it from its current location? We'll make everyone think the prophecy has been fulfilled, which should, in itself, have a positive effect on the energy?'

'That's the theory.'

'But what happens after that? What if it doesn't have the desired effect on the energy, or if we can't return the Relic for real? Surely that would have a significant adverse effect?'

'Truthfully, we have no idea. If Bass' theory doesn't work, then it's likely we'll have total chaos on our hands, pretty much overnight. If it does, then we'll turn all our efforts to sending it back properly. If we can't do that, then who knows what'll happen. We've survived for hundreds of years living with the Relic and the prophecy, so it stands to reason we'll have time to work this out.'

'So long as Bass' theory is correct, and the energy responds as he thought it would…'

Helena shrugged.

'What if the Gods punish us?' said Marcus.

'I can't deny it's a risk, but apart from sending us the prophecy and Relic, the Gods have always stayed out of our affairs; there's no reason for them to start meddling now. And anyway, it feels a lot like they're punishing us at the moment, so maybe they'll like the fact we're finally trying to overcome the challenge they sent us.'

CHAPTER 16

'Descendants, councillors, children of the Temples of the Mind, Body and Spirit…,' Alexander's smooth, reassuring voice sailed out from the radio. Anita and Elistair were sitting in the observatory (Patrick had been mysteriously absent for weeks now), waiting with bated breath to see what would happen next.

The start of the energy fall had corresponded with Austin's announcement about Christiana's death, so it wasn't beyond the realm of possibility to think an upturn could begin with this announcement. Anita's energy was taut, her body ridged, and she read from Elistair's energy that he was feeling the same way. They'd been working for three weeks on perfecting Bass' theory, considering all angles and conducting small-scale experiments to test the finer points of the execution. All had gone according to plan, and they were ready to announce it to the world.

'… it will have escaped no ones' notice that our world has been in severe energy decline since the death of the Body Descendant, Christiana. Not a single one of us has escaped the consequences of that decline.

'For this, I am deeply sorry; sorry the Descendants could not do more, sorry you have all had to suffer, and sorry I could not make this announcement sooner.

However, today marks a turning point, because today, I can finally tell you that we have a solution.' He paused, Anita's eyes fixated on the dashboards in front of her. 'We have found a way to return the Relic to the Gods.'

Another long silence spilled from the radio, Alexander letting the news sink in, Anita willing the dials to respond. Nothing happened as Alexander's voice pierced the silence once more. 'One week from today, at eleven o'clock, at the temples in Kingdom, the Descendants will return the Relic. We welcome all of you to attend this most exciting and momentous occasion.'

The transmission cut out, Elistair and Anita continuing to sit in apprehensive silence, not wanting to look away for a second, lest they miss some small indication that the energy was responding. They sat for a full hour before noticing any signs, and when they did, they couldn't even be sure they were witnessing something concrete; one or two of the most sensitive receivers showing a slight uptick.

'I suppose it's a start,' said Elistair, wearily.

'Barely,' said Anita, 'and nothing like we saw when they announced Christiana's death.'

'That's because people always respond to bad news more violently than good. People are sceptical; it'll take them a while to believe it's really happening. It might even take until after they've seen the Relic sent skywards for them to truly believe.'

'I suppose so,' replied Anita, tapping a couple of dials, making sure they were working.

Elistair laughed. 'Come on,' he said, 'there's nothing more we can do here. I'll come back later to check if there's any movement. Let's go and meet the others.'

Anita nodded. It felt good to finally be back in Empire. She welcomed the prospect of a couple of escapist hours, drinking some crazy new cocktail, and gossiping about whatever scandal Cleo had unearthed today.

* * * * *

Anita returned to the observatory later that evening, insisting Elistair go home, reassuring him that she would call if there was anything to report. He reluctantly agreed, Anita relieved when he did, relishing the prospect of spending some time by herself, in the quiet of the great brass observatory.

She climbed the stairs to the middle level and sat down at the dashboards, recording the readings methodically, one by one. Her energy pulsed at the increasing evidence of an upturn. The most sensitive dials had moved more dramatically now, less sensitive ones showing signs as well. Her spirits lifted as she moved along the dials, finally feeling like what they were doing might really work.

She finished recording the readings and decided against ringing Elistair. He needed some respite too, and anyway, nothing all that significant had happened. She headed to the third floor, her favourite level, to look out over Empire. Now that winter had them fully in its grips, the sky was pitch black, the lights of Empire punching violently upwards, the stars standing aloof above them, twinkling majestically, unconcerned by the competition below.

Anita stood mesmerized for several moments, recalling the hundreds of times she and Bass had stood or sat together in this spot, laughing about something Patrick had done, or working on an energy problem. She moved away from the edge and lay on the largest of the energy receivers, the lolloping waves reverberating through her, providing a strange sort of comfort. With

Bass gone, there was nobody to tell her off about the effect this would have on the readings below.

She leaned her head back against the smooth, cold brass and closed her eyes, dropping her hands so they rested on the roof either side. She brought her hands together underneath the metal, stretching out her tense shoulders, feeling a wave hit her, energy pouring through her, helping with the stretch.

Knowing she shouldn't linger too long, lest she have a meaningful impact on the readings, she released her hands and made to sit up, but as she did so, her right hand brushed against a piece of paper stuffed into the lip on the underside of the brass. Anita's skin prickled with intrigue; maybe this would explain where Patrick had disappeared to so suddenly... but when she unfolded the paper, all thoughts of Patrick were forgotten; it was a note from Bass, and it was meant for her.

She scanned the writing, rereading it several times, lowering it when she finally thought she understood the meaning of Bass' words. The message was cryptic, taking steps to obscure its point, but it certainly related to the plan to send the Relic back, and seemed to contain some kind of warning.

From what she could make out, some part of Bass' calculation had been troubling him, although he couldn't put a finger on why. He thought it was something relating to the Relic itself... but if she were deciphering the message correctly, he hadn't discussed it with anyone else, not fully trusting some specific person within the Institution, although who, it didn't say.

The hair on the back of Anita's neck stood on end. Something was wrong, and she didn't know who she could trust to help her work it out.

* * * * *

Anita sank down beside Alexander, leaning into him, putting her feet up on the sofa as he pulled her towards him, his arm around her. They'd retreated to Alexander's cottage on the outskirts of Empire, the fire crackling across the cosy sitting room. They were full of beef stew, tired and a little fuzzy headed, having recently moved onto their second bottle of rich red wine.

All they had talked about for days were the arrangements for sending back of the Relic. From security measures, to viewing screens, to the exact positioning of each Descendant, to crowd control, given the number of people expected to attend, to the strange disappearance of all protestors from the temples after the announcement. But Anita couldn't let go of the nagging feeling that something was wrong, and Alexander felt her tension.

'You're still thinking about the note?' he asked, as she wriggled into a more comfortable position.

'Aren't you?' she said. 'Bass wasn't dramatic. He wouldn't have left something so cryptic if there was nothing to worry about, and he didn't share his concerns with either Patrick or Anderson, which means he didn't trust them.'

'But neither Patrick nor Anderson are working on returning the Relic any longer, so we don't need to worry about them, and if Bass was genuinely concerned his plan wouldn't work, he wouldn't have kept it to himself.'

'Well, there's something he wasn't happy with.'

'And you still can't find what it is,' he said, caressing her arm.

'No.'

'What does Elistair think?'

'We've been through everything with a fine-tooth comb, and we can't find anything that looks odd, although, seeing as no one has attempted this before, we don't know what we're looking for.'

'Maybe Bass was being overly cautious? Or maybe the note is from ages ago, and it's a problem he overcame before he died? Or maybe there isn't a problem at all? Is it possible you've misinterpreted his meaning?'

'Anything's possible, but I don't think so. I've looked it over a hundred times, and I can't think of any other conclusion.'

'And Elistair's looked at it too?'

'Yes. He can't decipher it at all.'

'I'm not sure there's much you can do then,' he said, kissing the top of her head. 'We're setting everything up tomorrow, and the big day's the day after. I pity anyone who tries to put the brakes on at this stage; the mob would take over Kingdom before I could get halfway through the announcement!'

'I know,' said Anita, sitting up in frustration, 'it just feels like there's something we're missing.'

* * * * *

There was a frost in the air the following morning, Anita and Elistair at the station in Empire, carefully packing the equipment they needed onto the first train of the day. The sun was still struggling to break across the horizon when they finished, Cleo turning up with flasks of tea, and containers filled with porridge, topped with honey.

They sat in the rickety wooden waiting room, green paint peeling off the walls, and ate greedily as Cleo filled them in on who would be coming with them, versus who was already there.

267

Gwyn and Marcus, had, of course, already gone ahead, but Helena, and the rest of the Institution members, including Peter—scandalous, seeing as he should have gone with Gwyn—would travel to Kingdom with the three of them. The Spirit Leader and a few of his monks would join them when they arrived in Kingdom, and most of the councillors were already there.

'What about your new boyfriend?' asked Anita, provocatively. 'Will we be seeing him there?'

Cleo shot Anita a dark look. 'As you well know, I don't have a new boyfriend. I shan't be expecting anyone in Kingdom.'

'What about your father?' asked Elistair, also shooting Anita a look. 'Will be he joining us there?'

'Of course,' said Cleo, clearly happy to move away from talk of her mysterious man. 'Dad will be there; it's too good an opportunity to sell stuff for him to miss,' she said gleefully. 'He's coming back from the Wild Lands with a bumper load of beer that he's intending to sell to the crowd at exorbitant prices.' She smiled. 'Knowing him, he'll probably succeed.'

They waited for another twenty minutes for everyone else to arrive, and then boarded the train, filling multiple carriages. Anita, Alexander, and Cleo hung around outside for as long as they could, making sure they were the last to board, meaning they could avoid the carriages already occupied and sit away from the others.

The train doors banged shut, the whistle blew, and to Anita's surprise, just as they were gliding away from the station, the carriage door slid open, and Cordelia stepped through. Alexander immediately jumped up to help her place her luggage in the rack above them.

'Oh good,' said Cordelia, ignoring the startled look on Anita's face, 'I am glad you've secured a carriage away from those dreadful Institution people. And that means we won't have to share the picnic I've brought with me. Now, let me see,' she said, settling herself down next to Cleo, pretending to be oblivious to the obvious, unanswered question floating between them.

'I've got flasks of tea, apricot flapjacks, and cheese and ham sandwiches; thought that would all travel well, don't you think? And a couple of apples, much more boring, but just in case; you never know when someone's going to be on a health kick,' she said, disapprovingly.

Cordelia finally stopped talking when they reached the outskirts of Empire, countryside whipping past, the first orange rays of the rising sun casting soft light across frost-covered fields. Silence fell in the carriage and Cleo and Alexander looked to Anita, silently pressuring her to speak next.

Anita took a deep breath. 'That sounds lovely, thanks,' she said, then paused, racking her brain for the least offensive way to ask what in the world Cordelia was doing here. 'I was just... wondering,' she said, as sweetly as she could, 'um... why are you here?'

'Don't know if you realize,' said Cordelia, fixing Anita with a look which told her this would be a short conversation, 'but this will be, easily, the biggest event in living memory. I may not like the Institution, to put it mildly, however, I am not about to pass up the opportunity of front row seats, which I am assuming you can provide to me,' she said, turning to Alexander and waiting for an affirmative head nod before continuing, 'because I dislike the organization that happens to be organizing it. Now,' she said finally, 'who would like a cup of tea?'

* * * * *

They reached Kingdom by lunchtime, everyone spilling out of the train, heading in separate directions. Alexander, Elistair, Helena, and Anita headed to the Relic, where they would set everything up and conduct a couple of final tests. They reached the temples to find the whole area a hive of activity, scores of people flitting this way and that, some unclear but urgent purpose driving them.

'Who's done all of this?' asked Anita, not sure which way to turn in the pandemonium.

'I don't know,' replied Helena, sounding both surprised and a little put out that such a well-oiled machine was whirring away, entirely without her knowledge.

They made their way to the very centre of the temples, to where the Relic stood, as ugly and unassuming as ever. They found Marcus and Timi huddling over some drawing, deep in conversation.

Helena's annoyance blazed to full anger when she saw who was responsible. 'What, in the name of the Gods, is going on here?' she demanded, Marcus and Timi turning in unison towards the source of the attack.

'We're overseeing the arrangements for tomorrow,' said Timi, calmly, not even a little concerned by Helena's furious energy.

'This is an Institution event,' said Helena.

'And if I'm not mistaken,' said Timi, his tone still blasé, 'I'm also a member of the Institution.' Helena's face contorted and Timi's eyes flashed. 'A more senior member than you,' he added.

'Right,' said Elistair, irritated by the pettiness, 'we're here to set up the apparatus for tomorrow, and then we need to do some tests. If you could lend us a couple of your helpers, we would very much appreciate it; it will make things go much more quickly. Then you can continue, unburdened by us, with whatever it is you're concocting.'

'Of course,' said Marcus, 'let me find you a couple of our best.' He returned moments later, with two large, muscled, keen-looking men, who Elistair immediately put to work.

'We'll need to clear all of this stuff out of the way,' said Elistair, taking control, motioning towards the flower decorations around the base of the Relic. 'And you're going to have to remove at least the first five rows of chairs. No, actually, make that seven rows, just to be safe.'

'Seven rows?' exclaimed Timi. 'That means there won't be enough room for all the councillors.'

'My heart bleeds,' said Elistair, barely looking up from the brass tripod he was erecting on the Body Temple side of the Relic. He and Anita, with the aid of Marcus' two helpers, put up another tripod on the Spirit side and another on the Mind side. They placed several brass energy meters and other contraptions inside the triangle this created.

Once the heavy lifting was done, Elistair sent away the helpers. He and Anita worked all afternoon, taking measurements and tweaking the positions of their equipment. All around them, the large song and dance created by Timi and Marcus continued. Flowers arrived, a lectern and microphone placed on the Mind side of the Relic, names laid on seats, ropes erected around various other areas to contain the masses.

At one point, two men appeared with staging, and started to put up platforms for each of the Descendants to stand on. Elistair and Anita gave each other an exasperated look before Elistair quickly sent them on their way. Minutes later, a flustered Marcus turned up to insist, rather pompously, that the platforms be used.

Anita explained this wasn't possible; they hadn't factored platforms into the measurements. Marcus finally accepted the explanation, especially when Anita pointed out that, if the Descendants looked too far removed from the apparatus, or if people could scrutinize them too closely, it was more likely that someone would realise they weren't actually doing anything.

They finished setting everything up just as everyone arrived for the dress rehearsal. Gwyn, Marcus, Timi, Peter, Elistair, Helena, and to everyone's surprise, Anderson, descended on the Relic in quick succession, Timi seizing control. 'As you all know,' he said, condescendingly, 'tomorrow is a momentous occasion for the world. So we reasoned,' it wasn't at all clear who this 'we' involved, but he continued assuredly, as though it were self-evident, 'that there should be at least a modicum of pomp and circumstance about the day.'

'A modicum,' Anita whispered to Alexander.

Timi's head whipped around towards her, his energy losing, for only a moment, its usual unaffected air. Anita smiled openly at him, willing him to say something. He ignored her and continued.

'Marcus and I have gone to great lengths to ensure the day tomorrow has a sense of magnitude; flowers, seating plans, music, carefully placed people in the audience, as well as overt security measures to ensure no trouble makers. In addition, the day wouldn't be complete without someone to chair the whole occasion, a master of ceremonies, if you will.'

Helena stepped forward, having assumed this role would fall to herself, but before she could intervene, Timi went on, 'Anderson, please step forward.'

Anderson did so, taking up a position at Timi's right shoulder. Timi looked with glee at their confused faces. 'You all know Anderson? As the world's leading

Relic expert, I'm sure you'll agree, it's only right for Anderson to lead proceedings. He also has a delightful theatrical flair, which I am sure will do much to rouse the spirits of the crowd.'

'But surely it should be Elistair,' said Anita, talking over the end of Timi's sentence to get a word in. 'Elistair has been central to pulling everything together for tomorrow, and Anderson has been absent from the planning for quite some time now. Elistair is a trusted and respected councillor, so he brings a certain gravitas that Anderson does not.'

'But, of course, Elistair will be here too,' said Timi.

'Unlike you,' said Gwyn, venomously. 'In fact, what are you doing here?'

'Anita has played a fundamental part in setting up the experiment,' said Elistair, brushing Gwyn's comment aside as though she were insignificant. Gwyn scowled. 'We couldn't have done it without her.'

'However,' said Timi, his energy, again, showing signs of fury, 'Elistair will be here in his capacity as an energy expert, paying full attention to the technicalities. Anderson will direct attention away from Elistair, ensuring the crowd focuses on the Descendants and their role, and not Elistair and all his brass instruments.'

Anita had to admit, he had a point; it was in everyone's interests to ensure nobody realised what was really happening. However, that person being Anderson sent a ripple of discomfort down her spine. Bass hadn't trusted Anderson with whatever had been troubling him, and Anita had never liked him. She looked over at Elistair, who shook his head when their eyes met, clearly telling Anita she should let it go.

'That's fine,' said Elistair, smoothing over the tension. 'Now, if you don't mind, we need to do some test runs, to ensure everything's set up correctly.'

'Of course,' said Anderson, 'anything I can do to help?'

'No,' said Elistair, pointedly, as he stepped towards one of the two huge boulders they'd brought with them. The boulders were significantly larger than the Relic, however the Relic was far denser, so their weight was the same.

They'd agreed to send the Relic to the great mineral sea in the Wild Lands. If everything went according to plan, the boulders today, and the Relic tomorrow, would land right in the centre of the large expanse of water. That way, if there was something unexpectedly different about the Relic, they had as much tolerance as possible for it to still land in the sea.

They'd already sent Institution members there, to track where the Relic landed, pick it up before anyone else could find it, and take it to an Institution safe house not too far away. The same Institution members were standing by now, waiting to send a radio message when the boulders landed.

Elistair directed each of the Descendants to the tripod in front of their respective temple. He instructed them to place their right hand, outstretched towards the Relic, in the horseshoe shaped holder at the top of their tripod. He gave Anderson a radius around which he could walk when addressing the crowd, right back by the chairs, so he wouldn't interfere with the energy waves. He instructed the others to stand back with him, by the first row of seats.

Elistair explained the importance of nobody getting in between him and the Relic, especially careful to make Anderson understand he had to sit down once the build-up was over, to be sure he wouldn't get in the way.

When Elistair was happy the others were where they should be, he picked up a brass instrument with a small, hook-like part in the middle. He turned the contraption on, ensuring it was hovering over the top of the first boulder as he did so, and then moved it to the ground, placing it carefully on a mark on the floor they'd made earlier. Once he was happy with its placement, he moved back to his seat and sat down, telling Anderson he would have about four and a half minutes from the point of turning the instrument on, to when the Relic would be sent skywards.

Unable to contain his curiosity any longer, Timi interrupted. 'How exactly does it work?' he asked, eagerly.

Anita inwardly rolled her eyes, but Elistair told him.

'When I turn on the instrument,' said Elistair, 'it finds and then pinches a specific type of energy wave. When I move the machine to the floor, that energy wave is stretched. The instrument holds the pinch, meaning on one side, the wave's energy stacks up, while on the other side, it stretches out.

'At the four and a half minute point, the force of the pinched wave will become too much for the machine to withstand. It will release the wave, which will spring back to its original course.

'We've taken great care to precisely position the machine underneath the boulder, so when the wave springs back, the force of the wave will send it where we want it to go.

'So long as we've done our sums correctly, the boulder will fly with the correct force, on the correct trajectory, and will land in the Salt Sea.'

'Fascinating,' said Timi, shooting Anderson a look.

'That's the plan anyway,' said Elistair. 'It's worked perfectly every time we've tried it so far, but as we've never been able to test it on the Relic, Anita and I will hold our breath tomorrow, along with everyone else.'

The remaining minutes ticked by in silence, Anita's mind wandering. If Elistair had positioned the machine incorrectly, the boulder would fly in the wrong direction, taking out anyone in its path. She looked over at Alexander and her blood ran cold... too late now to suggest the first trial run take place without the Descendants in place.

Alexander turned towards her, a worried look on his face, feeling her energy change but not knowing why. It was too late to tell him; all she could do was hold her breath and pray.

A large crack thundered through the silence, the energy hook releasing, the boulder rocketing upwards. A burst of wind blew flowers out of place, knocking Gwyn backwards as the boulder disappeared into the darkening sky.

It was sunset, the earliest they'd dared test the experiment, in case the boulders flying through the sky caught too much unwanted attention. They hoped that, in the fading light, even if people saw the spectacle, they wouldn't be able to make out what it was. Even so, two trials were all they could risk, to keep the threat of discovery to a minimum.

'I think that went well,' said Elistair, only a little caution in his voice. He turned on a radio receiver and waited anxiously for news.

A few minutes later, a crackly but distinctly excited voice leapt out of the speaker. 'It's here!' the voice screeched. 'By the Gods, it just landed right in the centre of the sea! You should have seen the splash!'

'Many thanks,' said Elistair, calmly, Anita stifling a chuckle at the impressive spike in his energy that contradicted his tone. 'We'll send the other one shortly; please stand by.'

Anita smiled at Elistair, who gave her a reassuring nod. 'Right.' Elistair snapped back to business. 'This

276

time, Anderson, I think you should try walking around and addressing the crowd, making sure you don't go within the circle I've specified.'

'Fine,' said Anderson, suddenly sulky for some bizarre reason, 'but I don't think I'll practice the speech itself. It's always better if these things are spontaneous.'

'As you wish,' said Elistair, paying him very little attention as he reset the energy hook, carefully placing it on the floor under the second boulder. 'Over to you, Anderson,' he said, returning to his seat. 'Tomorrow, it would be a good idea for you to distract the audience while I'm setting up the hook. We don't want anyone to focus on me.'

'Fine,' said Anderson, busy parading around the perimeter, every now and again checking his watch, sitting down at just under the four-and-a-half-minute mark.

The second boulder went exactly the same way as the first. The same loud crack reverberated off the stone of the temples, the same gust of wind followed, although this time, Gwyn braced against it, much to Anita's disappointment.

The boulder hurtled into the sky, and five minutes later, the same voice came over the radio to confirm it had landed in the middle of the Salt Sea, this time, a little less excited.

'Right,' said Elistair, 'our work here is done. Time for dinner and a stiff drink, I think. Marcus, I take it your men will be here overnight, and can be relied on to guard the equipment?'

'Of course,' said Marcus.

Elistair picked up the hook and put it in his satchel. 'This one's coming with me,' he said, to no one in particular. 'We're in a bit of a pickle if this goes wandering off.'

* * * * *

They had dinner in Monty's back room. Helena, and the other more senior Institution members, reminisced about how it had been when they were young, Cleo, Alexander, and Anita chatting about what tomorrow would bring. Marcus, Gwyn, and Anderson were absent, but the drinks flowed, the mood spirited, everyone seemingly relaxed about the event that would take place in the morning.

Anita and Alexander departed early, wishing the others a good evening, and lazily wound their way back to the temples via Kingdom's cobbled streets. They were staying at Alexander's rooms in the temple, so they would be close to the action in the morning. Seeing as Anita had never been into this one of her boyfriend's domains, she was excited to see what the place was like.

They reached the middle of the Spirit Temple, and Alexander placed his hand on a stone to the right of the door, applying a little pressure before they heard a click and the door swung open. 'That's all it takes to get in?' asked Anita, concerned for their privacy.

Alexander smiled as he took her hand, pulling her in after him. 'That's all it takes if you have the right energy for the monitor in that stone,' he said, pushing the door closed behind them.

'Oh,' said Anita, feeling a little foolish, 'that's good.'

It wasn't at all what Anita had been expecting, and in stark contrast to the small rooms under the temple in Empire, this was one large, almost haphazard space. The ceiling was the same height as the rest of the temple, acres above them, a sheet of glass all that stood between them and the night sky above.

'Wow,' said Anita, craning her neck to look upwards, 'I never imagined this is what it would be like in here. Are the Mind and Body chambers the same?'

She wandered around, but her eyes kept flitting back to the ceiling.

'I don't know, I've never been in them,' he said, moving to the drinks cabinet and pouring two glasses of wine. The cabinet was one of several items placed against the walls of the open room, which was split up into sections.

The drinks cabinet was next to a partner's desk, piled high with books and papers. Then came an L-shaped seating area facing outwards into the room, a low coffee table in the middle. On the other side of the space stood a plush, canopied, king sized bed, with almost unnoticeable doors in the wall on either side. Anita presumed one was a bathroom and the other a wardrobe.

A small kitchenette was next to the seating area, with a tiny square table and two spindly chairs, but the whole point of the room was in the middle, where a large area had been left clear, aside from a few well-worn meditation mats.

Anita found the room oppressive; something about the big open space, enclosed on every side, the only light coming from above, windows too far away to reach.

'I agree, it's horrible,' said Alexander, reading Anita's energy as he handed her a glass, leading her to one of the mismatched sofas. 'We can stay at the house if you'd prefer?'

'No, it's fine,' said Anita, leaning into him, taking a sip of wine and rolling it around her mouth, 'it's just such a strange space.'

'I know,' he said, stroking her arm, 'made stranger because all the Spirit Descendants have hated it, but nobody's ever done anything to try to improve it. It's like they know it's a lost cause!'

Anita smiled. 'Dinner was better than I thought it would be,' she said. 'Everyone was well behaved.'

'Helped by the fact Gwyn, Marcus, and Anderson didn't turn up,' laughed Alexander. 'It's strange that Anderson's suddenly back, and that he seems to be best friends with Timi.'

'It makes me nervous, seeing as Bass didn't trust him,' said Anita. 'But it's not surprising he wants to get in on the action; he's supposedly the world's leading Relic expert, after all. If you ask me, he's a shameless narcissist.'

'Harsh,' said Alexander, giving her a playful squeeze, 'I'm not sure I'd go that far.'

'Well, Bass didn't trust him,' she said, pointedly.

'We don't know why though.'

'We don't know a lot of things we'd like to,' she said, her tone taking an exasperated turn. 'We've made no progress with the note Philip left you, or with opening the cylinder in my head, or with the meaning of Bass' note. And then there's the mystery around Cleo's nameless new friend, what the Magnei are, where they live in the Wild, and how we find them?'

'True,' said Alexander, 'but we have to focus. Tomorrow we send the Relic back, the day after that we start to rebuild our political system, democratically, and after that, we work out the rest, including how to actually return the Relic.'

'Which is all well and good, so long as tomorrow goes according to plan.'

'It will,' he said, reassuringly. 'The tests went like clockwork, and so will tomorrow, given the levels of precision applied by you and Elistair.'

'If you say so,' she said, not convinced. 'Timi and Marcus is another strange partnership.'

'Yep,' said Alexander, but he wasn't really paying attention. He took her wineglass, putting it and his on the floor, then leaned in and kissed her lips. 'I don't want to talk about them.'

'What if I do?' she said, looking up at him encouragingly.

'You don't,' he said, kissing her again, pushing her back onto the sofa.

She huffed out a breath as his weight came down on top of her, her body arching into him, tipping her neck back so he could reach it with his lips. 'I suppose you're right,' she said.

CHAPTER 17

They woke early the following morning, the room lit by dazzling sunlight. Anita now understood the canopy above the bed: it was shelter. The room felt different now, like walking on the inside of a light bulb, too close to the element for comfort, but restrained by the glass from breaking free. The room was stifling. She breathed a sigh of relief when they exited in search of breakfast, Alexander clad in his floor-length Descendants' cloak, ready for the ceremony.

To their surprise—although, when Anita thought about it, it wasn't surprising at all—the temple was already packed full of people who'd arrived early to secure a good spot. They'd planned to go to one of Alexander's favourite cafes for breakfast, only a couple of minutes' walk from the temple, but, as they emerged, it was clear that wasn't going to happen.

Outside the temple was a horde of people, all queuing for the security checks Marcus and Timi had put in place. As soon as they spotted Alexander, their attention switched to him. Thankfully, the security guards acted quickly, ushering Anita and Alexander through the crowd and into the council building across the road. With all the grabbing hands and the press of bodies, they were both thoroughly shaken when they got there.

'Should have realised that would happen,' said Alexander.

Anita took his hand and squeezed it, her attention moving swiftly to the raft of lingering councillors in the entrance hall. 'Is there anywhere in here we can go?' she said, keen to get away from public scrutiny.

'Yes,' he said, leading her towards a door to their right. 'Descendants' drawing room,' he said, as they emerged into a stuffy room with a large fireplace, heavy curtains, several formal sofas, and a couple of tables, laid with crisp, white linen. 'This room is for the sole use of Descendants, so as long as none of the others decide to show up, we should have the place to ourselves.'

Anita sat down at one of the tables, Alexander walking to the side of the room, pulling a cord for service.

Moments later, a waiter, clad in a restrictive morning suit, crisply entered the room. 'How can I help, Sir?' he asked, standing stiffly in anticipation of instruction.

'We'd like some breakfast, please,' said Alexander. 'Coffee and orange juice for me, and a sausage sandwich made with fennel rye bread and onion chutney. And for you, Anita?' he asked, sending the waiter's attention her way.

Anita raised an eyebrow at his specific and demanding request. 'Orange juice and tea please,' she said, 'and Eggs Royale, if that's possible?'

'What bread would you like that served on?'

'Seeded brown?' she asked, hopefully.

'Very good,' said the waiter, 'anything else I can get for you?'

'No, that's all, thank you,' said Alexander, taking the seat opposite Anita.

'Rationing doesn't apply here?'

A guilty look crossed Alexander's face. 'Not currently. It's on my list of things to change... if today doesn't go according to plan...'

Breakfast arrived rapidly, but they ate at a leisurely pace. The ceremony wasn't until midday, so they had several hours before Alexander had to be there; before Anita had to make herself scarce. They had barely finished eating, Anita relaxing back in her chair, cradling her tea, when the door opened, and in walked Marcus and Gwyn, with Timi and Anderson.

'Oh,' said Marcus, as he spotted them, his energy wary, 'I didn't think you would be here for ages.'

'We weren't going to be,' said Alexander, 'but the unruly crowd outside made our decision for us.'

'You have to leave,' said Gwyn's sharp, snippy voice. She was looking directly at Anita. 'Now,' she added, turning to Alexander and saying, 'that's what we agreed.'

'We agreed I wouldn't be at the ceremony,' said Anita, furious at Gwyn's audacity; waltzing in and issuing dictates, 'not where I could or could not be several hours beforehand. But if you find it so difficult to control your emotions, I'll leave. I hope you manage more composure when you're standing in front of the entire world, pretending to have a legitimate role in our plan.'

Nobody replied, although Anita was pleased to see from Gwyn's energy, that she was beside herself with anger. Anita got up to leave, and Alexander followed her out of the room.

'Go back,' said Anita, continuing before Alexander could protest, 'I don't know what they're up to, but whatever it is, they don't want either of us there. I don't think we should grant them that luxury. In fact, I'm going to get the others. I'll tell them to come and join you; that should really ruin their morning.'

'What do you think they want to discuss?' asked Alexander, with an edge of scepticism.

'I don't know. Maybe nothing. Maybe they want to coordinate outfits. Or maybe they're discussing how to take control after we send the Relic back. Either way, I'd rather not make it easy for them.'

'Fine,' said Alexander, looking pointedly at the growing number of councillors who were finding a reason to linger. 'I'll see you afterwards,' he said, pulling her into an embrace, then kissing her enthusiastically goodbye, not caring about the watching eyes.

'Good luck,' she said, as he pulled back.

'All I have to do is stand there and pretend,' he said in a low voice, 'I think I can handle that.' He called over a councillor to show Anita out of the back entrance, to avoid the crowd.

She kissed him one final time before turning to leave, determined to find anyone she could who Gwyn might not like, and send them in her direction.

* * * * *

Several hours later, Anita made her way down to the beach, finding the secret path Alexander had shown her the first time she'd come to Kingdom.

She'd gone to the hotel where Helena and the other Institution members were staying, and after telling them of the meeting between Timi, Anderson, Marcus, and Gwyn, found they needed no encouragement to head for the council building.

Anita was smug, before emptiness took hold. She had been working on Bass' theory with Elistair for weeks, but would be the only one not there to witness it

285

in person. Worse, she felt like an outsider, like she had no connection to what was going on at all. Even those in the crowd would be part of something that Gwyn had shut Anita out of; it hollowed out her insides.

She walked around the market for a bit, looking at all the exotic merchandise. She imagined which stalls her mother had done business with, when she'd returned from the Wild Lands after meeting Jeffrey. But the market, almost empty when she got there, was like a ghost town by the time the event was due to start, all the stalls closed, not a single person to be found on the usually packed streets.

So she made her way to the beach, where at least the waves kept to their usual rhythm, pounding the shore and sending up white froth. Anita sat just above the waterline, picking up pebbles and throwing them into the sea as she ran over everything in her mind. Try as she might to concentrate on something more productive, she kept coming back to the image of Gwyn falling backwards as they'd sent the first test boulder into the sky. She smirked cruelly every time she thought of it.

She couldn't put the day's events out of her mind, so decided to meditate. She still needed to open the brass cylinder, and hadn't tried since they'd returned from the Cloud Mountain. And maybe, if she looked closely at the hall in her mind—the Great Hall of the Magnei, apparently—she might glean some clue as to where it was located, or what took place there.

She closed her eyes and concentrated her energy, arriving at the hall on her first attempt. It looked just as it had the last time she'd been here, although it felt shaky under the strain of the solo meditation.

She'd meditated by herself only a handful of times, and it still felt strange without the support and comfort of someone else's energy. She walked around the room and looked out of the windows, seeing nothing but woodland beyond. Large, old, haphazardly spaced trees grew where they wished, huge and ancient branches bowing this way and that, but nothing that gave any clue where the hall was located.

She reached the end of the room where two thick, heavy doors covered with ironmongery stood. She pulled on the rings to open them, but the doors wouldn't budge.

Becoming frustrated, she circled the room again, hoping some detail would jump out at her. Maybe she'd missed an inscription on a wall, or behind a tapestry she would find a hidden map. Or maybe she'd find an object originating from a specific region in the Wild. She had no such luck, so turned her attention to the box and brass cylinder instead.

She picked up the box, removed the brass cylinder, and sat on a throne as she turned it over in her hands. She studied every detail for anything she might have missed. She looked at the ends, then tried to pull and twist them. She rubbed the sides, hoping for hidden words, or grooves invisible in the low light. She even hurled it at the floor. Nothing worked, her exasperation reaching new heights, Anita having to restrain herself from launching it through the nearest window. The only thing that stopped her was the worry that she'd never get it back.

She gave up, leaning back in the throne, letting her mind wander, trying to calm down and reflect. This inevitably led to thinking about what was happening at the temples. She ran through how she thought proceedings would go; Alexander, Gwyn, and Marcus, clad in floor length Descendants' cloaks, hoods up as they processed in, each through their own temple.

They would emerge, somehow in perfect unison, and stand before their tripod, in front of the Relic. The councillors would have already processed in, also clad in cloaks, all solemn and self-important. There would be music; something serious and dramatic, giving an air of intensity and significance, riling up the crowd, creating a tense and expectant atmosphere.

Everyone would be on tenterhooks, waiting anxiously for the main event. And then, after a meaningful pause, leaving time for everyone to dwell on the magnitude of what they were about to see, Anderson would stand. He would draw the crowd's attention, providing a cover for Elistair setting the energy hook.

Anderson would continue to wind up the crowd, describing what they were about to see, the effects it would have on the energy, and most importantly, would paint a picture of how the future might look. He would describe change of extreme proportions; democracy and elected leaders, equality and prosperity. Then, when his vision of the future was so real it was almost palpable, he would carry his show to a quiet, deliberate conclusion. He would instil a calm, anticipatory trance. The crowd would be silent on the surface, but something would bubble almost uncontrollably underneath, just waiting to be given the chance to break free.

Anderson would take his seat, and all eyes would move to the Descendants. They would lower their hoods, outstretch their arms, furiously focus on the ugly rock in front of them. And then there would be a small click that would sound like a great crack across the eager silence, and the Relic would catapult skywards, and the crowd would silently watch it go.

They would not believe what they were witnessing, that it was really happening, and then, when it settled into their bones, they would erupt into roars of celebration. They would clap and hug and begin to really believe a better future was near.

And at the front, at the epicentre, Anita imagined the Descendants looking cautiously at each other, Alexander turning to Elistair, sharing a look that meant they had succeeded. But as she took in the warmth of Alexander's victorious smile, the image of Gwyn falling over in the back draft popped once more into Anita's mind.

She found a smile spreading inadvertently across her lips, before something snapped forcefully into place in her mind. She dropped the cylinder, the shock of the realization so great, her only desperate thought that she had to get to the temples. She had to stop everything. But as the cylinder hit the floor, it bounced back up in front of her. It hovered in mid-air, the metal unrolling before her eyes, revealing its secret.

It looked like nothing more than a sheet of brass unfurling, becoming flat. It contained nothing physical, but somehow, Anita now knew the location of the Magnei. She knew who and what the Magnei were. But more than that, she knew, with certainty, that the Magnei held the key to returning the Relic to the Gods.

She didn't know why the cylinder had opened now, but she had no time to consider it; she had to get to the temples. She couldn't get the image of Gwyn falling over out of her head because it was the answer to the question in Bass' note. His calculations didn't properly account for the level of energy backlash when moving the Relic, because the Relic was a unique object, whose powers they didn't even begin to understand. Bass had made a guess, but that was all it was. Something that powerful could have a terrible backlash, so large that it might not simply knock over, but could even kill those close to it. And Alexander was one of the closest of them all.

Anita pulled herself out of the meditation and sprang to her feet, sprinting toward the temples. She didn't stop until she reached the security guards at the entrance to the Body Temple, who, recognizing her, refused to let her pass. 'Sorry,' said a small, particularly officious guard, 'we've had strict instructions from the Body Descendant not to let you in. I'm afraid we're going to have to ask you to leave.'

Anita considered arguing, but quickly threw this notion aside; they had their orders, and she didn't have time to convince them, nor would she be able to fight her way through all the guards in time. Instead, she forced her way around to the entrance of the Spirit Temple, weaving her way through the thick crowd, who, having been unable to secure a place inside the temple, were rapturously watching a projection. They didn't appreciate Anita's attempts to push past.

Anita looked up at the screen to see Anderson in full flow, and redoubled her attempts to get through, their time nearly up.

She finally reached the entrance to the Spirit Temple, and although the guards gave each other a meaningful look, they reluctantly let her pass. Anita promised that Alexander would reward them for their actions. She ran for the aisle leading to the front, spotting Cleo's nameless friend leaning casually against a pillar. 'You,' said Anita, her voice accusatory as she faltered beside him. 'What are you doing here?'

He looked her up and down. 'Watching,' he said, simply. 'You *know*.' His eyes went wide with unexplained excitement.

'I know what?' demanded Anita.

'You know,' he replied, a mysterious smile playing about his lips.

Anita gasped, sprinting for the front of the temple, her footsteps the only sound, the crowd waiting in silent expectation, just as she had imagined. People turned to see the source of the noise, but Anita ignored them, screaming, 'Stop! Elistair, stop!'

She neared the front, Anderson in his seat, Alexander, Gwyn, and Marcus playing their roles to perfection, but faltering when they saw her. Alexander removed his arm from his tripod, looked to Elistair, started moving. Elistair was already on his feet, his concerned expression freezing when he saw it was Anita. He whirled towards the energy hook, had taken two paces towards it, when a seemingly inconsequential click rang out across the temples. Anita screeched to a halt.

The Relic responded perfectly, its uneven form taking to the sky with faultless grace, and for a moment, everything was calm and silent, all eyes watching it go. Then, after what seemed like an age, time slowing, as it only did when something awful was taking place, a colossal force hammered down on the temples. Stone that had stood for hundreds of years leap into the sky.

Those at the front were thrown outwards as the backlash rippled away from where the Relic had stood, across the floor of each of the temples. It tossed people aside like rag dolls, nobody able to withstand its awesome force. Marcus and Gwyn were thrown backwards, Elistair disappearing into a cavernous hole in the floor. Anita lost sight of Alexander as it knocked her off her feet.

She hauled herself up and struggled towards the Mind Temple, where she thought Alexander had been thrown. She pressed on, seeing, to her relief, Cordelia, on her feet, heading for the exit. Her heart was pounding, adrenaline and fear coursing through her, pushing her onwards, despite the people lying dead or screaming in pain all around. And then, a deafening boom cut across the madness.

Anita stopped, frozen to the spot, trying to make sense of the noise, when a fracture appeared in the floor. A dreadful creaking, cracking sound accompanied it, a great fissure opening to the left of where she stood. '*Alexander,*' she screamed, as a section of the Mind Temple fell away into the chasm, a pair of unwelcome hands clamping around her torso, pulling her back as she tried to go further into the chaos.

The hands were unrelenting, pulling her in the direction she'd come, demanding that she follow them. Anita resisted furiously, clawing at the hands to make them let her go, to let her find Alexander, to help him.

A pillar fell in front of them, blocking their path, a cloud of dust billowing up, engulfing them. A voice screamed in her ear, 'We have to leave. Alexander went through the Mind Temple. He was helping get others out. We have to leave now!' It was Marcus' voice, but not as she knew it, full of urgent terror, and Anita knew they had to go.

She stopped resisting, giving him a look that told him she would comply. He released his grip, and they followed the length of the pillar until they found a place where they could climb the debris. They pulled others along with them, helping as many as they could.

An earth-shattering crash boomed out from just behind them, a chunk of the temple falling from above, trapping countless bodies below. Anita frantically pushed those around her back into motion, pressing on with renewed resolve, Marcus' energy close behind.

They finally made it, emerging from the Spirit Temple into bedlam. People ran aimlessly this way and that, others lying injured on the ground, some screaming for help, some silent, the shock too much to endure.

Anita looked around her, searching urgently for any trace of Alexander; his red cloak, blond hair, someone taking control and directing people to safety. There was no sign anywhere, and everyone looked the same, covered in dust and blood, confusion and disbelief.

But what happened next was beyond anything anyone could have imagined. A deep rumbling filled the air, silencing the people. Anita spun towards the temples, her mouth gaping open as the soaring spires wobbled. The noise got worse, rumbling joined by cracking, booming explosions of sound. And then they collapsed, the Mind Temple first, followed by the other two.

Pillars fell, the roofs, which had always seemed so majestic, grand, slid off their supports to come crashing down on those left inside. Anita watched it happen in slow motion, titanic slabs of stone hurtling towards the ground, and then landing, sending a new shock wave of destruction outwards, a tsunami indiscriminately sucking up everything in its path. The wave plunged towards her, a wall of power that no one could outrun. And then nothing. Then only blackness. Then only the dark.

EPILOGUE

A hooded figure sat in a small, wooden rowing boat in the middle of the great Salt Sea, scanning the sky and smiling as she finally saw a large object hurtling towards her. Her heart momentarily skipped a beat, the reckless mass looking as though it were coming straight for her, although it landed, thank the Gods, fifty feet away, a great splash marking its arrival.

She took up the oars and rowed towards the spot where the Relic had landed, waiting patiently for it to float back to the surface. The Institution had not expected that; they'd had divers waiting to scour the seabed for the precious stone, not that she needed to worry about them any longer.

She'd known it would float, and sure enough, float it did. She picked up the net laid out on the base of her small vessel and hooked it around the Relic. She couldn't haul in on board, it was too heavy for that, but she could pull it behind her. She secured the net, checked the tether, then sat back and enjoyed the sun on her face, taking her time as she rowed her treasure ashore.

I hope you enjoyed Temple of Sand. Book three, Court of Crystal, is coming June 2021. In the meantime…

*   *

ARE YOU A MIND, BODY, OR SPIRIT?

SIGN UP TO MY NEWSLETTER TO TAKE THE OFFICIAL QUIZ!

IT'S ALSO THE FIRST PLACE TO HEAR ABOUT MY NEW RELEASES, GET BOOK, FILM, AND TV RECOMMENDATIONS (ESPECIALLY FANTASY ROMANCE!), AND FOR THE OCCASIONAL FREEBIE…

SIGN UP HERE: HTTPS://WWW.SUBSCRIBEPAGE.COM/R2A0N6

*   *

I'd really appreciate it if you left a review on Amazon US, Amazon UK, Goodreads, Instagram (#TheRelicTrilogy   #TempleOfSand #FantasyRomance), or any other place you can think of… authors aren't fussy! Just a few words, or a line or two would be perfection. Thank you for your support.

CONNECT WITH HR MOORE

Are you a Mind, Body, or Spirit? Sign up to HR Moore's newsletter and find out! You'll get all the latest news about releases, book recommendations, and freebies too! Here's the link:
https://www.subscribepage.com/r2a0n6

Find HR Moore on Instagram:
@HR_Moore
#TheRelicTrilogy
#TempleOfSand
#FantasyRomance

See what the world of The Relic Trilogy looks like on Pinterest:
https://www.pinterest.com/authorhrmoore/

Follow HR Moore on BookBub:
https://www.bookbub.com/profile/hr-moore

Like the HR Moore page on Facebook:
https://www.facebook.com/authorhrmoore

Follow HR Moore on Goodreads:
https://www.goodreads.com/author/show/7228761.H_R_Moore

Or check out HR Moore's website:
http://www.hrmoore.com/

ABOUT THE AUTHOR

Harriet's British, but lives in New Hampshire with her husband and two young daughters. When she isn't writing, editing, eating, running around after her kids, or imagining how much better life would be with the addition of a springer spaniel, she occasionally finds the time to make hats.

TITLES BY HR MOORE

The Relic Trilogy:

Queen of Empire
Temple of Sand
Court of Crystal (coming June 2021)

In the Gleaming Light

Printed in Great Britain
by Amazon

68867191R00177